OVERLAND

RAMCY DIEK

FROM THE TINY ACORN ...
GROWS THE MIGHTY OAK

ACORN
PUBLISHING

Overland

First Edition
Copyright © 2020 Ramcy Diek

Book cover by Damonza.

www.acornpublishingllc.com

ISBN—Hardcover 978-1-952112-23-2
ISBN—Paperback 978-1-952112-22-5
Library of Congress Control Number: 2020916840

Acknowledgments

For months, I struggled with the genre of this novel. Is it drama, a thriller, suspense, or romance? In the end I decided that Overland falls best under the ~~romantic~~ *dramatic*-suspense category and hope you'll agree when you finish reading.

But I not only struggled with the genre and want to send out big hugs and lots of gratitude to my editors, Lindsey Carter from Acorn Author Services, and Laura Taylor, who made it into a story I can be proud of.

Credits also go out to my beta readers Catherine Van B., Luci O., Theresa R., Becky C., Caren G., and Heather S. It's amazing how much your input improved the story. I can't thank you enough for your feedback, suggestions, friendship, and encouragement.

Thank you, Damonza, for creating my beautiful cover.

And as always, my never-ending appreciation goes out to Jessica Therrien and Holly Kammier from Acorn Publishing.
I might not always follow your instructions, but believe me, I know I should, and couldn't have done this without you.

Last, I want to thank my husband and two sons, my biggest supporters. I love you more than anything in the world.

Author Note

Dear Reader,

If you fell in love with
Storm at Keizer Manor and *Eagles in Flight*,
I want to let you know that,
unlike these two clean romance novels,
Overland, a dramatic, romantic suspense thriller,
contains sexual and mental abuse.
I'm not explicit but because I know some people have high
sensitivities to anything involving this kind of trauma, I want to
make sure you're aware of it before you dive in.

But don't let this scare you away. Throughout the pages, there
will still be romance, and I truly hope you'll enjoy the story of Skyla
Overland as she struggles to survive and escape evil.

If you do, please let me know by leaving a review on Amazon,
Goodreads, or Social Media.

Warm Regards,

Ramcy Diek

PROLOGUE

THE TRIP INTO THE CITY took him almost three hours. Rage dominated his already ugly frame of mind.

"Asshole!" he yelled, honking his horn at the unexpected car that suddenly pulled out right in front of him. "Who taught you to drive, slowpoke? Hit that throttle!"

He looked at his fuel gauge. Empty. A stream of curses spewed from his mouth. He wanted so much and had so little. Life was unfair. Everything he'd ever cared about had been taken away from him and all that remained were responsibilities. The upcoming holiday season only added to his misery. He hated Thanksgiving. It brought out too many people, the spirit of Christmas already in their eyes as they clogged up the streets, sidewalks, and parking lots. Beyond pathetic, they were blind to other people's misery, pretending the world was one big happy place. It was not. Not for the likes of him.

He drove first to the post office. With any luck, his welfare check was waiting for him. After finding a parking spot, he got out of his pickup truck. The frigid November blizzard immediately hit him in the face, and he pulled up his collar against the snowflakes whirling around. The sidewalk was just starting to turn white, his boots leaving footprints in the slick layer. As he rounded the corner to Edison Street, the force of the cold westerly wind slammed into him. He took a quick hold of his baseball cap, drawing it further down to keep it from flying away, and shuddered. His threadbare camouflage jacket was no match for the almost below freezing temperatures.

Other pedestrians hustled by, all bundled up and eager to escape the cold. He envied them their warm coats. He needed one of those rugged waterproof parkas. Preferably one with a hood and lots of pockets. That would make life a little better.

At the post office, he opened his box and pulled out the small stack of mail. The first item that caught his attention was a red note, informing him his rent for the box was overdue. He mumbled a harsh word, crushed the note in his hand and tossed it onto the floor. "That check better be there," he mumbled, searching through the stack of letters and advertisements until he found it. On his way out, he dumped the rest of the unopened mail in the garbage bin. Whatever it contained, he didn't care.

Continuing his drive on fumes, he headed downtown to cash what had become his only source of income. Without a phone or a watch, he had no idea of the exact time. The darkening sky suggested it had to be close to five. When he reached the bank, it was already closed.

"Damn you people," he shouted. He banged his right fist several times against the glass door, leaving dirty smudges all over. "Lazy sons of bitches! Can't you work a few minutes longer?"

He looked around with wild eyes filled with wrath, his hands still balled into fists. Several pedestrians hurried to get out his way. He didn't even notice their shocked reactions as he continued to rant and rave. "Get out of my way!"

He lumbered back to his truck. His stomach growled, and he hadn't had a cigarette in more than two weeks. He craved the nicotine more than anything. What now?

Frustrated, he stepped in and slammed his palm against the steering wheel. He'd spent his last few bucks on gas and didn't even have a penny left in his pocket, the mental image of the double burger and large fries beyond his reach. Dammit, he needed cash. He needed it now.

All over the city, lights sparkled. Store windows glowed, filled with decorations and signs, trying to lure in customers with discounts. The holiday season would kick off with Thanksgiving only a few days away, followed by Black Friday, Small Business Saturday, and Cyber Monday. All the cheerfulness and brightness fueled his resentment. What a way to spend your time, buying useless gifts nobody wanted or needed. Didn't they have anything better to do with their money? Why not give it to the poor and needy, to someone like him?

Traffic crawled. The snow stopped, turning into a light drizzle. With luck, he might just make it to the Westside Soup Kitchen. He'd been there several times in the past. Run by several priests, or some other religious dudes, the food was decent. They even served a second helping if someone asked. With the holiday season, people were more generous to the hungry and donations to shelters increased. Who knew? They might even offer dessert.

He left his truck and walked the last few blocks. On the way, he passed an All-American diner, an Italian restaurant, and two burger joints. The delicious smell of roasted meat and french fries tickled his senses and made him salivate. His anger against the bank flared up again. He would have given anything for a juicy burger smothered in cheese and several thick strips of bacon, or for a bucket of fried chicken with mashed potatoes and gravy. Instead, he would probably wind up eating spaghetti and cheap white dinner rolls, or Spanish rice with sticks of celery and iceberg salad.

One of the city buses came to a halt next to him, the screeching brakes drawing his attention. The doors opened and people streamed out on the sidewalk in front of him. Others waited to climb on board, blocking his path. He stopped and waited, his hands deep in his pockets, until he noticed the colorful advertisement on the side of the bus.

It read – 'Protection for all you hold dear. Call Overland Insurance' - in bold lettering, with two men and two women on either side, all four dressed to perfection, smiling brightly with their too white, orthodontia-enhanced teeth.

He felt sucker punched in the belly and his blood started to boil. He knew that insurance agency too damn well. The Overland family! Definitely the last name he needed to see today. Acid-filled resentment flooded his throat, and disgusted, he spat on the sidewalk. He detested those people, hated them. They'd caused his troubles. They were to blame for his misery. Somebody should destroy them, make them burn in hell. That's what they deserved.

CHAPTER

1

A STRANGE SENSATION crawled up Skyla Overland's spine as she crossed the busy parking lot toward the grocery store. Slightly on edge, she looked from left to right, and then over her shoulder. Nothing seemed out of the ordinary, with cars pulling in and out, and others looking for a spot to park. Shoppers pushed their carts, loaded their groceries, or hurried to the entrance. Everyone went their own way, all bundled up in heavy coats, hats, and scarves. Winter had come early this year. People wanted to finish their shopping and get home as soon as possible, to escape the persistent drizzle and near freezing temperature on this bone chilling and dreary evening.

Skyla shivered and pulled the faux fur-lined hood of her red parka closer around her face. She'd bought the thigh-length, well-insulated coat on a whim three weeks ago, while she still walked around in shorts. It turned out to be a smart decision. They'd gone from summer straight into winter.

At the entrance, she found a shopping cart and walked inside. With Thanksgiving only a few days away, the store was extra crowded. People rushed along with huge shopping lists, wanting to get a head start to avoid long lines with overloaded shopping carts at the last minute. Skyla had a list herself. She'd promised her parents to bring a fruit salad for Thanksgiving and wanted to surprise Edmond with a home-cooked meal tonight. They'd met just before Thanksgiving last year and she wanted to celebrate. She wondered if he remembered.

Her earlier unease forgotten, she melted inside her coat and undid the zipper as she walked through the aisles. After she found the basics, like almond milk, bread, eggs, and garbage bags, she pulled out her cell phone to check her list. Lasagna was one of Edmond's favorite dishes, especially if she added spinach and mushrooms. It was five-thirty. If she hurried, she could have dinner ready by seven.

As Skyla made her way through the produce department, she noticed a small boy wearing a red Santa hat and a green raincoat. He stood by himself, next to the bags of green and red grapes. His bottom lip trembled, and he had tears in his frightened blue eyes. He seemed lost, searching for a parent.

An eerie feeling crept over her as she recalled a similar incident six or seven years ago in the exact same store. She'd gone in for a few groceries and noticed the grapes were on sale. Before deciding to buy them, she'd sampled a juicy green one.

"Can I have one, too?" someone had asked.

She'd looked down and found a boy standing next to her, his hand raised, blue eyes hopeful. He couldn't have been older than four or five. She'd smiled, handing him two.

A grateful grin appeared on his smudged little face as he

popped one in his mouth and chewed.

"Aren't they delicious?" she'd asked. "What do you think? Should I buy them?"

"My dad always eats half the bag while we're still in the store," the boy had told her, munching on the second grape.

His remark had made her look around. "Where are your parents, sweetie?"

He didn't seem worried and shrugged. "I don't know."

Although she didn't know the boy, there was no way she would leave him alone in the huge store. "What's your name?" she'd asked, taking his sticky hand in hers.

"I'm Tom," he said.

"Well, Tom, let's try to find them."

Together, they'd walked up and down a few aisles until they reached the meat department.

"There they are." Tom pointed toward a couple sorting through packages of ground beef. In their shopping cart sat a toddler. Her red face was covered with cookie crumbs, dirty streaks, and snot. It looked like she'd been crying.

"Lexi had a tantrum. My dad got mad. That's why I walked away," Tom said.

A frail woman stood beside a bull-necked man in a black muscle tank and army fatigue cargo pants. He wasn't bad looking with the broad torso of a bodybuilder, a strong jawline, straight nose, and a high buzz cut. His legs and arms looked like tree trunks.

The couple looked up when Skyla approached. It seemed they hadn't missed their son and weren't concerned to see him accompanied by a stranger.

"Are you bothering that woman, you little brat," the man

had growled, grabbing Tom forcefully by his arm. He then looked at Skyla, taking her in with slimy unconcealed appreciation and lust. "Well, look who we have here. If it isn't the pretty lady from the gym."

A cold hand had squeezed her heart when she recognized him. The boy's father was the macho man who'd kept making unwanted advances at the gym. She'd even contemplated changing gyms, or quitting her workouts altogether, because he kept pursuing her, not taking no for an answer. That man was trouble. She'd been sure of it.

Ignoring his family, the macho man had taken several steps in her direction, a calculated, smug look on his face. "This can't be a coincidence, seeing you here. Are you following me?"

She recalled backing away as he lifted his finger, intending to raise her chin.

"Not in a million years," she'd replied, a nervous nausea forming in the pit of her stomach.

A woman's voice brought Skyla back to the present.

"Oh, Vincent, sweetheart, there you are!"

The woman rushed toward the boy with the Santa hat, tears brimming in her eyes. "I was so worried when I couldn't find you." She scooped him up in her arms, hugging him tightly and kissing him everywhere.

At least this woman cared, Skyla thought, relieved to see mother and son reunited. She turned her attention to the apples, bananas, and melon she needed for the fruit salad. I'm not buying grapes, she thought. They would only remind her of Tom and his atrocious father.

She headed to the register, loaded her groceries on the belt, and paid for them. But no matter how hard she tried; she couldn't shake off the unwanted memories of the encounter with Tom's father years ago, and everything else that had ensued before and afterwards. She gritted her teeth, her fingers tight around the handle of the cart as she exited the store. *It happened so long ago. She should be over it by now.*

The cold drizzle still fell, the store lights reflecting in the wet asphalt. She shuddered involuntarily, her excitement about the planned romantic evening faded. Hopefully, Edmond would bring a good bottle of wine to help her relax.

A car drove by, splashing up water and she cast an angry glance after the driver, her foot soaking wet. *Some days are just like that*, she thought, *don't let it get to you.* She opened the trunk of her Jeep Compass when sudden movement caught her peripheral vision. In the shadows, a dark figure moved away, or was it just her imagination? With quick frantic movements, she threw in the groceries and hurried to return the shopping cart to a stall. *Why are you suddenly such a scaredy-cat?* she scolded herself. Was it because she recalled that creep from years ago, or because of the episode of Forensic Files she'd watched last night, where a woman got kidnapped from a parking lot? All it had taken for her to vanish off the face of the earth was a guy asking directions with a map in his hand.

Shrugging off her anxiety, Skyla climbed into her Jeep and drove off. *Something like that would never happen to her, right?*

CHAPTER

2

SKYLA'S FATHER, Harold Overland, owned an insurance agency in Rosehurst. The small town, once surrounded by open farmland, was now completely swallowed up by the ever-growing Portland metropolitan area. No one could distinguish any longer where the town ended and the city began. Skyla and her sister had both worked for their father since graduating college - Skyla for six years and her older sister Taylor, for nine.

The day before Thanksgiving, Skyla and her father walked into the office building at exactly the same time.

They waved at Taylor behind the reception desk, her petite frame almost invisible behind the bouquet of purple and pink dahlias brightening up the hallway.

"Good morning," they said in unison.

Taylor shoved a stray lock of blonde hair behind her ear and looked up with a stern expression on her face. "You're late.

Don't let it happen again."

Taylor liked to joke around and sometimes said the craziest things.

"It won't," they replied, grinning as they proceeded down the hall.

"Have you noticed how much she looks like your mother?" Harold Overland reflected not for the first time. "While I always think you're the one who takes after me, with your raven black hair."

"I hope so," Skyla said, glancing at him. She was proud of her tall and distinguished looking father. "But without the facial hair."

Her father smiled back into her teasing hazel eyes. "I love you. You know that?"

She took his arm and gave it a warm squeeze. "I love you, too, Dad."

Before they reached his office, Harold Overland turned to her. "Troy offered to help with the setup for the Thanksgiving get-together this afternoon."

"I don't need any help," she said. "I have it all under control."

"We all need help now and then," he replied. After an affectionate pat on her shoulder, he disappeared into his office.

Skyla headed further down the hallway, the aroma of fresh-brewed coffee pulling her into the break room. Lori, one of the secretaries, poured the dark liquid in her twenty-ounce coffee mug, which displayed a collage of photos of her husband, children and two dogs.

"Can I pour you one, too, Skyla?" she asked, before getting cut off by a violent sneeze, her eyes watery and her nose red.

"Sorry about that. It looks like I'm developing a terrible cold this morning." She grabbed a napkin, blew her nose a few times, and tossed the wet wad into the garbage can.

"I'm glad you didn't call in sick," Skyla remarked, knowing the party that afternoon wouldn't be well attended. "We already have enough employees at home with flu-like symptoms."

Troy, the office manager, sat at one of the round Formica tables in conversation with someone she'd never met before. Both men were drinking coffee. Skyla nodded politely in their direction.

"This is Tim Anderson," Troy said. "We just hired him to fill the vacant janitor position."

With his long blond curly hair and wrinkled suit, Troy didn't look like the average insurance agent. But with his friendly smile and pleasant demeanor, he brought in more business than anyone.

"Nice meeting you, Tim. I'm Skyla Overland." She filled her mug and followed Lori out of the break room, closing the door behind them so that the two men could talk in private.

"I pulled that old Henderson file you requested out of storage, Skyla," Lori said in the hallway, still sniffling. "It smelled musty and ancient in the basement, and some of the boxes were wet. Do you want me to scan it in for you?"

"No thanks, Lori. This time of the year, it's not so crazy busy. Most people have other things on their mind than taking out a new insurance policy. I'll take care of it myself."

"Well, let me know if you need anything," Lori replied and walked away.

Skyla took the stairs to the second floor and opened the

door to her office.

Her father had spoiled her, giving her the corner office with windows on two sides. It provided an incredible view over Portland and the Willamette River with its many bridges.

"Good morning, Grandpa," she said, pausing for a second to look at the portrait of Charles Overland hanging on the wall. Her grandfather stood with his arms folded, his black hair woven with silver, his mouth curved in a courteous smile. It had been his office until he retired four years ago at seventy. If it had been up to him, he would have continued to work. He was very proud of the insurance agency he'd founded thirty-five years ago, especially with Skyla and Taylor working there, too. But her grandmother insisted. She wanted to see Rome, Alaska, Thailand, and all kinds of other exotic places.

After Charles Overland's retirement, Skyla's father hired Troy as the new office manager to help with the workload. Despite their eight-year age difference, Skyla and Troy immediately became good friends. She found him kindhearted, his sense of humor infectious. Her father called him hardworking, smart, and to the point, traits he respected and welcomed.

Skyla sipped her coffee as she looked outside. The grey sky and gloomy clouds promised the arrival of yet another low-pressure system and several days of forecasted rain. The Pacific Northwest was known for its high amount of precipitation. She turned her back on the gloomy horizon. The view only added to her unease, the creepy feeling of being watched still lingering.

To distract herself, she sat behind her desk, booted up the computer and opened the first case of the day. It was a dispute over a disability claim, and she stiffened, the issue immediately bringing her senses back on edge. *If this is about another macho looking guy pretending to be injured, I'm passing it on to Troy,* she thought, not wanting to be reminded of that stressful case for the entire day. The words, forty-two-year-old woman, mother of three, jumped at her. She let out a sigh of relief. She could handle that.

Several hours later, Skyla looked up from her computer and stretched her back. Today, the insurance agency would close at three, so all the employees could gather for a holiday snack and a drink before they all rushed home for the four-day weekend.

Skyla's father had given her the task of organizing the office party this year. As daughter of the owner, she felt extra pressure to arrange a fun and relaxing get-together. Clicking with her pen, she went over her to-do list, to make sure she'd thought of everything. A recommended caterer would deliver fresh fruit and cheese trays served with fruit dip, Muenster, Gouda, and Havarti cheeses, and crackers. She'd also ordered garden fresh vegetables with ranch dip, lightly seasoned crispy zucchini chips, roasted nuts, golden raisins, and plump cranberries. With the stuffed eggs, potato salad, salmon spread, and various sliced meats, Skyla knew there would be more than enough food for the entire staff. For drinks, she'd brought in eggnog and fruit juices, and two twelve-packs of the new seltzer water she'd just discovered.

An hour before the party was planned to begin, she headed to the break room to meet with the caterer.

"Thanks for offering your help, but I got it handled," she said, glancing at Troy who had followed her in.

"Are you sure?" he asked, bobbing his eyebrows in an exaggerated way.

Skyla chuckled at his antics.

"Yes, there's nothing left to do other than telling the caterer where to put everything. But you could help with pouring drinks when everyone gets here."

"I would be honored," Troy said, bowing with respect.

She enjoyed his teasing. It helped lift her spirits and forget about her persistent unease, the creepy sensation of someone watching her constantly there.

Instead of leaving, Troy lingered around as the caterers brought in box after box and set out gorgeous decorated platters. "Do you have any plans for the holiday weekend?" he asked.

Skyla tore the plastic off a stack of heavy-duty paper plates and put them on the table. "The usual," she replied. "Sleeping in, going to my parents' house. I'm bringing a fruit salad and found this recipe for a sweet potato casserole with streusel topping. My mom and I want to try to make it."

Troy raised his eyebrows. "Just you and not Edmond?"

"Yes, it'll be different than normal. Edmond's parents have family coming over from New Zealand. There'll be several cousins Edmond hasn't seen in years, and he wants to spend time with them. So, I decided to help Mom and then join Edmond at his parents' house later. It'll be fun. How about you, Troy?"

"Me?" he asked, fretting with his skewed tie, only making it worse. "Oh, I've nothing planned. My mother booked a last-minute flight to Palm Springs to celebrate the holiday with her new husband's daughter. They'll fly out tonight at eight."

"Is everything to your liking, Ms. Overland?" the caterer asked, interrupting their conversation.

Skyla inspected the buffet and make-shift bar. "Looks amazing. Thank you so much."

"We'll leave the boxes for leftovers and pick up the empty platters after the weekend. Happy Thanksgiving," the caterer said and headed out.

"Same to you," Skyla replied before turning her attention back to Troy. "Do you have to take them to the airport?" She took a bite out of a chocolate-dipped strawberry and smiled. "Try one, Troy. They're delicious."

"Chocolate? Not for me," he said, pretending he didn't care about it.

She knew he loved dark chocolate and held up the tray.

He took one and rolled his eyes upwards, feigning he was in heaven.

Skyla laughed out loud. Troy was kind and easy-going, and unlike Edmond, who was always dressed immaculately, his jet-black hair cut to perfection, Troy never seemed to care much about his appearance. It looked like he dressed each morning in a hurry, opting to sleep in an extra half an hour rather than to get up to style his hair. She found it endearing.

"You can't show up like this at the party," she said, taking a step closer. "Let me straighten that tie of yours."

He sunk his teeth in his bottom lip and held his breath as she fussed over him.

It made her aware of her own body and how close they stood. She looked at him, and her laughter died when she caught his intense stare. For the first time since they met him, she couldn't think of what to say.

The sudden arrival of two coworkers made her take a quick step back. Despite that there was nothing going on, she felt like they'd caught her with her hand in the cookie jar.

"Hey, everyone," she said. "Glad you made it."

CHAPTER

3

"WHY DID EVERYONE leave so early?" Skyla asked, surveying the barely touched platters on the tables in the break room. She glanced at the wall clock. Not even five o'clock. "Look at all the leftovers!"

"Must be that terrible flu bug going around," Troy replied, consigning a pile of used paper plates to the garbage can. "Or perhaps everyone's just stressed out or tired. Whatever the reason, no one seemed to be in the mood to celebrate."

"Let's hope we'll all be able to relax and recover over the holiday weekend," Skyla remarked, beginning to organize. "I need a couple of days off myself."

"That doesn't sound like you," Troy remarked. He looked genuinely surprised. "Are you all right?"

"I'm just a little on edge, and I don't know why," she confessed, rinsing off the first empty platter at the sink. "Maybe I'm coming down with something, too."

Troy's gaze traveled from the top of her head, down her blue blazer and matching dress pants, to her elegant T-strap black pumps.

"You look lovely, as always," he remarked. "What should we do with all the food? We can't leave it here to spoil or throw it in the dumpster."

"I agree," Skyla said. "How about we empty the platters into the boxes and bring them to the homeless shelter around the corner? I don't know if they'd take it, but anything's better than letting it go to waste."

Troy glanced at his watch. "I promised to pick up my mother in about thirty minutes, so I can't go with you to the shelter, but I'll help you load everything into your car."

"That would be great. Thanks, Troy. I'm sure there'll be someone there to help me unload."

They boxed up the food and were ready to leave within five minutes. She looked forward to a quiet evening on the couch with a good book and a glass of wine. Pauline, her best friend and roommate, left last night, to spend the holiday weekend at her boyfriend's house. Edmond had to pick up his relatives, and she wouldn't see him until tomorrow.

"When does the new janitor start?" she asked, seeing the mess they'd left behind. There were wine stains, spilled food, and breadcrumbs on the tables and the floor.

"Not until Monday, but don't worry about it," Troy said. "It'll be his first day at work, and he'll be happy to show off."

"Show off his cleaning skills?" She grinned. "Right!"

They walked out of the office, both carrying two boxes. When they reached her car, they put them into the trunk.

"Should I set the alarm for the security system so you can be on your way?" Troy offered.

"No, I'll take care of it. I still need to get my purse." Skyla closed the hatch, ready to hurry back inside to escape the persistent drizzle.

When Troy didn't leave, she gave him a playful swat. "Go," she said. "You don't want to be late picking up your mother. With the holiday rush, it'll be crazy busy on the road and at the airport."

"Are you sure? I hate to leave you by yourself."

"Now don't start acting as if this is the first time I need to close the office." She nudged him toward his own car, laughing. "Stop worrying! I'll be fine."

Troy spun back around so abruptly that she lost her balance and landed in his arms. Startled, she looked up, her hands on his chest. "What is it, Troy?" she said, noticing his flushed face. "Did you forget something?"

In answer, he slid his arms around her waist and pulled her close. "I did."

Uncomfortable under the intent way he studied her, she wriggled to free herself from his embrace. They were friends. This wasn't supposed to happen.

Instead of releasing her, he lowered his head, his mouth curved into a dreamy smile. When his lips found hers, he let the tip of his tongue linger, as if waiting for permission.

A soft prickle of sensual tension formed in her throat, and she swallowed it back. This wasn't right. Her fingers clutched the lapels of his double-breasted overcoat coat. "What are you doing?" she asked breathlessly.

The slight movement of her lips was enough encouragement for him to boldly explore the softness of her mouth, a deep, content grumble resonating through his body.

Her blood churned under her skin and she gasped for breath, her head spinning. Nobody had ever kissed her with such passion, longing, and tenderness, the overall effect strangely mind-boggling. It wasn't right. For the second time, she tried to push him away, but found her arms had lost all strength. Still trying to decipher her mystifying, inappropriate reaction, her hand crept up around his neck, while her other hand cupped the back of his head pulling him closer. He immediately responded, molding his lips with hers, tasting, exploring, enjoying.

A moan of pleasure escaped her throat. For the first time in her life, her entire body came alive. She arched against him, pressing herself more closely into his warmth and strength.

"Troy," she whispered. "We shouldn't do this."

He pressed his face against her neck, his mouth scorching a path down her throat. "Oh, Skyla, I've been wanting to do this for so long."

A car alarm went off nearby and he drew in a deep, shuddering breath, then straightened and quickly released her.

"I'm sorry. I lost control. I didn't mean to do that." He slowly backed away, his body tense, as if he was ready to bolt. Raindrops had accumulated in his hair and threatened to spill down his forehead. With an impatient gesture, he raked his hand through his wet hair. "All I wanted to do was wish you a Happy Thanksgiving." He met her gaze, his expression subdued. "I hope this doesn't change anything between us. I mean, it shouldn't."

It took a moment to collect herself enough to speak. "I don't know," she replied, still recovering from her shocking response. They were friends, colleagues, and she'd never considered him as a boyfriend or a potential lover. With the taste of his passionate kiss still lingering on her lips, she wondered why. He was one of the kindest and most honest men she'd ever met. He was attractive, tall, and kept himself in shape. Not always easy for a man who worked in an office.

"I'm sorry. I really have to go," he apologized again.

She reached out to touch him, but he didn't notice, and she watched him flee to his midsize SUV. Before he climbed in, he turned and waved. A moment later, he drove off without a backward glance.

As his taillights disappeared, the prickling sensation at her nape reemerged. She glanced around. She was getting soaked, and if there was someone lurking around, she needed to go, right away.

Back in the brightly lit hallway, she felt safe and lingered for a few minutes. Troy's unexpected kiss had touched her more than she could have ever imagined. She was glad she wouldn't see Edmond until tomorrow. She needed time to sort through her emotions.

After straightening out her desk, she took her handbag and cell phone, and punched in the code for the security system behind the reception desk. At the front door, she hesitated, the alarming sensation of being watched terrifying.

Was someone out there, hiding in the shadows? Should she stay inside the safety of the building? Or should she call the police?

Chiding herself for cowardice and an overactive imagination, she pressed her lips together, straightened her back, and hurried across the pavement. Fearfully glancing over her shoulders from left to right, she unlocked her car with her remote. Her Jeep chirped back, and the headlights came on. When she reached it, she flung the door open, tossed her handbag and cell phone on the passenger seat, jumped in, and locked the doors, her nerves singing with anxiety.

In the safety of her car, she released a deep sigh. She clutched the steering wheel with both hands. At least no one had witnessed her frantic behavior. She was sure it would have been unusual to see her running in her high heeled black shoes, trying not to lose her balance. Her heartbeat slowed, and she pressed the start button. She was tired and stressed out. A hot shower, a change of clothes, and a glass of wine would take care of all that the moment she got home.

She put on her seatbelt, shifted the automatic transmission in reverse and glanced in her rearview mirror. Her eyes filled with dread when the face of a stranger grinned at her from the backseat. Nearly paralyzed with fear, she cried out. "What the hell are you doing in my car?" Before she could turn around and face the intruder, a strong hand covered her mouth and nose.

"How nice to see you again," he hissed close to her ear.

Terrified, she reached up with both hands and clutched at his arm to break free. Immediately a second hand slid around her throat and began to close off her windpipe with enormous force. She gagged, unable to catch her breath. Her eyes bulged and her stomach protested in full force. She thought she would throw up or die, whatever came first. Arms flailing in desperation, she dug her nails into the skin at the back of his hand and tried to scratch out his eyes.

"Stop fighting, or I'll break your neck," he hissed, his hot breath against her ear. He stank of feces, garlic, alcohol, and tobacco. Too panicked to coordinate her thoughts, she kept fighting until the tight hold around her neck released slightly. She gulped for air. "What do you want? Money?"

She could feel him move in even closer, her eyes bulging when he applied more pressure around her neck, choking her again.

"Listen, bitch," he hissed. "I'll take away my hand so you can breathe. But I promise I'll kill you if you scream or try to fight me. You understand?"

Her chest burned from oxygen deprivation and stars danced before her eyes. Choking back sobs, she nodded. She had to be smart. For now, he had the upper hand.

The moment he released his grip, she sucked in air and stayed quiet, her hands searching for the door handle. When she found it, she pulled on it and pushed the door open. Mad with panic, she tried to climb out. Her seatbelt immediately jerked her back.

"You stupid bitch," he growled. His hand came back around her face. With primal survival instinct, she bit his finger.

"Fuck!" he howled. "I told you to stop fighting!"

He could tell her all he wanted. She would not become his victim. With one hand, she struggled to release the seat belt. With the other, she hit the horn of her car, pressing down as hard as she could. The noise was so deafening, she knew it had to attract someone's attention. From the corner of her eye, she caught him raising an arm. He held a heavy object, and it came in her direction. She felt the pain on her forehead for only a split second before descending into unconsciousness.

CHAPTER

4

SKYLA HAD NO IDEA how long she'd been unconscious.
When she woke up, immediate panic constricted her throat.
She was lying on the backseat of her own moving car. She was
being kidnapped.

The car's heater ran at full blast, the air suffocating. Despite
the heat, she shivered convulsively. Her teeth chattered as
horrible images of her discarded mutilated body, raped and
beaten, flooded her mind. Drenched in cold sweat, her long
hair half covered her face and blocked her vision. She wiggled
her arms. They were numb, bound behind her back at the
wrists.

She lowered her legs to the floor of the car. A sharp pain
shot through her right temple as she tried to push herself up
into a sitting position. Overcome by a wave of nausea, she
gasped and almost burst into tears. With her eyes squeezed
tightly, she waited until her dizziness subsided. Don't panic,

keep your head together, she ordered herself. As long as your heart is beating, you'll have a chance. You can do this.

She reopened her eyes and caught a glimpse of the man behind the steering wheel. He was wearing a baseball cap and a dark coat, and his hair was shoulder length. She couldn't see much else and had no idea who he was. She shifted her gaze to look outside. The windshield wipers swished back and forth, and all she could detect was that he was driving in complete darkness. Other than the raindrops in the beams of the headlights, she couldn't see anything. Realizing every second brought her further away from home, she moved her attention to her tied wrists. He'd used thin rope. If she could get her hands free, perhaps she could find something to hit him over the head with?

The man shifted position and glanced over his shoulder. "Did sleeping beauty wake up?"

She half-leaned against the backdoor, her attention more focused on the rope than on him. As long as he was behind the wheel, he wouldn't be able to see what she did. This was her best chance.

"Who are you?" she spat at him, trying to free one of her hands, but the harder she pulled the deeper the rope cut into her skin. "What do you want from me?"

He emitted a harsh bark of laughter. "I'm the prince who's rescuing the princess."

Was this guy crazy? What the hell was he talking about? "Where are you taking me?" she demanded.

He laughed even louder. "I'm taking you to your new home. Isn't that what happens in fairy tales? Prince Charming and his white horse taking the princess to her castle."

She tried to make sense out of what he was saying. This wasn't a fairy tale. It was a nightmare.

"And it's so nice of you to bring dinner," he went on. "That doesn't happen very often."

Her situation got worse by the second. The guy was obviously out of his mind.

"I'm talking about those boxes you put in the back," he explained. "I peeked inside and took a few bites of the cheese and crackers. I hope you don't mind."

The party. The boxes with leftovers. She'd wanted to take them to the homeless shelter.

Outside the car window, the dark silhouettes of trees and bushes flashed by, including a guard rail. She sensed he was driving on backroads.

"Where are we?" she tried again. Every time she moved her hands back and forth, she had the feeling there was a little more slack. It gave her confidence she would have her hands free soon.

"You'll find out soon enough," he said and slowed down to take a sharp corner in the road.

He seemed highly amused with the situation. Her fear, overlaid with anger and resentment, let her throw caution in the wind. "I want to know exactly where you're taking me, and why. Otherwise you'll come to regret it." She came up further on her seat to give her words more power.

"Enough talking!" he growled, giving her a warning glance over his shoulder. "I hate women who make empty threats."

She got a quick glimpse of a gaunt face, dirty blond hair, a bushy beard, and a baseball cap, which was half mesh, half camo, and had a chainsaw embroidered on the front. He looked like any other homeless man or drug addict, who wandered around the neighborhood since the local shelter had opened several years ago. The increasing homelessness remained a difficult problem for the city.

"Do you want money? Is that what you're after?"

"Shut the fuck up!" he thundered. His large hands clutched the steering wheel and his neck swelled up. "Why are all women the same? They never know when to shut their mouths!"

His sudden rage and hatred shocked her, and she sucked in a terrified breath. He was a big man, broad shouldered and bull-necked, who didn't hold women in high esteem. If she wasn't careful, he would snap her in two.

The car slowed down and bounced around as the tires rattled over a washboard stretch of road. They left the pavement and drove down a dirt road. She assumed they had left the city a long time ago and were in a rural area. All she'd seen so far were trees and not a single car, road sign, or structure, let alone a house. Fear spread through her entire nervous system, and there was a hollow space where her stomach should have been. She needed more time. The rope was starting to give way; she was sure of it.

The car came to a sudden halt, and she cursed under her breath. If she only had another minute. Her abductor opened the door and got out. "Don't worry, honey, I'll be right back."

Hope gave her renewed courage. With her back against the door, she raised herself up to unlock it and pulled the handle. Her bodyweight pushed the door wide open. The next moment, she tumbled off the seat and onto the wet ground. It was still raining, and she cried out in pain when the back of her head hit something hard. Not allowing herself to wallow, she rolled over and crawled onto her feet, ready to take off. A powerful hand on her shoulder stopped her in her tracks.

"Are you so eager to get to your new home, sweetheart?" he said, pulling her up against his chest.

The blast of his foul breath across her face and his nauseating closeness made her heave.

"Let me go!" she cried out as she kicked him hard against his shins.

He glared daggers at her. "First you bite me, and now you kick me. I warn you, Skyla, you've about used up my patience. Behave, or you'll come to regret it."

He released her so abruptly, she almost fell for the second time and stumbled to stay on her feet. "How do you know my name? Who are you?"

The only thing that literally stood out in his face was his nose. It was big and crooked and looked like it had come in contact with someone's fists more than once.

A sinister look appeared in his eyes. "You'll find out who I am eventually. But there's no fun in telling you. Figure it out yourself."

A sinking feeling formed deep in her gut. He was bat-crap crazy!

"For now, I suggest you stay calm. We're in the middle of nowhere. Your best chance for survival is to do exactly what I say. Got it?" He opened the back hatch of her car. "What do you want to bring?"

Rain splattered the boxes and soaked her hair, rainwater streaming down her face and neck. She shivered. "What do you mean? I'm not taking anything."

"Fine," he replied, and shrugged. "You better think twice. Your car will end up on the bottom of that pond over there, along with everything in it."

For the first time, she noticed a small body of water next to where he'd parked, its ink dark water shimmering in the headlights of the car. If she'd taken off, she would have run right into it. "No, you can't do that," she cried out, horrified by the thought of her beloved Jeep under water. "You can't dump my car in some pond!"

"Although it pains me to see this beauty disappear, I damned well will," he vowed, unloading the boxes and the emergency blanket from the back. "I can't afford to keep it out in the open."

She stared at him, utterly dumbfounded as she tried to make sense of his intentions and her situation. He intended to take her belongings from her car and then dispose of the vehicle in the water? No way would she let that happen.

"I was supposed to meet up with friends right after work. I'm sure they already miss me and called the cops." She lied, but that didn't matter. All she wanted was to persuade him he'd made a monumental mistake by abducting her, so he would let her go. "Anyone!" she cried out at the top of her lungs. "Anyone out there! Help!"

Her scream died in her throat when he backhanded her. "I told you several times to shut up, bitch!" His voice sounded as hard as tempered steel. "Don't mess with me, or you'll regret it."

Her skull rang from the force of the brutal blow, and she tasted blood. She slid her tongue over her teeth to make sure they were all intact. "You asshole!" she moaned, tears flooding her eyes.

He ignored her and slammed shut the back hatch. "Okay, if there's nothing you want. Suit yourself."

"My purse," she replied in a trembling voice. "It's on the front seat."

As he rounded the car and opened the passenger door, her heart pounded so hard, she feared he could hear every beat. The moment he reached in to grab her bag, she took off running toward the tree line. Her bound hands constricted her movements, the rope cutting into her skin.

He cursed loudly as he pounded after her in the pitch-black night. Seconds later, she heard his heavy footsteps right behind her. He seized her by the arm, but she jerked free and took off again until a half rotten tree trunk blocked her way. She tried to jump over it but lost her footing. Not able to break her fall, she crashed to the ground and descended into darkness.

CHAPTER

5

SKYLA WOKE WITH a splitting headache, sprawled on a hard, bumpy surface. For a second, she didn't know where she was. Reality soon hit. She lay on the floor, on the passenger side of a moving vehicle, her hands still tied behind her back, and something solid poked her in the ribs. It hurt.

Lacking the strength to move, she moaned. All she wanted was to fall back into unconsciousness, the pit of her stomach on fire, and the pain in her head unbearable. But her sense of self protection kicked in, her need to survive too strong. She couldn't allow herself to be vulnerable and completely at his mercy. Giving up was not in her DNA, and her mind struggled to find options. She didn't have many. Her entire body hurt, and her arms and legs were numb. Barely able to move, she wiggled her toes and fingers to stimulate the blood flow. It only made everything hurt more.

"Are you uncomfortable, honey?" the hated, but already

too familiar voice asked.

With one eye, she vaguely noticed a muddy boot next to her own feet. One of her shoes was missing, her toes covered in dirt.

"I'm fine," she replied, mustering up bravery. "Except for something working its way between my ribs."

The vehicle bumped and bounced, throwing her around like a ragdoll. An expletive escaped her lips.

He slowed down and reached over just far enough to remove a metal object from beneath her. "You were lying on one of my traps." He tossed it onto the seat. "That better?"

The tires hit a deep pothole, and the side of her head banged against the glove compartment. The continuous jolting became almost too much to bear.

"Don't worry, we're almost there," he said. "When we get home, you can clean yourself up and pamper your wounds." He chuckled as the car hit another pothole. "I live in a beautiful area. There's a stunning view from the top of the hill behind our house. I'm sure you'll like it once you're used to your new surroundings."

Her stomach lurched painfully in her chest and she could barely register his words. She'd never felt so out of control and humiliated. I'll never give in to this creep, she vowed. I'll fight to the end.

"We're home!" he said, turning the engine off.

She raised her head. Although she'd tried hard to stay alert, she'd slipped off again.

He opened the door and got out. A rush of frigid air swept over her, and she shivered, anxiety threatening to choke her.

A moment later, the door of the passenger side opened. Two powerful hands grabbed her arms and pulled her out.

Her legs immediately gave out and she landed on the snow-covered ground. It was pitch dark, the moon and stars hidden behind a thick cloud cover. Terrified, she tried to squirm away.

"Ho, lady, what you doin'?" he smirked, pulling her back up. "We're a little stiff, aren't we?"

The stench coming off him was rancid, and she fought him off with what little remained of her strength.

"Damn, woman! I'm getting sick of your attitude."

He hooked his arm around her waist, picked her up, and threw her over his shoulder, like a bag of potatoes.

"Let me go," she screamed. All fight, she kicked her legs in thin air, her bound fists pounding his back. But his coat took the brunt of her effort. He didn't even seem to notice.

After covering less than ten yards, he put her down. Her legs had regained some of their strength, and she stayed upright, battling waves of terror as they crashed over her.

"For your own sake, you better be done fightin'," he growled. "Or you'll spend the night outside in the freezing cold. They're expecting more snow tonight with temps in the twenties. You won't make it 'til morning."

She shriveled under his evil glare, only two inches away from her face. All she wanted to do was make her escape but knew she wouldn't get far.

He grabbed her by her upper arm, shaking her. "The last warning. No tricks!"

Only then did she notice faint light glowing softly from behind a single window and in between the cracks of what appeared to be the wooden boards of a door.

He pulled Skyla forward onto the jagged wooden boards of what may have been a porch. Hinges squeaked as the door opened and rough hands dragged her further inside.

"I brought you something for Thanksgiving," her captor yelled. The door slammed shut behind them. "Why is it so dark in here, boy? Light another candle."

Skyla noticed a young boy standing in the middle of a dimly lit room; a blanket wrapped around his body. It was freezing inside.

"Did you bring something to eat, Dad?" the boy asked, rubbing sleep from his eyes. He let go of the blanket and tried to light a match at a table.

"You bet I did, Son. It's still in the car. I'll get it as soon as I put this little lady in a safe place."

When the boy caught sight of Skyla, his mouth fell open, the box with matches falling to the floor. His tiny shoulders shuddered when he glanced at his father. "Sorry, Dad." He dropped to his knees, gathered the matches from the floor, and lit a candle, his hands shaking.

The man pushed her closer to the table and pulled a knife from his pocket. "Turn around."

She just about had a heart attack when she spotted the serrated blade. "Why would I?" she hissed, straightening her spine.

"Cause I want to cut you loose."

Despite her bravado, she let out a sob like a dry heave and turned around. With one swift movement, the rope came off, and she rolled her shoulders, massaging her wrists.

"Now, sit down and don't move." He pushed her toward the table and forced her into a chair, before he thumped towards the door, the rough wooden floorboards protesting under his heavy boots.

When the door closed behind him, Skyla looked around the candle-lit room. Inside there was only a table and four chairs, a woodstove, and a workbench against the rough wall, and it smelled like smoke.

A shudder overtook her. One moment she felt cold, the next blistering hot, the effort of suppressing her fear exhausting.

The boy stood only a few feet away from her, his face ghostly white in the flickering light. "Are you cold?" he asked. "I can add another piece of wood to the fire."

The last thing she'd expected to see was a child, but his presence gave her confidence a boost for a good outcome. Although her abductor seemed insane, he wouldn't hurt or rape her in the presence of his son, right? Emotionally drained, she nodded. "Yes, that would be nice."

He opened the door of the woodstove with an oven mitt and added two pieces to the smoldering ashes. Bright flames immediately flared up and she could already feel the warmth.

With her blood flowing back in her veins, the tingling sensations in her arms and legs subsided, and her strength and courage returned with it. Warily, she ran a hand over the side of her head, just above her right ear. Touching the huge bump on the spot where he'd knocked her out, she winced. Next, she let her fingertips trail over her forehead and felt dried up blood from a cut that seemed at least an inch long. Overall, she wasn't in as bad a shape as she'd thought only ten minutes ago. It had also become clear he didn't want to kill her. With that large knife, he'd had ample opportunity. Instead he'd brought her to his home, which led her to believe his reason for kidnapping her had to be money. He was obvious poverty stricken, knew her name, and who she was. *But why her?* Her family was well-off, but not rich in the sense that they could hand over a kidnapping ransom.

Whatever he was after, she would figure it out. In the meantime, she had to find a way to escape. Her captor didn't seem too smart. It wouldn't be too difficult to outsmart him.

The door of the shack opened. She held her breath as he carried in two boxes filled with leftovers from the office party.

"Get your sister so we can eat," he told the boy.

"We were so tired. Julia kept on crying, keeping us up. She must not have heard you come home."

"Wake her, boy," the man said, opening one of the boxes. "I'm sure she doesn't want to miss dinner." He sat down and popped a cracker with salmon crème into his mouth, followed by a second one.

The boy opened a door at the dark end of the room. Skyla heard voices, then an excited scream. A moment later, a young girl rushed through the door and jumped into her father's lap. She was barefoot, but fully dressed in jeans and a sweatshirt.

"I'm so happy to see you, Dad." She smiled, pushing her long, unkempt mop of hair out of her face. "We were so worried you wouldn't come back."

"Hello, Pumpkin." He hugged her briefly, before he shifted her into the chair next to him. "I brought you some food."

Reluctantly, she let go of him. "I was so scared, Daddy. You left us alone for so long, and I was so hungry!" She seemed close to tears.

With his mouth full, he glared at her. "Stop whining, Girl. I haven't been gone for more than three days."

The girl cringed away from him, her bottom lip quivering.

Unfazed by her obvious distress, he pointed at the boxes. "I brought you food. Didn't I?"

Skyla couldn't believe her ears. Had he left these two small children by themselves for that long? No, that wasn't possible. Their mother had to be around.

"Come on, eat!" he said. "I don't know what all this is, but it smells damn good."

The girl got on her knees to look closer and reached in with two hands. So did the boy. They both started eating so fast, it looked like they were starving. Knowing the kids had been left alone for three days, she realized they probably were.

When her captor had his fill, he belched and swiped his sleeve across his mouth. "Good stuff."

"Thanks, Dad. This is the best food ever," the boy smiled with his mouth full. Juice from one of the chocolate-covered strawberries trickled down his chin.

"Don't thank me. Thank her." He folded his arms in front of his chest and leaned back in his chair, a stupid grin on his face.

She gave him a blank stare, although her insides were shaking.

"Believe it or not, kids. Along with the food, I brought you a new mother. What do you think of that?" He slapped his thigh, showing two missing front teeth as he laughed out loud.

It seemed he found himself hilarious, but all she saw was a terrifying and delusional individual with the physical power to do whatever he wanted. He disgusted her.

"A new mother?" the girl asked. Her blue eyes looked too

big in her small pale face as she peered at Skyla.

"Yes, isn't that a wonderful Thanksgiving surprise?" He let his chair fall back on its four legs, bringing his face almost next to Skyla's.

Stoic, she looked away, not wanting to give him the satisfaction of revealing how shocked she was at his outrageous statement.

"I'll get the rest of the stuff from the truck," he said, raising his hand in a fist, right in front of her face. "You behave! Or else..."

She recognized the warning gleam in his eyes and nodded in consent. She didn't plan to do anything. At least, not tonight.

CHAPTER

6

"I'M VERY THIRSTY. May I have some water?" Skyla asked after her abductor closed the door behind him. Her mouth felt as dry as the Sahara Desert.

The girl climbed off her chair and grabbed a chipped cup from a shelf attached to the wall with two simple brackets. Giving Skyla suspicious side glances, she dipped the cup into a pan filled with water and handed it to her.

"Thank you," Skyla said, bringing the cup to her lips. The water tasted fresh and cooled the burning acid in her stomach. She gave the girl a weak smile, hoping she didn't scare her with her blood-covered face. "My name is Skyla. Are you Julia?"

The girl looked at her with a guarded expression, stuck two of her fingers in her mouth, and shook her head.

The boy had stayed quiet, observing her. At her question, he stood and took a protective stand in front of his younger sister.

"Her name is Lexi. I'm Tom."

"Hi, Lexi and Tom, nice to meet you," she said. "Now, I hope you don't mind me asking, but you didn't eat for a while. Is that right?"

The children looked at each other and shrugged.

"I believe you said something about Julia, who kept you awake because she cried so much. Don't you think she needs to eat, too?"

Lexi pulled her fingers out of her mouth. "Julia is sick. She can't eat."

"Couldn't we try?"

"I guess," Tom said, but stayed where he was.

"I really think you should wake her. There's still plenty of food left," Skyla persisted.

"Why don't you get her, Lexi?" Tom said, still reluctant. "Maybe she's right. Maybe Julia should eat something."

"But she doesn't want anything," Lexi protested. "I tried. All she did was cry."

"I know, but get her anyway," Tom ordered, glancing at Skyla. "Maybe she can do something about it."

Dragging her feet, Lexi headed toward the door.

"Julia cried for days," Tom explained. "We didn't know what to do and were glad she fell asleep."

Skyla didn't know what to think. The entire situation was so surreal.

Lexi returned, carrying a life-sized doll partially wrapped in a dirty pink baby blanket. Skinny legs with two bare feet hung free, pale and limp.

Julia is a doll and not an infant, Skyla thought, relieved. Her blood still ran cold at the very thought of that possibility.

"Is that Julia?" she said, deciding to play along. "Can I hold her?"

She held out her arms, and the moment she felt the weight of the baby, she realized the children had told the truth. Julia was a real baby. She bit her lower lip to keep from crying out in shock as she stared at the baby's face. Her eyes were closed, the tiny lips white, her pale cheeks smudged with dirt and dried up drool. "For heaven's sake, where's your mother?" she shrieked, tossing the children a look of utter disbelief.

"It's not our fault," Tom replied, shriveling within himself.

Lexi started to cry and Tom wrapped his arm around her shoulders, throwing Skyla a heartbreaking glance. "Dad said you're our new mother. You should make her better!" His bottom lip trembled, and his eyes filled with tears. "Do you think you can?"

Skyla found herself at a loss for words. They couldn't possibly believe she'd come here of her own free will to take care of them? She looked from one child to the other, their bodies scrawny underneath their double layers of rags. They both had dark circles around their eyes, their cheeks sunken in. She could tell they were severely neglected, powerless, and beyond vulnerable. Her heart broke. How could she reveal their father had kidnapped her? That she was here against her will, and had no idea what to do?

The door opened and her abductor stumbled back into the room. "Good, you guys are getting acquainted," he said, carrying two more boxes of food. She recognized the emergency blanket from her car hanging over his shoulder. After he set the boxes on the table, he pulled Lexi's fingers from her mouth. "Didn't I tell you to quit sucking your fingers?"

Skyla couldn't believe his cruelty. "Did you really leave your children to fend for themselves for three days?" she snapped angrily. "Where's their mother?"

"Dead," he replied.

"But Julia's just a baby!" she cried out. "Look at her!" Though her tears, she stared at the lifeless child in her arms. "She's sick, very sick, and who knows how long it's been since she had anything to eat. Don't you see that she might die if she's not taken care of properly?"

The room was warming up and she started to sweat, feeling she might suffocate.

"What else am I supposed to do when I have to go into town?" he countered. "They need food, don't they?"

The situation was so unreal. Surely, she would wake up soon, finding out it had only been a horribly vivid nightmare.

"They need a mother!" She regretted the words the moment they slipped from her mouth.

"Finally, we agree on something." He gave her a smug look. "Now, shut up about it. Children are women's business." With that he left the cabin, slamming the door behind himself so hard, the walls shook.

Skyla nearly burst into tears but swallowed them back. Breaking down in front of the children was not the answer. Something needed to be done. The baby's life depended on it.

"Do you have a bottle and formula somewhere?" she asked Lexi. She knew nothing about babies, but believed it wouldn't be too hard to figure out how to warm a bottle and change a diaper.

Lexi nodded. "We tried to give her the powdered milk, but

I told you she doesn't want any."

Skyla mentally reviewed the contents of the boxes. Stuffed eggs, potato salad, cheese, asparagus, and sliced meats. Nothing suitable for a baby. "Please, get the bottle so I can try," she said.

Then she turned to Tom. "When your father took me, I had a purse in my car. Could you check his truck and see if it's there?" She had a bottle of ibuprofen in her purse. If the baby was in pain or had a fever, maybe she could crush one of the tablets and administer it to her.

Lexi returned from the bedroom with a bottle. It was completely full.

"Fold the blanket in two and spread it on the floor close to the woodstove?" she instructed.

Eager to help, the young girl did what she asked.

"Good job," she complimented her and sat down on the blanket with her back against the rough wall.

Lexi sat down next to her, stroking the baby's head, her fingers back in her mouth.

"Please, drink, Julia," she said as Skyla gently pried the baby's lips apart with the nipple. Holding her breath, Skyla waited for a reaction. Nothing happened, and she only knew the baby was alive due to the slight movement of her chest, her breathing shallow. She squeezed the bottle to force a few drops of milk into her mouth. Without opening her eyes, the baby swallowed.

The door of the cabin opened, and Tom walked in, carrying her purse. She couldn't believe her good fortune. Next to ibuprofen, she also had her cell phone in there. That would be her way out. She opened her purse with one hand, and quickly hid the cell phone beneath the blanket, deciding to use it later. She needed to take care of the infant first.

With the children's help, she crushed one of the red-coated pills on a saucer and dissolved it in water. "This is medicine for Julia," she explained.

Two fat tears rolled down Tom's gaunt face.

"Are you all right?" she asked.

He took a couple of shaking breaths. "Yes, it's just that you're so nice."

She could only imagine how relieved he had to be, to have someone else take over the responsibility for his baby sister. He couldn't be older than ten and shouldn't be in charge in the first place. Instead, he should be playing with toys, hanging out with other boys his age, and going to school, without a care in the world.

Lexi pressed her little fists into her eyes and yawned.

"Maybe you two should go to bed," Skyla suggested. "I've no idea what time it is, but I imagine it's past your bedtime. You both look very tired."

Tom hesitated.

"Don't worry about your sister," Skyla said. "She seems to be doing a little better already. I'll take care of her tonight."

Before following Lexi into the adjacent bedroom, Tom grabbed several pieces of firewood from the pile stacked up against the wall and put them in the stove. It was a task he was probably used to.

Her abductor was still gone, and she had no idea what he could be doing outside at this time of night. Convinced she was in for a rough night, she leaned her head against the rough wallboards of the cabin. Stress took its toll. Exhausted, she closed her eyes.

CHAPTER

7

WITH EVERY SOUND, Skyla expected her kidnapper to walk in, the temptation to pull out her cell phone almost impossible to resist. But she didn't want to take the chance that he strode in while she made a call. He would probably return any second and be enraged. Who knew what he would do besides destroy the only lifeline she had?

It wasn't much later that the door opened and he marched inside. She didn't move from her spot against the wall, pretending to sleep. His footsteps stopped next to her. She felt his stare. Then he sighed, added more wood to the stove and disappeared into the bedroom without saying a word.

She counted the seconds, tensely waiting until she was convinced he'd gone to sleep, before she pulled out her phone. Her hands were cold but sweaty as she dialed 911, the three tiny beeps piercing the silence of the night. She cringed with anxiety as she waited for the connection to establish.

Nothing happened. Her fingers trembled when she redialed two more times, tears of frustration filling her eyes. Damn phone. She had to be out of range. It was a blow she almost couldn't take.

With the phone clutched in her palm, she fell asleep only to wake up about an hour later. She immediately turned it off, to save her phone's battery, and hid it beneath the blanket. At first daylight, she hoped to get the chance to pick up a signal outside.

By the soft glow of a candle, she dripped more milk into the baby's mouth. Throughout the rest of the night, she kept feeding her, her neck muscles and lower back protesting. It was impossible to get comfortable on the hard floorboards, the emergency blanket not thick enough. She constantly shifted position, thinking about the ultra-plush king-sized mattress in her apartment. The salesman had told her the gel-infused memory foam with multiple layers of the softest and most supportive materials helped to relax the body and offered ergonomic support and spine alignment. At the time, it sounded like way more than she needed, and she'd laughed about it. Thinking about it now brought her to tears.

After another hour, the temperature in the room had dropped. She got up to stretch her muscles and added more wood to the stove. The floorboards were freezing below her feet, her thin nylons torn, with several holes. She watched the fire come back to life and closed the stove door.

At the window, she pressed her hand against the glass and stared outside in the pitch-dark night. The heavy silence around her was deafening. She wasn't used to it, the constant noise from street traffic, the humming of her fridge, people talking, or one of the neighbors shuffling through the hallway a comforting part of her life. Unnerved, she sunk down on the blanket, propped her parka underneath her head and tried to sleep.

Sunrise finally crept up and for the first time Skyla could take in her surroundings. The room and furniture were just as dismal as she'd expected, the two single pane windows filthy and lacking curtains, the bare walls rough and unfinished. Through the cracks between the floorboards, she could feel the draft weasel its way inside, the trim around the door missing and letting in even more frigid air. The cabin looked more like an abandoned shack than a home.

"Why are you living under such terrible conditions, Julia?" she whispered. The baby was still breathing, but she'd barely moved all night and seemed to be in the same heartbreaking condition as the night before. It scared her. One of her friends had just given birth, telling her the newborn needed to be fed every three hours. The bottle with milk powder was still half full. It surely couldn't be enough to sustain her.

"You have to drink, sweetie," she whispered, gently touching the baby's lips with the silicone nipple. Julia responded to the slight pressure and Skyla's heart skipped a beat. Was it her imagination or was she trying to drink? "Please, Julia, drink." First nothing happened, but suddenly several tiny air bubbles made their way up through the white liquid. Kissing the baby's smooth forehead, she prayed, "Please Lord, save this child and let her live."

Harsh morning light crept in through the dirty windows. While her abductor still slept, she wanted to go outside with her phone. The sound of movement in the bedroom made her reconsider. It was too risky. Prepared for anything, she stayed put and waited, the muscles of her shoulders so tense that it hurt. A loud fart and deep groan scared her half to death, and when the door opened and her abductor thumped his way in, she coiled up like a rattlesnake.

"You look like shit," he sneered. "Must have been a rough night."

He was dressed in the same clothes, and she assumed he'd slept in them.

He picked up several pieces of firewood. The fire already burned brightly, and he glanced at her over his shoulder. "You're settling in nicely," he said, throwing the wood back on the stack. "I like it."

She had her first good look at him but didn't recognize him at all. *Who was he?*

Yawning, he scratched the back of his head with both hands, his long brown hair a tangled, greasy and unkempt mess. "I'm going to take a leak." A rush of frosty mountain air blew in as he opened the door and walked outside.

Skyla looked down at the baby in her arms. She seemed to sleep; the bottle almost empty. That was a positive sign. She wet her finger in the diluted ibuprofen water and let a drop fall between her tiny lips, hoping she didn't hurt her by doing so.

When her abductor returned a few minutes later, she stood. After protesting for hours, her own bladder needed relief, too. "I need to go," she said. "Is there an outhouse?"

His laughter sounded like a howling hyena. "The great outdoors not good enough for Ms. Overland?"

The bastard! "Oh, no problem," she replied. "Except for the

fact I only have one shoe and hoped the other one might be in your truck."

He pulled a pack of cigarettes from his vest, stuck one between his lips and lit it with a match. A smart remark about secondhand smoke causing health problems in infants and children wouldn't be appreciated. She kept her mouth shut.

"I don't know where it is," he shrugged, blowing smoke in her direction.

Given no other choice than to go outside on one shoe, she donned her parka and opened the door. It was a relief to escape the dank, claustrophobic cabin, and breathe in the crisp morning air. Careful to avoid big rocks, she walked over the frozen, snow covered soil and took in the uneven terrain. Tall grasses and weeds grew everywhere, and low-growing shrubs extended up to the towering evergreens. Above the tree line she spotted the tops of snow-covered mountains in the far distance. The hope of finding a neighboring house, farm, or homestead went up in smoke. She was in the middle of nowhere.

Desperately trying to keep it together, she lowered her pants behind some shrubs, out of sight of the windows of the cabin, and emptied her bladder. Without toilet paper, she had no other choice than to pull up her pants. She felt beyond filthy, but knew that if there wasn't a toilet, there wouldn't be a shower either. She would have to find another way to freshen up.

The freezing cold penetrated her bare foot, and she limped back to the cabin, her elegant T-strap black pumps no match for the rugged terrain. If she made her escape, she needed a good pair of sneakers or hiking boots. But first she needed to figure out her location, to get a rough idea in what direction she had to go to find civilization.

Then she remembered it was Thanksgiving. Would someone miss her already? Probably not. She'd promised to visit her parents for several hours before going to Edmond, but that wouldn't be until one in the afternoon. A torrent of sadness welled up inside her. How she longed to be with her loved ones. How worried they would be when they found out she'd gone missing.

The next moment, she stepped with her bare foot on a sharp rock and fell. "Crap!" She pushed herself up until she sat, rubbing the puncture wound at the bottom of her foot vigorously with both hands. When the pain subsided, she gathered enough courage to struggle back up. No matter what she faced inside the cabin, she intended to live through this ordeal and do whatever it took to survive.

CHAPTER

SKYLA RE-ENTERED THE CABIN, her fingers and toes numb from the cold. Tom and Lexi sat at the table; the boxes of leftovers open in front of them. They looked up with their mouths full, eyes huge in their sunken faces. On the floor, wrapped in her blanket, the baby slept. Their father paced the room, a mug in his hand.

"Julia drank from her bottle this morning," she told the children, grabbing a few crackers. They were soft, but she didn't care. She was hungry and needed to eat.

"I like the eggs with the weird stuff," Lexi said.

"And I like everything," Tom added.

She turned to her abductor. "I don't know who you are or why you picked me to take care of your children," she said in a low voice. "But I'd really like to know how you think I can do that without proper food, a kitchen, or running water."

He slammed his mug on the table, and the children paled.

"Do I look like the kind of guy who can afford to buy them anything?" he roared. "Why do you think I live here in the first place? Do you think I like it? That I want to live like this?"

She watched him put on his coat and head to the door. "I have money."

"That's right," he replied with sarcasm. "Why didn't I think of that? Misses Overland is rich."

"Isn't that the reason I'm here?" she asked. "For ransom or blackmail?"

He narrowed his eyes. "Since you mention it, that might not be a bad idea. Your family cost me dearly, and I deserve payback. Glad you pointed that out."

So, he held a grudge against her and her family. *Was it personal or business?* "Care to explain?"

"No! Figure it out for yourself." He grabbed his baseball cap from a nail in the wall functioning as a coat hook, ready to head out.

His superior, scornful attitude pissed her off. If it wasn't for Julia, she would have stayed silent and let him walk out, but the baby needed formula. "Wait! Please! Go shopping for the baby. You can use my credit card. It's in my purse."

He scoffed. "How do you expect me to pay for anything with your credit card? You think I'm stupid? They'll know right away it ain't mine."

She gave him her most convincing and sincere smile. "I'll make a shopping list. All you have to do is go to a store and show the list to a clerk. Tell them your wife sent you, and they'll believe it."

He hesitated. Going on a shopping spree with her credit card appealed to him, but he didn't trust her.

"It'll be fine," she tried to convince him. "Do you have pen and paper?"

He turned his back and walked out.

Skyla took off her coat and pulled a chair next to the woodstove, to warm her frozen and painful foot. She needed socks and shoes more than anything.

"I have pencils and a coloring book you can use," Lexi said, nibbling on a piece of cheese.

"That would be wonderful, Lexi," she replied.

A few minutes later Skyla sat at the table to make a list around the black outlines of a dragon exhaling a flame. Lexi had started to color it red and orange. She wrote down diapers, baby formula, a toothbrush, toothpaste, and soap when the door banged open. "Your fucking purse is gone! Who's been in my truck?" he yelled like a raging bull.

Her heart contracted and all she could do was stare. "It's here. I asked Tom to get it," she finally managed to say. When he took a threatening step toward his son, she flew up to block his way. "It's not his fault. The baby needed ibuprofen, and I carry a bottle in my purse. She's sick. You know that."

He lowered his arm. "The baby. Ha! Don't give me that bullshit. You were after your cell phone." He laughed without mirth. "I would've loved to see your face when you tried to use it. There's no reception around here for miles." He stuck out his hand. "Give it to me!"

He followed her glance and noticed the cognac colored leather purse on the floor, next to the baby. With a triumphant smirk, he yanked it up by the shoulder strap and turned it upside down above the table. The entire contents came tumbling out and several items landed on the floor, including her lip balm, sunglasses, and mascara. He searched through the items, glaring at her when he noticed the phone was missing. "Just what I thought! Where is it?"

She didn't answer. She refused to offer it on a silver platter.

He grabbed her coat and searched the pockets, pulling out a handkerchief, a few dollar bills, her gloves, and a fleece ear warmer headband. After that he jerked at the emergency blanket, taking his semi-unconscious infant daughter with it.

Too shocked to speak at his crude behavior, her jaw dropped. Didn't that bastard care about his children at all? How could he behave like such a brute? She jumped into action to protect the child and picked her up just before the blanket sailed across the room, revealing her cell phone.

"I knew it!" he sneered, trying to crush the phone beneath the heel of his worn work boots. Skyla gloated secretly when nothing happened, the tempered glass screen protector holding its own, until she noticed the two terrified children. They stood frozen in place, hugging each other. It broke her heart.

Bellowing curses, her captor grabbed the hand ax next to the stove and smashed the sharp edge right into the face of the phone. After a few more strikes, it broke in two. That was the end of that.

Barely able to breathe, Skyla wondered what he would do next. The man was insane, his ruthlessly erratic behavior beyond comprehension. How would she ever survive this ordeal?

He moved to the table and grabbed her wallet with his filthy, calloused hand, dirt caked beneath his long nails, yellow nicotine stains on several of his fingers. "You done with the list yet?"

"Almost," she said, sitting down with the baby in her lap. After adding a few more items, she tore it from the coloring book and handed it to him. "You can use the cash in my wallet to buy gas and the Visa card for other purchases. The limit on the card is $6,000. Be my guest."

"If it wasn't for the baby, I wouldn't even consider it," he said, glaring at her with suspicion. "You understand?" Her wallet disappeared in the front pocket of his quilt-lined Carhartt duck coat.

"Of course," she replied.

On his way out, he grabbed her by the back of her neck and pulled her from her seat. He held her so close to his face, that she could see the pores in his crooked nose. "If I come home and don't find you here, you'll regret it for the rest of your life, because I'll blame the children for your disappearance and punish them for it. I'm sure you don't want that on your conscience, seeing as how much you already care about the little runt." He let go of her so abruptly, she fell back onto the chair. The baby whimpered in her arms. It was the first time she'd heard her make a sound, and she immediately loosened her tight grip.

After he walked out, she slumped forward, with her head on the table, waiting for the shaking to stop. He scared the hell out of her, and it took her a few minutes to compose herself.

In the taut silence, an engine came to life, roaring loudly. She got up and walked to the window to peek outside. Tom and Lexi joined her, just in time to see his lifted beat-up pickup truck bounce through the potholes down the dirt road away from the cabin. Together, they watched the taillights disappear through a small opening in the trees.

Resentment for the man rose in her throat, and she swallowed hard to stifle her cry of rage. Everything around her was complete chaos, her life turned upside down, the horrifying situation making her feel hollow and terrified.

She stared at the hostile landscape outside long after the truck was gone. She wanted to scream, put her coat on, and run as fast as she could. Back to freedom.

CHAPTER

9

"WHAT WAS THAT my dad broke?" Tom asked, pulling Skyla's attention away from the window.

She looked at him with an attempt to hide her feelings. She didn't want him to know how outraged she was. The children were defenseless victims, their childhood a living hell, and their father deranged. She couldn't take her frustration out on them.

A single tear escaped from her eye, and she brushed it away. "My cell phone," she explained.

From the questioning look on his face, she realized he had no idea what she was talking about. It made her wonder how long the family had lived here. "It's a device you can use to talk to people far away. But it's broken now. We might as well throw it away."

Still trying to recover from the horrific scene and losing her phone, she sat down next to Tom. He had gathered the pieces.

They lay spread out over the table and he studied them with interest.

Lexi sat on the floor next to the woodstove, feeding Julia. "The bottle is almost empty," she said.

Both children looked pitiful, their blond hair unkempt, their faces dirty, and their clothes no more than rags. They needed her help and protection. Not her wrath.

"Where do you get your water?" she asked.

"From the stream out back," Tom explained. "But we boil it first. Mom told us if we don't do that, it could make us sick because it can carry diseases from dead stuff upstream."

Relieved she hadn't fed the baby contaminated water, she looked at the woodstove. It had to weigh a ton, and she had no idea how they could have gotten it inside. It was wider than the door and produced a tremendous amount of heat. On the floor next to the stove stood two heavy black cast-iron pots, one smaller than the other. "Did your mother use the woodstove to cook?"

"Mommy always made us yummy pancakes." Lexi grinned, letting her tongue slide over her upper lip.

"I love pancakes, too," Tom agreed

Skyla yawned, the weight of everything that had happened pressing down on her, but pancakes for lunch sounded good. Exhausted, she forced herself up on her feet and opened the doors of the cupboard to check the contents. A percolator to make coffee, a teakettle, two frying pans, a stack of chipped plates and bowls, and a tray with silverware, among several plastic and metal cups. It wasn't much. She also noticed bags of sugar, oatmeal, and rice, and a carton of elbow-style noodles, almost all empty. Was that what the children had survived on?

If so, the boxes of leftover food from the Thanksgiving party must have been a godsend.

"Do you think Julia will get better?" Lexi asked, tucking her two fingers back into her mouth. Skyla guessed she had to be about seven. A bit old to still suck on her fingers, but since it seemed to soothe her, she wasn't going to deny her the comfort.

"I honestly don't know, honey," she answered, filling up the small cast-iron pots with water. She'd found a threadbare rag and wanted to use it to freshen up. "I don't have a baby of my own and don't know much about them, but I'll do whatever I can to help her. How long has she been sick? Do you remember?"

Lexi shrugged, glancing at Tom for help.

Skyla wondered if the children had any concept of time. If not, asking how long they'd lived here might be futile. "Do you know how old you are?" she asked instead.

When Lexi shook her head, Skyla wondered if they'd ever attended school. "Did your mom and dad teach you how to read or write?"

"Our mom used to tell us stories," Tom answered instead of Lexi. He remained engrossed in the cell phone parts.

"Did you ever go to school, Tom?"

"I was in kindergarten once," he answered. "I remember they taught us the days of the week, and they had a huge sandbox."

Skyla's heart ached for him. Wasn't anybody keeping track if children attended school, or could they just drop out of sight without being noticed? That shouldn't be possible this day and age.

Waiting for the water to warm, she allowed herself for the first time to think of Troy. As a single parent of two boys, his mother had worked two jobs to pay the bills, and they still often had to go without. Helping children who grew up under similar or worse circumstances had become one of Troy's passions. He talked about it often, and she knew it would shock him to see Tom, Lexi, and Julia, so malnourished and shabbily dressed, their eyes filled with fear and sorrow.

"The water is boiling, Skyla," Tom said, bringing her back to the harsh reality.

She added some cold water from the bucket to cool it off and freshened up. The wound on her forehead started to bleed. There wasn't a single Band-Aid in the house, and all she could do to stop it was to press her handkerchief against it. She also didn't find flour, making pancakes out of the question.

"There's enough food left in the boxes," Tom said, trying to cheer her up.

As young as he was, he'd picked up on her sour mood. "You're right," she said, pulling herself together.

With the baby in her lap, Skyla sat at the table, deep in thought, a fresh bottle of powdered milk in her hand. She guessed her abductor had left about three or four hours ago.

"Is your father always gone for so long, Tom?" she asked.

"He's usually gone all day, but sometimes two or three," Tom said.

"That must be difficult for you," she said, thinking she couldn't care less if he dropped dead along the way, but she assumed the longer he stayed away, the more remotely they lived. That idea didn't sit well with her.

"It's okay," Tom said. "He only leaves to get food."

Julia made a sputtering sound and squirmed a little. Skyla quickly looked down at the child. Was she waking up?

"She sometimes does that," Lexi said. The girl stood next to her, staring blankly, as if she was in her own little zone.

Skyla longed to hug her, to wipe the heart-rending expression off her cute little face. "I think Julia might feel a little better," she said.

Lexi moved in a little closer and stroked the baby's cheek, her bottom lip quivering. "Go on, drink," she whispered.

Skyla returned to the previous conversation. "Do you know where we are, Tom?"

He munched on another piece of toast, most of the food beginning to spoil in the warm cabin. "We live in the Clifford Forest," he said. "Mom told us they named it after a big red dog. We have a book about him."

Skyla's heart sank. She'd never heard of a forest with that name.

"Can you show me the book about the big dog?"

He disappeared into the bedroom and returned with the tattered copy.

The three of them cuddled on the blanket on the floor. With a child on each side, and the baby sleeping peacefully in her lap, Skyla read the story of Clifford, the huge red dog, who saved a house from a storm by lying in front of it to protect it from the waves of the ocean.

"The end," Skyla said after she finished.

"That's the letter C," Tom said, pointing at the first letter of Clifford's name.

"That's right," she replied. "You know what? Since I'm

here, I'll teach both of you a few letters." She pointed to the second letter. "The first one is the C, and this is the L. Can you repeat that?"

As the children practiced writing the letters C and L with their finger in the air, Skyla realized it had to be late afternoon. Her parents would be worried, trying to call. When they failed to reach her, they would first get ahold of Edmond and then Pauline, perhaps even drive over to her apartment. After that, it wouldn't take long before they'd call the police. Her ordeal would be over soon. Real soon.

CHAPTER

10

"COME ON, SKYLA. Why aren't you picking up?" Harold Overland muttered when her cell phone went straight to voicemail for the third time. "Clara, didn't you say Skyla planned to be here at three?" he called to his wife, who was in the kitchen cleaning Brussel sprouts.

Drying her hands on a kitchen towel, Clara walked into the living room. "Yes, Skyla planned to be here no later than that, but probably earlier, Harold," she replied. "She's expected at Edmond's house around four and wanted to finish the fruit salad before going over."

Harold looked at the clock, a worried frown creasing his forehead. "It's already three-thirty. Don't you think it's strange she isn't here yet?" He lounged in his recliner, the Insurance Journal Magazine in his lap.

"Don't worry," Clara said, laughing off his concern. "She may have changed plans at the last moment."

"It's not like her to change plans without telling us, especially not on Thanksgiving," he disagreed.

"She's not a teenager any longer, Harold, and she's in love. Things change. Don't forget that," Clara said.

Harold knew his wife well enough to know she wasn't as convinced as she pretended to be. Skyla was punctual and always kept them informed. They were a tight-knit family, their relationships built on love, trust, and mutual respect.

Noise from the kitchen announced the arrival of his other daughter Taylor, her husband, and their two young children. He put his phone and magazine on the side-table next to his chair and stood to welcome them. The quiet house immediately filled with laughter and excited voices. Taylor's boys were one and three years old, and a handful. Nothing would be safe for the next four hours.

"It smells so wonderful here," he heard his son-in-law remark. The turkey had already been in the oven for several hours and the signature scent, mixed with the delicious aroma of cinnamon and fresh baked apple pie, filled the house.

His youngest grandson reached out to him. Taylor looked overloaded with two children and a backpack filled with diapers and other items the children required. Her husband carried a casserole and placed it with obvious pride on the kitchen counter. "This year, I made the Holy Casserole and gave it a Mexican twist by adding roasted green chili salsa, kidney beans, corn, and cilantro."

Harold hated beans and cilantro but kept his opinion to himself. He could work his way through several bites.

After the adults settled in the family room, the kids playing with their Duplo blocks at their feet, Taylor looked around. "Wasn't Skyla supposed to be here?"

Nearly four o'clock now, Harold couldn't ignore the inkling that something wasn't right. Taylor immediately agreed.

"Skyla always answers her phone!" Taylor pulled out her cell phone and tried three times to call her sister. Each time it went straight to voicemail. "Either she turned off her phone, her battery died, or she's out of cell phone reach. None of that makes sense. Something's up."

"Or she's on her way," Harold suggested, trying to sound unconcerned. "Doesn't she have a new feature on her phone that automatically goes to 'do not disturb' when she's driving?"

"I hope you're right," Taylor said. "Otherwise, I may not get to see her at all since she's having dinner at Edmond's."

"She may already be at Edmond's. You know how young lovers can be," Clara added. She got up from her chair. "It's time to put the rolls in the oven."

Trying not to worry, the adults busied themselves with pouring drinks, nibbling on a few appetizers, keeping the children out of trouble, and setting the festive table when Harold's cell phone rang.

"That must be her," Harold said and hurried to retrieve his phone from the side table.

"Mr. Overland? This is Edmond. Is Skyla still at your house? We're ready to start dinner in a few minutes, and she hasn't arrived yet."

Harold felt as if a sledgehammer had hit him in the stomach.

"No, she's not here," he answered, trying to catch his breath. "We've tried to call her multiple times. When she didn't answer, we assumed she'd changed her plans and might already be with you."

"No, she planned to be at your house first before coming over. I haven't heard from her, and I'm surprised she's not here yet," Edmond answered.

"That's exactly what she told us, but she never arrived," Harold said. "I don't understand. Where could she be?"

A tense silence fell until Harold sighed heavily. "Something's definitely wrong."

"Maybe you should drive to her apartment," Edmond suggested after another pause. "I can't leave here. We have family over from New Zealand."

Harold Overland stiffened. Were those family members more important to him than Skyla?

"Yes, I will," he replied tersely, and disconnected.

"What did he say?" Taylor asked from the edge of her seat, her back straight.

"She didn't show up at Edmond's house either," he said, his voice clipped. "Why don't you start dinner without me? I'm driving to her apartment."

"Take her spare keys so you can get in," Clara said, her eyes worried. "They're on the hook in the hallway closet."

In twenty minutes, Harold pulled into the parking lot of a three-story apartment building. Skyla rented a spacious two-bedroom unit on the third floor together with her best friend, Pauline, splitting the expenses.

He looked around the parking lot for Skyla's Jeep. It wasn't there. Too impatient to wait for the elevator, he took the stairs to the third floor and banged on her door. When nothing happened, he let himself in.

He stood in the middle of the sparkling clean living room. It smelled like a lemony cleaner and bleach, and it was cool, the thermostat set on low. That wasn't unusual. It had automatic settings and Thursday was normally a workday, so the heat pump wouldn't kick in until five. He also knew Skyla didn't like clutter, although even to her high standards, the apartment was spotless.

Horrible images of someone cleaning up blood after committing murder whirled in his mind. He'd seen enough forensic investigation shows to know not to touch anything, to prevent contaminating a potential crime scene.

His heart banged rapidly in his chest and perspiration beaded on his forehead as he checked her bedroom. The bed was made and the bathroom unused. Pauline's bedroom was empty, too.

He raked his fingers through his short gray hair. Had anyone been here this afternoon, this morning, last night? Had she come home at all? And where was Pauline? Did they go somewhere together?

Against the wall below the bedroom window stood a wooden desk. He settled into the uncomfortable plywood desk chair, convinced nobody could sit in it for more than five minutes without getting a backache. He shook his head, his own leather office chair comfortable enough to sleep in. But he knew better than to argue with her. She was from a different generation, fascinated by non-GMO, vegan, gluten, and everything green.

He opened Skyla's laptop. It wasn't password protected, and he clicked on her calendar app. All it said on today's date was "Thanksgiving".

Next, he opened her Gmail account, clicked on her contacts for Pauline's number, and called her with his cell phone.

While waiting for her to answer, he gazed at the framed picture on Skyla's desk. It was from him and his wife, taken while they were on a cruise in Alaska the previous year, their hair windswept, and behind them a massive bluish glacier.

After five rings, Pauline finally picked up. "Hello?" Her voice sounded aloof.

"This is Mr. Overland," he said, drawing swirlies on a yellow pad with a pencil. "Is this you, Pauline?"

"Oh, yes, sorry, Mr. Overland," she replied. "I didn't recognize the number. Is everything all right?"

"Skyla didn't show up at our house today. Edmond hasn't seen her, either. We tried to call her numerous times, but she didn't answer. Do you have any idea where she might be?"

"I don't know, Mr. Overland," Pauline replied. "I tried to call her last night. When she didn't answer, I assumed she might be in the shower or that she'd gone to bed already."

"Last night?" He pushed down so hard on the pencil in his hand that the tip broke. "That's not good."

Pauline told him what he already knew about Skyla's plans for the holiday. "Why don't you go over to our apartment?" she suggested. "I'm in Seattle and won't be back until Sunday."

"I'm in her bedroom, sitting at her desk. Nothing seems out of the ordinary, but her car is gone, and from what you're telling me, it looks like she didn't sleep here last night. Please call me if anything comes to mind. I'm very worried."

Overwhelmed by a sense of foreboding, he disconnected and called his wife.

Clara picked up right away.

"Oh, no," she cried out. "Something must be wrong, Harold. This isn't like her at all."

He heard the alarm in her voice and knew she was close to tears. "I agree. I'll call the police right away."

CHAPTER

11

SKYLA BATTLED MOOD SWINGS. One moment she was desperate and choking up, the next she felt confident the perilous situation would end soon, with her family looking for her, aided by the police. It was already dark, and twenty-four hours since her abduction. Recalling the frightful event, she shivered. Had he really driven her car into that pond? It was only a few years old and in excellent condition.

The loud noise of a truck's engine and tires crunching on gravel shook her out of her dark mood. Why had it taken him so long to get back?

Tom rushed to open the door. "What did you get us, Dad?"

"Lots of good stuff, son," he grinned, carrying in two large brown bags.

He was bigger and uglier than she remembered, and she broke out in a cold sweat.

"What are you gawking at?' he growled with malice in his

pig-like eyes. "You could be a bit more cheerful." He dumped the bags with a loud thud on the table, right in front of her.

All she wanted to do was hide.

"You need help, Dad?" Tom asked.

"Yes, why don't you give me a hand. There's a lot more stuff in the back of the pickup. Grab what you can, but make sure you don't drop anything. It's a sodden mess out there."

Skyla took a deep breath to steel her nerves and opened the first bag. Two big cans of baby formula. She pulled them out, to read the label. Brain building, with probiotics and iron. That sounded much better than instant nonfat dry milk.

"There's a measuring scoop inside," Lexi told her. Together they prepared a bottle of formula with lukewarm water and shook it several times until the powder was dissolved. Hopefully, the formula would provide the nutrients the baby needed and help her recover.

Tom and his father walked in and out of the cabin until the table was full.

"I bought new sleeping bags and pillows for everybody," her captor said, throwing them on the floor. He disappeared into the bedroom and returned with a pile of disgusting looking blankets, the sour smell nauseating. "These are for you," he said and threw the pile at Skyla's feet. His eyes glittered with malice.

Skyla shot him a look filled with disgust.

Her reaction brought a satisfied grin on his face. "No? Okay, suit yourself, but if you change your mind, they're in the shed."

Relief washed over her. She would rather sleep on the barren wooden floor than cover herself with those filthy blankets. The sadist!

"Skyla, look at all that food!" Lexi shrieked in delight.

He'd bought an enormous amount of supplies and it must have cost her a lot of money, she thought. But she couldn't care less. It was a small price to pay to see a little happiness in this atrocious place. The fact she had formula for Julia was an even greater relief.

Her abductor returned and dropped a sleeping bag and a pillow on the floor. "These are for you," he said.

Skyla touched the warm thick fabric and couldn't help but feel grateful. She was dead tired, and longed to lie down and close her eyes, to forget her sorrow and fear, if only for a few hours.

"Thank you," she said.

Tom and Lexi peeked in all the bags, squealing with excitement.

"Opportunity came knocking on my door. I decided not to ignore it," her kidnapper said, winking. "Tom, Lexi, I bought you happy meals from McDonalds."

"McDonald?" Tom asked, uncomprehending, but as soon as he smelled the food, he opened one of the colorful bags and pulled out a cheeseburger, a small carton of fries, and a toy wrapped in plastic.

These kids have missed so much in their lives and deserve so much more, Skyla thought, squeezing her tired eyes shut to keep from crying.

Something hit her right leg and she looked up. Her abductor towered over her like a terrifying grizzly bear. "I picked you up a burger, too," he said.

She picked it up, noticing it was cold.

"You better eat it, because this is dinner."

The moment he came home, she'd lost her appetite, her stomach one giant knot. "Sorry, I'm not hungry," she replied.

"Fine, more for me," he snickered and snatched it out of her hand.

Ignoring him, she shifted her attention to the baby in her arms. To her surprise, the bottle with formula was half empty.

"Good girl," she whispered and kissed her softly on her forehead before positioning her against her shoulder.

"Are you letting her burp?" Lexi asked.

Skyla smiled. She'd done it without thinking and wondered if her maternal instinct had taken over.

After all the burgers and fries were gone, her abductor pushed back his chair and stood. "I'm leaving," he said. "Don't forget the woodstove, Tom."

The moment the door slammed closed behind him, the atmosphere in the cabin improved. She could breathe again.

"Are you excited to sleep in your new sleeping bags?" she asked.

Emotionally drained, she wished them goodnight, snuggled with the baby in her own sleeping bag, and wept.

During the night, she woke up several times, her heart squeezed in a recurring nightmare about missing shoes, piles of snow, emaciated children, dirty clothes, and her desperate family searching for her. They would be frantic by now.

And Troy. What would he say if they saw each other again? He'd run off so fast in the parking lot. Did he regret kissing her? Or would he do it again? She let her fingertips trail over her lips, the sizzling electricity coursing through her at the memory of his kiss startling.

Heavy footsteps outside made her squirm in fear. Just like the night before, her abductor had been gone for several hours and came back home, with a lot of noise.

She made herself as small as possible, her heart pounding with adrenaline as her survival instinct kicked in.

When it all got quiet again, she fed Julia, added a few pieces of wood to the smoldering red coals in the stove, and tried to fall back asleep, only to awaken a few hours later.

The baby fussed a little and moved her arms. Groggy and stiff-limbed, she prepared another bottle and dozed off, until someone kicked her in the ribs.

"Fix me some breakfast, woman," the hated voice growled.

Tempted to refuse outright, she thought of the children. He was quick to anger. Afraid of what he might do if crossed or challenged, she kept her mouth shut and forced herself up.

He sat down at the table and watched her rifle through the bags.

"How about pancakes?" she asked, pulling out two big bags of waffle and pancake mix.

"I wouldn't mind having a piece of that," he said.

She turned around to look at him, her suit pants hugging closely around her hips. There was no mistaking his interest, and her blood turned to ice. She quickly donned her blue blazer to block his view.

He chortled. "You're a beautiful woman, Skyla, and I like watching you."

It would be impossible to avoid him in the close confines of the cabin. She had to make sure not to draw too much attention to herself and considered this a warning.

With the frying pan in her hand, she studied the

woodstove. She'd never cooked on one before. Not even on an outdoor grill or barbeque. As a true city girl, it hadn't been part of her life; her vacations spent in luxury resorts, hotels, or B&B's.

"I'm not much of a cook," she said. "But I'll try."

She took out a bowl, added flower and water, and stirred. Next, she put the frying pan on the stove, added olive oil, and poured in the batter.

Tom and Lexi appeared in the doorway, rubbing the sleep from their eyes. "Help your mother, Lexi," her captor ordered. "She clearly doesn't know what she's doing."

If he hoped to get a reaction, he would be disappointed. So far, it had gone remarkably well, and the first three pancakes looked perfect. It gave her a little sense of control. "Give me a plate, guys. Breakfast is ready."

After breakfast, her abductor walked out, leaving them to clean up. Lexi and Tom did the dishes, and Skyla prepared a bottle. When she bent over to pick Julia up, she noticed she looked at her with curiosity.

"Hi, Julia," she smiled, the words exhaled from her mouth in relief. "I'm Skyla. How are you?"

She lifted her up in her arms and carried her to the children.

"You saved her!" they both cheered, their eyes shining with gratitude.

If she'd made a difference, she didn't know, but seeing the baby alert lifted her spirits. She sat down at the table to feed her, and the baby sucked vigorously, her fingers wrapped around Skyla's thumb. A rush of affection overwhelmed her.

What a precious little girl. So sweet, so innocent. It didn't take long before the bottle was empty, and she lay her down on the sleeping bag next to the stove.

"Let's organize all the supplies," she said, spreading out the canned food. He'd bought bags of potatoes, onions, and beans, jars of peanut butter, and grape and strawberry jelly. There were also two bags of oatmeal, loaves of bread, several cans of coffee, sugar, walnuts, salt, pepper, and cinnamon, and more milk powder. Enough to last them for weeks.

With the baby doing better and Tom and Lexi playing on the floor, Skyla walked into the bedroom. She hadn't had the courage earlier, the sour stench coming from the room too horrendous. But with the nasty bedding gone, it was slightly better - either that or she was getting used to it.

She looked around in the dark room. Someone had nailed a heavy blanket to the wall, to cover the window, blocking all light. Other than that, the room only contained a king-size bed the family shared and a rickety chest with six drawers. Clothes spilled out of the drawers and dust hung heavily in the air. She pinched her nose to keep from sneezing. How could they live under such primitive conditions? It wasn't anything better than in the early eighteen-hundreds, when the settlers first arrived in this part of the country. They participated in the fur trade, and claimed land to farm in the fertile Willamette Valley, living off the land by growing their own food and hunting for game. They'd done it without electricity and running water. It had to have been just like this.

She pulled out some of the unfolded, wrinkled, and dirty clothes. There were several dresses that must have belonged to his wife, and a pair of sneakers that had seen better days. Most of the clothes belonged in the trash.

Since her abductor seemed quite at home spending her money, she decided to start another shopping list, adding candles, writing tablets, pens, crayons, children's books, lots of winter clothes, and the toiletries he'd conveniently forgotten.

Despite the steady rain and intermittent wet snow, her abductor stayed busy all morning with a chainsaw, cutting a dead tree in slabs, and swinging an axe to cut firewood.

As soon as he walked in later that morning, a lighted cigarette hanging from his lips, Skyla presented him her list.

"We'll see," was all he said. He pulled a percolator from the cupboard. "Now, it's time for coffee."

He impatiently tapped his foot against the floorboards while she followed his instructions on how to use the percolator. He liked it pitch black with sugar. After it perked for fifteen minutes, he poured himself a mug and lit another cigarette. Her look of disapproval only generated a conceited smirk.

They all sighed in relief when he walked out, only to come back an hour later. "Ever cleaned a hare before?" He pulled a dead animal from a burlap bag by its ears and smacked it on the table. A hideous grin split his face, showing several missing teeth. "Finally, one of my traps paid off."

"Oh my God," Skyla shrieked "What's that?"

"Fresh meat," he replied. "How about a stew tonight with onions and beans?"

"I don't know how to clean a dead animal," she protested weakly. Her stomach churned at the prospect of having to eat rabbit, and the beans were another type of food she disliked.

Tom walked over to the table. "Dad's a great trapper," he

said.

The pride on the boy's face broke her heart. What would he think when he discovered his father was a criminal, and that poaching animals was illegal?

CHAPTER

12

HAROLD OVERLAND spent the night tossing and turning, wondering why he'd let Edmond convince him not to call the police. Yes, Skyla had moved out of the house six years ago, she was an independent, strong woman, and sometimes took off unexpectedly for a fun weekend at the coast or to get pampered at their favorite hot springs resort, but it didn't sit well with him. It was Thanksgiving, and she wouldn't pack up and leave without telling her family. What if she'd had an accident and was stuck in her car somewhere? What if she was in serious trouble, and he could have prevented something terrible from happening to her? The *what-ifs* drove him crazy.

At four in the morning, he couldn't take it any longer and went downstairs. Would it be possible that Edmond was hiding something? Did they have a fight, and did he know more than he let on? He'd seemed preoccupied and evasive.

His wife joined him in the kitchen, frazzled and tired. She

made coffee and after drinking a cup, he grabbed his car keys. "I need to find out if she's home, Clara," he said, hugging her tight before he left.

At six, he stood in Skyla's apartment, finding it just as he'd left it the day before. Without hesitation, he called 911. "I would like to report a missing person at the Rosehurst Apartment complex on Multnomah Street, apartment thirty-three. Could you send someone over?"

It didn't take long before two police officers showed up. One of them looked haggard, with bags under his eyes, his complexion greyish. The other one was an obvious rookie, messing with the straps of his first response vest.

"I'm officer Kirk. This is officer McKinney," the older man said. "You called about a missing person?"

Harold took a step back to let them enter. "It's my daughter. This is her apartment, and I realize everything seems to be in order, but I know for certain something is wrong."

"The police are hesitant to consider a person missing until they're gone for twenty-four hours," Officer Kern said in a stern voice. "How old is your daughter?'

"Twenty-six."

The officer put away his notebook, suppressing an annoyed sigh. "She's an adult, Sir, and adults often leave for periods of time without informing anyone."

Harold raked his hand through his hair. "She's missing since Wednesday afternoon. That's well over twenty-four hours. Besides, I know my daughter. She would never skip Thanksgiving dinner without telling us."

Shrugging, the officer made his way back to the door, the

rookie right behind him. "What if we had to track down every adult who hasn't been seen in twenty-four hours? What do you think our job would look like then?"

Harold's anger flared, and he nearly grabbed the indifferent man by the arm to stop him. "Please, don't leave," he gritted between his teeth. "You have to believe that I would never get the police involved if there was any doubt in my mind that something wasn't seriously wrong."

"All right," the man replied wearily. "Since I'm here anyway, I might as well write down her information." His notebook reappeared, and so did his pen.

Harold sighed in relief and invited the officers to sit down at the dining table.

"What's her full name? Has she been in trouble with the law? Any known drug use? Boyfriend trouble? When did you see her last?"

He told them about the Thanksgiving get-together at the office, about Pauline who'd tried to call her, and about Troy helping her with the cleanup.

"Who's Troy?" the officer demanded, suddenly alert.

"Troy Summerton is our office manager," Harold replied. It was only seven in the morning, but he didn't think Troy would mind if he called him this early, and on his day off. He knew how much he cared for his daughter.

After only two rings, Troy answered. "What's going on, Harold?" he asked, his voice thick with sleep.

"Sorry to wake you so early," Harold said. "But no one has seen Skyla since Wednesday and we can't get ahold of her. I have the horrible feeling that something is wrong and hoped you could provide any details about Wednesday evening."

He heard the sharp intake of breath and the rustling of sheets. "She's not home?"

"I'm calling from her apartment. I'm here with two police officers. We were wondering if you could tell us what time she left the office after the party, and where she might have gone."

There was a moment of silence on the other end of the line. "Sorry, I don't understand. Are you trying to tell me Skyla is missing, and that you called the police?"

Harold sighed, massaging his forehead as he spoke. "Yes, I guess I am."

"Give me five minutes," Troy said. "I'm coming over right away."

Harold let his arms fall next to his sides, deeply concerned about his daughter's wellbeing.

"I believe he hung up the phone. That's suspicious," the burned-out police officer said to the rookie, his implication clear.

"He didn't hang up," Harold replied, irritated by the superior tone of his monotonous voice. "He doesn't live far and should be here soon."

Troy threw on some clothes and rushed out the door. Skyla was missing. Skyla was *missing*. It was all he could think about. Buttoning his shirt, he ran out the front door and over the pebbled walk to his car parked in front of the garage. He'd bought his modest home several years ago with the hopes of having a family at some point. It only needed a few upgrades, including an additional bathroom. Other than that, the house was perfect for him, the garage huge, giving him enough room for his motorcycle and the classic sixties muscle car that had belonged to his father.

Frustrated with the heavy traffic, Troy suppressed the urge to honk his horn. It was much busier than he'd expected. When he passed the local department store and saw the over-crowded parking lot, he realized why. Black Friday brought people out in droves, to take advantage of the sales put on by all retailers.

By the time he pulled into the parking lot of Skyla's apartment building, he was beside himself. He'd kissed her, taking her by surprise, and then he'd run off, leaving her by herself. What could have happened? Was he to blame? He raked his fingers through his already disheveled hair. He should've never left her alone, without any regard for her safety. Taking his mother to the airport was no excuse to hurry off. But he was honest enough to acknowledge that hadn't been the real reason he'd left with his tail between his legs. He'd felt like a fool, and wanted to get away, afraid of how she might react or what she might say.

He took the stairs two at the time and knocked on the door. Harold opened and they grabbed each other by the arms. "I can't believe this," Troy said.

The two police officers sat at Skyla's dining table. One twiddling his thumbs, his eyes cast down. The other flipped through a notepad. "You must be the office manager, Troy Summerton?"

Troy's eyes instinctively searched for Skyla before sitting down. "I am."

"From what we gather, you might be the last person to see her, Mr. Summerton," officer Kern said. "Can you tell us more about that day, what time she left, and where she went?"

Troy couldn't tell them much, realizing it didn't look good for him. To not make matters worse, especially with Harold listening in, he left out the awkward kiss. It was none of their business.

"Do you remember what she was wearing?" was the officer's next question.

Troy remembered exactly how beautiful and professional she'd looked at the Thanksgiving party. "She was wearing her blue blazer and matching dress pants, a white V-neck button-down shirt, and her black pumps with tiny straps. And she put on her red parka before we walked outside." He realized they might find his detailed account suspicious, but didn't care. Unlike the kiss, this was important information and could help them find her.

The officers finished their questioning, took his name and cell phone number, and promised to be in touch.

Harold closed the door behind them. "Couldn't they have sent two smart guys instead of those uninterested pig heads," he burst out. "All they did was take notes and sit around, barely looking around the apartment."

"I believe one of them is on his way in the door, and the other one out," Troy commented. "We should contact their superior." He walked around the apartment, feeling like he invaded Skyla's privacy. His hand trailed over the kitchen counter where he'd seen her make apple-cinnamon margaritas last Christmas. The mixture had tasted horrible, and she couldn't stop laughing at the look of disgust on his face. He smiled at the memory, almost tasting the salt on the rim of the glass and the sugary flavor of the apples.

Harold paced the floor, his shoulders hunched. "What can we do?" he sighed, his words half question, half frustration.

"I think you should go home and try to get some sleep. You're in no condition to be of help. While you get some rest, I'll call around to local hospitals to find out if they admitted a Jane Doe. Maybe she was in an accident, is unconscious, and they don't know who to contact."

Harold's eyes lit up. "Why didn't I think of that? Thanks, Troy, I will. Just promise to call me the minute you find anything out."

They both left Skyla's apartment. But instead of going home, Troy drove to the office. He could think more clearly behind his desk, with a computer right in front of him and a landline at his disposal.

He pulled into the parking lot, hoping to find Skyla's car. It wasn't there. He parked where he'd last seen her and relived their kiss, as he'd done many times over the last thirty-six hours. Each time he remembered it differently, the only thing not changing was how his heart had raced when he felt her warm lips against his. Once she returned home, he would do everything in his power to win her heart. Something he should have done already years ago. Sorry Edmond, you're not the right man for her.

He stepped out and shivered in his dress shirt. It had rained non-stop for three days straight, the wind gusting from the west, the temperatures in the low thirties. Where could she have gone in this horrible weather?

He unlocked the front door, turned off the alarm. On any normal workday, there was a lot of activity, but since the office was closed, he was the only one there. His footsteps echoed in the empty hall, and it was cold, the thermostat set at low.

In his office, he donned the light grey cable sweater he kept on a hanger behind the door and sat down at his L-shaped desk. It was devoid of the usual family photos most people displayed. He only had his mother and older brother, no pets, and didn't care for knickknacks.

While the computer booted up, he made coffee in the break room. He needed the caffeine, his mind slogged with memories and regrets.

Two hours later, Troy had checked the security footage of the parking lot. The employee parking was at the far end of the lot and all he could see was her car driving off seven minutes after him. Everything must have been okay at that point. He'd also talked to administrative assistants at different hospitals, two clinics, and several medical groups. Not a single one was allowed to give him personal information and not one had admitted a Jane Doe over the last two days. He'd left his contact information with the hope to get a call if they did. It was frustrating and discouraging.

He paced back and forth across the carpet. Skyla had disappeared. *Where was she? What had happened to her?* He took a few aspirins to stave off the tension headache at the base of his neck. He hadn't eaten yet but wasn't hungry, the third cup of coffee making him jittery.

Agitated, he sank down behind the computer and called Skyla's number, hoping that by some miracle she was safely back in her apartment. That he'd worried over nothing. It went straight to voicemail. His fingers drummed impatiently on his desk. Could the police trace her phone?

He heaved a sigh. The hands of the clock on the wall didn't move. Time seemed to stand still. He hoped Harold had gone to bed and didn't want to call him. He'd looked sick with worry, the lines on his face more pronounced.

Instead of calling Harold, he called his wife. Clara Overland immediately answered her cell phone. "Hi, Troy," she said. "Did you find anything?"

"No, I'm sorry." He rubbed the back of his neck with one hand to relieve the tension. "How about you?"

"I called everyone I could think of. No one knows anything," she replied. He could tell she was ready to burst into tears. "Pauline is calling around, too. So is Edmond. We just don't know what else to do!"

His heart twisted, his emotions matching her desperation. "I thought about making flyers, to get her face in the public eye and make sure everyone is aware she's missing."

"Harold is taking a shower," she replied, her voice a little more hopeful. "I'll tell him you called. Thanks, Troy. That's a great idea."

One dead end after another.

Within ten minutes, Harold called and came straight to the point. "I assume you had no luck with the local hospitals?"

"No, I didn't," Troy replied. "Were you able to sleep a little?"

"Yes, for about three hours. Now, we're having something to eat. Clara mentioned you want to make a missing person's poster. We talked about that, too. Pauline and Taylor are posting on Facebook and other social media sites. It might be a good start. Shall we meet at the office?"

Troy didn't have a Facebook account, but he had Instagram and agreed using social media as another venue to reach out to the public was a great idea. "I'm already here," he said.

After disconnecting, he opened Instagram on his cell phone and typed in 'missing'. Right away #missingpeople and #missingpersons popped up. They both had thousands of posts from all over the world. It was heartbreaking to read the stories, some of them including videos made by friends and family members. Others had links to YouTube and hashtags to other posts. It gave him the idea to include a picture of Skyla's car on the poster, and to use several photos of Skyla instead of just one. It all seemed so futile. Wasn't there anything else he could do?

CHAPTER

13

"GOOD MORNING, JULIA," Skyla said to the baby looking at her with curiosity.

During the night, she'd fed her another bottle and changed her diaper, the adorable child now more alert and responsive. Something warm and fuzzy swelled inside her and she stroked her soft cheek with her fingertip. Taking care of Julia had stirred her desire to start a family of her own. Upon her safe return, she would talk to Edmond about it, convinced he wanted to have children, too. "Are you feeling better?"

Julia smiled back at her, showing several baby teeth.

"You must be hungry," Skyla said. In the morning's quiet, she prepared another bottle, the only sounds the wind outside and the occasional snort or grunt coming from the bedroom when her captor changed position. She already dreaded the moment he would wake up, his temper erratic, his mood unpredictable. At least he hadn't touched her. Had he only brought her here to take care of his children? They needed a mother. They were neglected and scared, their blue eyes haunted, their skittish behavior disturbing.

With Julia in her lap, sucking vigorously, she forced her thoughts away from her depressing surroundings and tried to bring on happier reflections, like her roomy apartment, Thanksgiving with her family, and the births of her sister's first and second child. Anything to get her mind off the present situation. Then she tried to imagine her future. She wanted to work in the accounting part of the business, get married in a stunning gown, and live in an older Victorian-style house with a porch, yard, and flower beds. The house would have a nursery for her first child, with brightly painted walls, a crib with matching changing table, and stuffed animals everywhere. In her fantasy, she saw herself with her back pressed against the sturdy body of a man, his hands smoothing over her pregnant belly as they gazed down into the empty crib, eagerly awaiting their baby's arrival. After he turned her around, her arms would slide up around his neck, her fingers buried in his long blond waves, before their lips...

Why was she thinking of Troy, his unruly blond hair soft under her touch, his kind eyes looking at her with admiration and love?

The bedroom door opened. Lexi walked out, followed by Tom. Skyla patted the sleeping bag, inviting them to join her. They sat down, one on each side, their warm bodies pressed against her.

"What do you think was wrong with Julia?" Tom asked.

Skyla thought for a moment. "I honestly don't know. Maybe she only shut herself off from the world for a little while."

The children nodded. They understood.

Loud coughing coming from the bedroom disturbed the short-lived peace in the room, and the lump of fear nestled solidly in the pit of her stomach tightened. She hurried to put the percolator on the woodstove for coffee. He'd told her he expected a fresh cup the moment he woke.

"It smells great here, woman," he said when he appeared. "This is going much better than I'd expected." He sat down at the table. "You made biscuits?" He glared into the pot and took them all, leaving none for her.

"Are you going out again?" she asked, pouring him a cup of coffee. "We need more supplies."

He stared at her with his deep-set eyes. She had no idea what he was thinking, his silence grating on her nerves. To evade his glare, she gathered the empty plates.

The tension in the room mounted. "What do you need?" he asked. She quickly gave him her ever growing list.

"You need shoes and clothes?" he smirked. "I rather see you go without."

Late last night, she'd washed her blouse and underwear. Having nothing else to wear while they dried by the stove had made her feel much too vulnerable. His words only affirmed her fear.

"I can't walk around barefoot," she snapped.

Half an hour later, he grabbed the list and climbed into his pickup truck. She waited for a good fifteen minutes, to make sure he was gone, before heading to the door. The sneakers she'd found in the bedroom were several sizes too small, but better than what she had.

"I need some fresh air. I'll be right back," she told the children. It was time to explore the terrain and form an escape plan.

Huddled in her red parka, Skyla walked over to the shack next to the cabin that he'd called a shed, the door almost falling off its hinges when she pulled it open. Inside the six by six foot space, she found the pile of blankets from the bedroom. Two of them seemed to be in decent condition. It would be nice to wash them, or at least air them out for several days, to create a mattress. Her limbs were stiff from sleeping on the hard surface. The other blankets were infused with the sour smell of unwashed bodies and cigarette smoke and were too far gone. They needed to be burned.

Below a grimy window stood a workbench. Two chainsaws lay on top of it, one of them taken apart, with the bar and the chain completely off. Plastic bottles of two-cycle oil and chainsaw lubricant stood next to them, and several dirty rags he must have used to wipe off his hands. She also spotted several axes, wedges, and other garden tools like shovels, shears, clippers, and a pick. All of those could be used as weapons, especially the pick. Heavy and long handled, it could kill a man easily if one hit him over the head. A grand idea, but she feared she lacked the courage or that she would get the chance to follow up on it. He was a massive man in his late thirties. Despite his smoking habit, he seemed in excellent condition, cutting firewood by hand and swinging an ax for hours without taking a break.

With every wind draft, an awful stench overpowered the

smell of the blankets and chainsaw oil. She left the shed, looking for the source.

A short distance away from the shed stood another small wooden structure. Expecting a rotten carcass or worse because of the stench, she opened the door to look inside. An outhouse with a non-flushing toilet. The lid of the white plastic seat was up, and several rolls of toilet paper hung from a rope attached to the wall. Although using the outhouse didn't appeal to her, it was better than using a spot in the snow and having her pants down. Why hadn't he told her about it? The bastard!

She'd seen enough and closed the door. Other than the shed and the outhouse, there was nothing to see besides firewood, unsplit rounds, and three metal garbage cans. Only one of them was half full, so he must be able to dispose of his garbage.

She shivered in her coat and her toes, curled up in the sneakers, were numb. It was much colder than the previous few days. The wind gusted and the sky contained a dark gray weight, with clouds hanging low over the mountains. Snowflakes brushed her cheeks. She pulled her gloves out of her pockets and put them on. They were a gift from Pauline, with Merino wool and a fleece knit, the back of the hands boasting a Scandinavian pattern Skyla really liked. Who could have guessed she would wear them for the first time under such dreadful circumstances?

Not finding anything else of interest, she left the clearing and followed the dirt road into the forest. Snow already covered the recent tire tracks from the truck, and more snow piled against the deep ruts.

Fingers of dread closed around her throat and the

desolation of her location brought tears to her eyes. "Are you out there, Daddy?" she moaned. "Why is it taking you so long to find me? Please come, Daddy. Please ... rescue me."

"Will you teach us more letters from Clifford's name?" Lexi asked as soon as Skyla stepped back into the warmth of the cabin. "You promised."

Something to distract her was just what she needed. "Of course," she replied, taking off her parka and hanging it over the back of a chair to dry. "Why don't you get the book and pencils, and we'll start practicing."

They sat down at the table. With Julia in her lap, she told the children to write Clifford's entire name on the brown paper bags twenty times. She already knew they could count and knew the months of the year and days of the week. At least their parents, or probably just their mother, had taught them something.

"I know how to write my name," Tom said with clear pride. He immediately began to scribble.

"Can you write my name, too?" Lexi asked right away.

They were both eager to learn, their young brains like little sponges. Skyla chuckled, enjoying their enthusiasm.

"That's not fair," Tom said when he found out Lexi had four letters in her name and Julia five, while he only had three.

"You have a point," Skyla agreed, tousling his hair. "Why don't you practice Lexi's name too? Or I could write down your last name. Do you know what it is?"

"Of course," Tom grinned, bouncing up and down in his seat. "It has a bunch of letters. Our last name is Rikkerson!"

"Rikkerson?" she stammered as memories flooded her

brain.

Memories of a big sweaty guy, dressed in tight blue shorts and a wife beater, who'd followed her around in the gym and kissed her against her will. Memories of a heavy file on her desk at the office; her testimony in the court case that never seemed to end; the murderous look in his eyes when he lost everything he owned. There was no doubt in her mind, her captor was that same man. Bjorn Rikkerson. And Tom was the toddler with the blue eyes, sharing her grapes in the supermarket that day.

Overcome by fury as everything fell into place, she handed Julia to her sister and got up from her chair. She wasn't a random victim. He wasn't after money. He was out for revenge, to settle old scores! Her hands formed fists at her sides. She wanted to punch him in the nose, knock him out. She wouldn't wait for her father to come and rescue her. She couldn't sit around any longer, like some docile recipient of whatever torture and abuse he devised. He apparently had a plan, and it wouldn't be good. She had to save herself, and she needed to do it right away.

"Oh, he'll be in for a surprise," she muttered, her heart racing. She was getting the hell out of this horrible place, right this minute.

"Skyla, what's wrong?" Tom asked.

"I'm leaving," she snapped.

Two pairs of blue eyes, filled with dread, stared at her. Overcome with guilt for her tone and her desire to leave them, she inhaled and slowly exhaled to steady herself and dampen her anger. "I'm sorry, but I must leave."

"You can't leave!" Lexi cried out. She sat in her chair with the baby in her lap, tears spilling from her startled eyes. "You're my new Mommy!"

Skyla's heart twisted with despair. "Listen," she said as kindly as she could. "I can't expect you to understand, but I'll try to explain. I've met both of you before, but you probably don't remember because it happened many years ago."

Tom looked at her with a blank expression on his face, his body tense.

"I was in a supermarket when I first saw you, Tom. We shared a few grapes, and I helped you find your parents. Lexi was just a toddler. Do you remember that?"

Tom's eyes lit up for a moment. "Yes, I remember. You were nice to me." Then he gave her an accusatory glare. "So why aren't you nice now?"

Skyla's vision blurred with unshed tears. "I did something that made your father very angry. I'm afraid he'll hurt me if I stay."

Lexi put the baby into her makeshift bed and hurried over to Skyla, wrapping her arms around her legs. "You can't leave us. Please, please, please," she sobbed.

Skyla gently loosened the girl's grip and grabbed her coat. "I'm so sorry," she said, looking down at them. "I have to leave before your father comes home. There's no other way."

In the doorway, she turned around one last time for a quick, loving hug. "Take care of Julia," she told them, fighting to keep her voice steady. "I promise I'll come back to get you. No matter what it takes, I'll come back for all of you."

Then she left.

CHAPTER

14

ON THE MONDAY MORNING, after the long holiday weekend, Edmond entered Troy's office unannounced. "How's the search going?" he asked.

The police had asked for a complete list of Overland employees, and they'd checked traffic cameras in the streets, following Skyla's car after it drove away from Overland Insurance in the opposite direction until it left the city limit a few minutes later. Due to heavy rain, it was impossible to get a good look at the driver. After the tracking of her phone and credit card had delivered no results either, Harold had called a meeting for eleven o'clock, to go over any further action they could take themselves. He contemplated to hire a private investigator and air radio commercials. He also wanted to discuss where they were with social media, the missing person posters, and a lot more. Skyla's entire family, Edmond, and most Overland Insurance employees would be in attendance. He'd also invited Pauline and her boyfriend.

Troy looked at the time. The meeting wouldn't start for half an hour. Annoyed with the interruption by a man who'd done little or nothing to help in the search so far, he said, "There's nothing new to report."

"Nothing?" Edmond's tone sounded accusatory.

Over the last four days, Troy had done everything he could think of, while Edmond spent most of his time entertaining his overseas relatives. Troy was eight years his senior and he wondered if he'd been so carefree at twenty-six. He didn't think so. No, he would've talked to Skyla's parents constantly, and he would've been a frequent visitor of the Rosehurst police station, instead of only going in once after they called him in for questioning. But being a frivolous, uninterested boyfriend didn't make him a kidnapper, or worse, and he knew Edmond was a dead-end. He had a rock-solid alibi, and couldn't tell them anything. No arguments, no trouble, and his relationship with Skyla going well as far as he could tell.

Troy sighed in an effort to suppress his distaste for the arrogant, good-looking man. "Can't this wait until the meeting? There's a lot of work on my desk." To make his point, he lifted the stack of files in front of him.

"I don't have a lot of time," Edmond told him, unimpressed. "That's why I came early to get a head start. Come on, I'm sure you have time to tell me the latest. After all, I am her boyfriend."

Yes, rub it in, Troy thought, and immediately pulled himself together. He couldn't let Edmond notice his inner struggles. They were his. "Well, let's see. You know there's been no activity on her cell phone, the phone either turned off or out of battery. We also haven't received any viable leads."

Edmond wiped some imaginary lint from the sleeve of his tailored business suit. He seemed completely in control and utterly relaxed, in glaring contrast to Troy, who'd worn the same shirt and blue jeans for days. He'd barely slept or thought one second about a shower or his appearance. That is, until ten minutes ago, or to be exact, the moment Skyla's picture-perfect boyfriend had walked into his office.

"I would've thought with her photo on the Overland Insurance ads posted all over the city, the television ads, and the website postings I created, Skyla would be a familiar face to a lot of people. That should've helped a great deal," Edmond remarked, easing his long frame into a chair and studying his nails. Edmond had a master's degree in marketing and worked for Randall Advertising and Marketing, his father's agency. Working for a parent was something Skyla and Edmond had in common.

"Do you want input for the article in the paper?" Edmond continued. He leaned comfortably against the back of his chair, his arms on the rests, as if in charge.

Normally Troy would have asked his secretary to bring in coffee, but Edmond's arrogance rubbed him the wrong way. "It's already submitted and will be in tomorrow's edition with her picture, description, and the details about her disappearance," he replied, coolly polite.

"Details? I thought that everything we know is based on speculation?" Edmond said.

"I mean where and at what time she was last seen, the make, model and license plate from her car, what she was wearing. Things like that."

Troy rubbed his forehead with his fingertips. They'd made no progress since Skyla had disappeared. It looked as if she'd gone up in smoke.

"Why don't you go home and clean up?" Edmond commented, regarding him up and down. "You look worn out, and don't have anything to report at the meeting this morning, anyway."

Troy couldn't believe the guy's condescending attitude. What was his problem? "I don't agree," he replied composedly. "I think there's plenty to talk about."

"Take a break, my friend," Edmond suggested, hiding a yawn behind his hand. "You look like you need one and I'm sure we can do it without you for the rest of the day."

Besides handling the marketing for the insurance agency, Edmond wasn't part of the business. He had no clue what kind of work Troy did or what his responsibilities were. Why Edmond presumed he could order him around and treat him as a doormat, he didn't understand, unless he already saw himself married to Skyla and as his future boss. "I don't think it's up to you to decide what I should or shouldn't do," he replied, struggling to hold his temper in check.

"I know what your problem is." Edmond slapped his knee and grinned, as if telling a joke. "You're in love with Skyla."

Dumbfounded, Troy stared at him. He thought he'd been able to hide his affection for her, that his secret was his alone. Damn it. Edmond was the last person he wanted to know about his private struggle. But since it was out in the open, he opted to face his adversary.

"Yes, I am," he replied, wishing that Edmond was anywhere else. On the moon maybe, or preferably even farther.

"Don't worry, I'll keep your little secret," Edmond responded with easy confidence. "I've heard that even love unreturned has its rainbow, so what the heck."

Edmond seemed so thoroughly amused, Troy's hands began to itch. He was ready to punch the guy just to get rid of his condescending smirk.

A knock on the door interrupted their conversation. Harold walked in.

"They just informed me the posters are done," he said. "Somebody has to go to the printer, pick them up, and hand them over to several employees so they can hang them all over town."

"On my way," Troy said to Harold Overland, thoroughly fed up with Edmond. Maybe he did need a break. Without saying goodbye, he walked out of the office.

⁓⤳ᘯ⤲⁓

After the door closed behind him, Harold rubbed his eyes and sank down in Troy's chair behind his desk. He looked weary and dejected, his skin an unhealthy grey.

"How're you doing?" Edmond asked.

"I can't think straight anymore," Harold admitted. "I'm tired but can't sleep. There are so many questions without answers, making it impossible to relax, especially at night, which is when I seem to lose touch with reality and take everything out of proportion, only thinking the worst."

Edmond got up from his chair and walked over to the window to look outside. The weather had been terrible during the last week, with steady rain, occasional flurries, and cold winds coming from the west. Today was no better. The sky was a claustrophobic gray, and tree branches whipped around in the powerful gusts. He hated the winters here. After they found Skyla, he intended to take her on a long vacation, maybe to San

Diego or perhaps Maui. He was convinced she would want to get away, to forget her ordeal, or whatever she'd landed in.

As he turned around to talk to Harold, he caught his own reflection in the window. His hairdresser had cut his almost jet-black hair to about two inches on the top and the short sides almost faded at the sideburns and the back. For him, it was a new style, and he liked it. It reminded him of Clark Gable and Cary Grant, two great actors from the thirties.

"Harold," he started, thinking how best to put it. "There's something important I have to discuss with you."

Harold rested his elbows on the desk, hunched over, and his head in his hands. He looked up. "What is it?"

"It's about Troy. Have you considered that he might be involved in Skyla's disappearance?"

"Are you out of your mind?" Harold frowned, straightening his back. "Whatever gave you that crazy idea?"

"Well, he was the last person who saw her," Edmond said.

"So?"

"And he's completely in love with her."

"And?"

Edmond scratched his head. He'd known for months how Troy felt about Skyla, his eyes following her wherever she went like a lovesick puppy. He'd found it amusing, and it gave him more reason to be extra attentive to Skyla when he was around. But he'd thought he was the only one who'd noticed.

"Well, everybody knows that unrequited love often leads to violence, sometimes even murder. He should be the primary suspect in her disappearance since he had both motive and opportunity."

"Listen carefully, Edmond," Harold said, his face stern. "Troy is probably very much in love with Skyla, but that would only be more reason for him not to hurt her. Not ever! You'd better remember that!"

Edmond straightened his shoulders. "I really believe your judgment is clouded," he said. "I'd at least let the police check his alibi."

"They already did! He took his mother and her husband to the airport that evening. After he drove off, the security footage shows Skyla reentered the office before driving off herself five minutes later. They also know Troy had ribs at that Famous Bills' Barbeque that evening after leaving the airport."

"Sounds premeditated," Edmond persisted.

"I don't want to hear another word about it," Harold said, his fury apparent. "Troy is trustworthy, honest, and reliable. He couldn't hurt a fly, let alone my daughter! And I'd rather not waste any more time on false accusations and assumptions. We should be a united front in this."

"That may be your opinion now," Edmond said as he stood and walked to the door. "But if I were you, I'd think about what you just said."

CHAPTER

15

AFTER GOING HOME to take a shower, shave, and change, Troy picked up the two boxes of posters at the printer. He returned to the agency not much later.

"Pauline offered to take care of the posters. She recruited several friends and wants to hang them all over town and drop them off in coffee shops, the library and a lot of other public places," he said when he walked into Harold's office. "I'm pleased with the result. The colors of the photographs are vibrant, and the font is bold and easy to read. Here, I brought several for you, too."

Harold pushed a stack of files aside and waved him in. "Could you close the door?"

Troy immediately picked up on the tension. "Did I miss anything important during the meeting? Was there bad news?"

Harold shook his head. Without Edmond and Troy, the meeting at eleven had been futile, the only productive discussion about the social media efforts he knew nothing about. He waved with his hand at the empty chair. "Sit down. We need to talk."

Troy swallowed. Something had happened while he was gone, and he felt it involved him. "Of course," he mumbled, trying to hide his apprehension.

"I won't beat about the bush," Harold said. "It's about Edmond. After you left this morning, he suggested the police should double check your alibi for Wednesday night. He believes you're involved."

"That jackass!" Troy cursed under his breath, squeezing the armrests, his knuckles white. "I knew he was up to something, but I didn't expect him to take it as far as trying to make me a suspect. What's he thinking? That I'm the Boogeyman?"

"I'm sorry to put you through this," Harold apologized. "But Edmond raised the question, and I don't want to have any problems or secrets between us."

"Don't be sorry," Troy said. "In most cases when someone is abducted or disappears, the suspect ends up being somebody related or close to the victim. If Edmond hadn't raised more suspicion, someone else would have."

"I trust you completely, even if you didn't have an alibi," Harold assured him. "I know you love my daughter, and that you would never hurt her."

"I would do anything for Skyla and will never forgive myself for leaving her by herself," Troy said, his voice choked. "But I did leave something out before..."

They went over the entire day. From the moment Harold and Skyla had walked in together, to the moment Troy had kissed her in the parking lot after the Thanksgiving party, driving off as fast as he could.

"She left the office by herself many times before, Troy. You know that," Harold replied.

Both men contemplated in silence for several minutes.

"I'll make a list with the names of all the employees who attended the party and email it to the police," Troy said. "And the name of the catering outfit, too."

The phone on Harold's desk interrupted them and he picked up. "This is Overland."

Harold abruptly straightened his back, the tension mounting as he carried out the conversation.

"Who was it?" Troy asked from the edge of his seat.

A smile appeared on Harold's face. "Finally, some news. That was the police. There was activity on Skyla's credit card. They're checking for security footage and asked me to come in."

"Thank God," Troy said.

Troy drove to the police bureau in his SUV with Harold in the passenger seat. It was pouring rain and his car handled deep puddles and slick roads much better than Harold's BMW Coupe. On the way, he noticed several posters for the missing Skyla were already mounted to nearby electric poles. They were soaking wet and curling up. Feeling hollowed out and sad, Troy wondered if anyone would even pay attention to them.

The drive took only ten minutes. Troy parked the SUV. He got out, pulled up the collar of his dark, double breasted, knee-length overcoat and hurried toward the entrance to escape the continuous rain. Troy had bought the coat, believing it was the right look for an insurance agent. Seeing his boss in the almost identical coat hurrying next to him confirmed his instincts.

The Parkhurst police station was recently built, with brick walls and small, reflective windows. The automatic doors opened as they approached, and they wiped their feet on a rug before stepping onto the tile floor in the reception area. Behind the enclosed counter stood two female police officers, looking at a file. One of them slid open the glass partition. "Mr. Overland?" she asked.

Harold nodded. A moment later she appeared in the doorway. "I'm Patrol Officer Duncan. Let me take you to the back."

They followed her down a hallway to what appeared to be the detectives' bullpen area. Troy counted five desks, all of them with a computer and stacks of paperwork. They were all unoccupied.

"We're a little understaffed this week," Officer Duncan said, pulling two chairs from the wall and placing them in front of one of the empty desks. "Please take a seat. Officer Weaver stepped out for a moment. He'll be right with you."

Almost at the same time, a door opened and a man with a bulging stomach walked in, in his hand a steaming cup of coffee. He placed the cup on his desk and extended his hand. Neither Harold nor Troy had seen him before.

"As promised by one of my colleagues, we're keeping a close watch on your daughter's bank and credit card activities," Officer Weaver said after introductions had been made. "I wanted to inform you that her credit card was used on Thanksgiving Day in a grocery store. That same day it was used a second time in a department store. I've received receipts from both stores by email and have printed them out." He handed them both a sheet of paper. "They total close to nine hundred dollars."

Harold shrugged. He didn't care about the amount. What he wanted to see was the security footage that had recorded those transactions.

Troy studied the receipts. On the first one were only groceries, with a lot of dried goods in bulk. The second was more interesting. "Sleeping bags, pillows, diapers, a flashlight, candles, batteries, engine oil," he read aloud. What could he make out of all that?

"He or she bought diapers and formula, so they must have a baby," Harold commented.

"It's a "he", gentlemen," Weaver informed them. "If you want to look at my computer monitor, I can show what's on the tape we picked up at the grocery store." He opened an attachment and pushed the monitor partly around so they could watch with him after a movie player opened.

The black and white film was grainy with white flashes, the quality poor. They could barely make out the figure of a man at a check-out register, wearing a camouflage jacket and what looked like a baseball cap pulled down over his forehead.

"It's impossible to identify the person," Harold said, disappointment written all over his face. "Can't that tape be enhanced or blown up or something?"

"I'm sorry, Mr. Overland. This is the best we have," Weaver replied.

"There's nothing available from the second store?" Troy asked.

The officer pulled his monitor back. "Unfortunately, the second store had nothing at all. It turned out to be a small department store without surveillance. The clerk, who also happened to be the owner, told my colleague he'd never seen the guy before. All he remembered was his facial hair, camouflage clothes, and baseball cap, which is confirmed by the tape from the other store."

"Any information is better than nothing," Troy said with optimism. It was more than they knew an hour ago. "Are you in charge of Skyla's case now instead of the chief?"

"No, I'm not. Police Captain MacMillen took the case over from Officer Brown the moment he heard about it He fine combed her apartment, talked to everyone who works with her, and he spent hours checking traffic cams. He has worked tirelessly on her case and I informed him right away about the latest development, but he's not here yet."

Not here? Why the hell not? Harold thought and sunk back in his chair, swamped with disappointment. He pressed his palms together, then decided. "I want to hire a private investigator." He'd toyed with the idea since the moment Skyla disappeared, the efforts from the police a letdown. "Is there someone you can recommend?"

"I know someone," Officer Duncan said from behind her desk in a far corner of the room. "Kim Lowe. She's smarter than hell and gets results. I have her business card."

"Actually, I had a man in mind," Harold said, hoping not to step on any toes.

"I wouldn't recommend her if I wasn't sure she would do an excellent job, Mr. Overland. I've seen her work firsthand. She's the best around. Trust me."

On his way out, Troy paused at Officer Duncan's desk and subtly asked for the P.I.'s card. Man or woman, it didn't matter, as long as the investigator went the extra mile, and if needed, he would pay for it himself.

CHAPTER

16

IT WAS STILL DAYLIGHT when Bjorn Rikkerson returned to the cabin. It had been a long day, and he'd had it with shopping, the stores overloaded with people he didn't want to see. He grabbed two plastic bags filled with groceries from the passenger seat, then lifted several more from the bed of the truck. He hadn't encountered a single problem when he paid with her credit card and didn't even need to feed someone the bullshit story about his wife being sick. Just in case they would question him, he'd thrown in a few items only used by women, like tampons and nylons, to make it more believable. He had to admit, it felt incredible to buy whatever he wanted, an experience he'd never had before.

"I'm home!" he shouted, his arms full. "Somebody open the door"

It only took a few seconds before his son appeared in the doorway. He looked scared.

"She's gone, isn't she?" he asked.

Exhilaration rushed through his veins. Finally, she'd made a move. He'd expected her to fight him from the get-go. Instead it had taken much longer than he'd predicted. All those days, she'd been docile, hovering over his children as though they were her own, and busying herself teaching them letters. Why, he didn't understand. They didn't need schooling. Their life was here in the woods, where no one needed books and bullshit like that.

He dumped the bags on the floor and grabbed his son by the shoulder. Wincing under his painful grip, Tom tried to move away.

"How long ago?"

Tom cried out in pain when his fingers dug even deeper into his flesh. "A long while ago," he whimpered.

Rikkerson released him. "Unload the rest of the stuff from the pickup," he barked, seizing his knife and a flashlight. "I'm going after her!"

He slammed the door shut behind him and circled the shack, looking for footprints, a broken twig, or any other sign that would tell him where she entered the forest. His entire life, he'd hunted. His father had taught him all the tricks from setting traps, tracking, skinning, butchering, and everything else about game-processing. Following the footsteps of a woman should be easy. The hunt was on.

Although they already had several bouts of winter, the snowpack on the ground wasn't too heavy yet. That was unusual so high in the mountains this time of the year, but it had been nice, making his trips into the city easier without having to battle several feet of snow. Not for the first time, he regretted dumping Skyla's Jeep into the lake. His initial impulse had been to get rid of it. He'd been stupid. It would've been great to go wheeling with it, see how it handled.

A few minutes later, he grinned. She'd run from the door straight into the nearest brush, a clear footprint of a running shoe in the mud between dead branches.

"Look out, Skyla! I'm coming for you!" he shouted.

Skyla prayed while she aimlessly ran through the woods. She'd left the cabin several hours earlier, deciding not to follow the dirt road, in case her captor would return and spot her. She also believed that's where he would look for her first. Safety would be in the forest, but she had no clue where she was. Everything around her looked the same, every tree, every pile of brush, and every clearing. The position of the sun, barely visible behind the thick cloud cover, not much help to get a feeling of direction. The idea to head downhill dominated her thoughts, believing it would be warmer on lower elevations, and that there might be a better chance to find a house or a road. In the mountainous terrain, it was impossible to tell if she'd made progress in the right direction, or if she only ran around in circles, not getting anywhere.

Pressing her hand to her side to suppress the constant stabbing pain, she looked up at the darkening sky. Was the sun really going down already? She'd lost all sense of direction, her path blocked by steep mountain sides, dense brush, and impassable rocky slopes and ravines. Panic filled her. Why hadn't she thought this through? Exhausted and fighting off the bitter cold, she climbed over a fallen log with soggy bark, leaving wet dirt all over her pants. On the other side, she pushed branches out of her way that were trying to grab her, and stumbled on. She needed to keep moving or she would freeze. But half an hour later, after the sun set in the west, she couldn't go on any longer and stumbled to a stop.

The closest she'd ever come to nature had been on a hike to see a waterfall, to reach a viewpoint, or a guided nature walk. Those outings had all been on designated trails, in the company of friends or family. In combination with basketball and tennis in high school, and her gym membership after she moved into her own apartment, she'd stayed in shape, and had found that to be sufficient exercise. Camping and the great outdoors had never been part of her life, every vacation spent in a luxurious resort in Florida, Hawaii or some other tropical destination. The most adventurous vacation she'd ever taken had been her trip to Indonesia with Pauline.

To find herself alone, in the middle of nowhere, surrounded by endless forest, terrified her. All kinds of dangers might lurk around, like bears or cougars. Without a weapon to defend herself, she was utterly vulnerable, and she regretted her hasty decision to leave the relative safety of the cabin without a sound plan of action.

Could she find her way back? And if she did, what would Rikkerson do? She could pretend she'd gotten lost while looking for berries or mushrooms. He might believe her, as long as Tom and Lexi hadn't told him otherwise. She drew in a deep, shuddering breath, struggling to keep from hyperventilating. What would be worse? To face Rikkerson or spend a night outside? She doubted if she would survive in the wilderness, in the freezing cold. Everything was wet, with patches of snow everywhere, and no place to hide. To take advantage of the last bit of daylight, she clawed up a hill. She had to find her way back. She had no other choice. To control her panic, she forced her mind in another direction. She began to count her steps and figure out the day of the week, the days blurring into each other as she struggled to make order out of the chaotic state of her mind.

Out of breath, she reached the top of the hill and stopped. The old sneakers were too small, and her heels hurt, her curled up toes numb and frozen. In a patch of snow, she noticed footsteps. She'd been here before. That meant she was on the right track back to the cabin. Her relief was short-lived when she heard the rustling of dry leaves and the sharp snap of a branch breaking in two, followed by the faint sound of something making its way through the underbrush in her direction.

She shuddered involuntarily, the metallic taste of fear oozing from beneath her tongue. Something big and tall came towards her. Her hand reached out to the tree she'd just passed, and she took several steps back to hide behind it, fear spreading through her entire nervous system. Then she caught the flash of a light, moving back and forth, as if carried by a human being. Relief washed over her. They'd sent search and rescue to scour the woods, to find her. She was safe.

She took a step forward and waved. "Thank God," she gasped. "I got lost..."

"Don't give me any crap!" a voice interrupted.

The beam of the powerful flashlight shone right into her face. She shielded her face with her hands.

"You tried to escape, and we both know it."

Rikkerson. From the looks of him, he was furious, his eyes

filled with ferocity, his entire demeanor threatening. "I got lost," he mimicked, grabbing her arm. "I know you did, slut. We're only twenty minutes from the cabin, and Tom told me you've been gone for hours. Nice going!"

"Let go of me," she whimpered, trying to break free.

He only tightened his grip and narrowed the space between them. "You're not going anywhere," he told her, his voice as hard as tempered steel. "You're coming with me."

Tears stung her eyes as she tried to free herself, but he ignored her futile protests and pulled her with him as though she was nothing more than a two-year-old throwing a fit. The beam of his flashlight danced in front of them.

"You're hurting me," Skyla protested. It was almost impossible to keep up with his long strides, his grip around her upper arm as tight as a vise. "Don't think I'm going back to the cabin. I know who you are and what you're up to. Bjorn Rikkerson!"

He stopped and whipped her around, the beam of the flashlight blazing bright in her face.

"Miss smarty-pants finally figured it out," he sneered. "I'm disappointed it took you this long. I expected more from you."

She sank her teeth so hard in her bottom lip, she tasted blood. "Your hair was short, and you didn't have a beard back then," she defended herself.

"Yes, rough times can change one's appearance," he agreed. "But I'm happy to hear you remember me so well."

"Don't get any ideas," she shot back at him. "You disgusted me then, and you disgust me even more now."

He gave a bitter-sounding laugh. "People got hurt for saying much nicer things than that, girl. You better watch your words."

"You're plain crazy, you know that!" she retorted, pushing the flashlight out of her face with an angry swipe of her arm. It landed on the ground. Her courage was short-lived. She backed away under his hard glare. "Stay away from me, or I'll scream," she cried out. Her eyes darted around, wild with fear. She was ready to run.

"That's it," he growled, reaching out to her. "I'm done playing games." Dragging her roughly against him, he tangled his hand in her long raven black hair, tugging her head back. His other hand pulled down the zipper from her parka. He pressed his face against the long vulnerable column of her throat, licking her skin. His facial hair scraped her skin. Revulsion and terror overcame her.

"Filthy pig!" She pounded at him, trying to hit him wherever she could. "Let me go!"

"Go on, Skyla, go on. I love it when a woman fights me," he urged, breathing heavily. He jerked on her hair, forcing her to arch her back. "Keep on struggling," he groaned, pressing his hard sex against her abdomen. "It turns me on."

She remembered seeing him lifting weights in the gym, the muscles in his arms and shoulders bulging. All that strength was now focused on overpowering her, taking her. She couldn't escape his brute strength. Her legs felt like pudding underneath her, and overcome with despair, she opened her mouth and screamed at the top of her lungs, intent on alerting everyone within a five-mile radius. It was the only way she could think of to defend herself.

"HELP!"

"Stop it!" he roared, yanking her head back even further.

Tears of anger and frustration stung behind her eyes. She wouldn't let him win, the bastard. "Jerk!" she screamed, clawing at his face, kicking, biting, spitting, and screaming, trying with all she had left to fight him off.

The next moment, he released his grip, drew his fist back and punched her in the face. A bright white starburst exploded inside her skull and her scream died in her throat, the pain so sudden and intense her knees folded.

Watching her stagger, a satisfied smirk appeared on his face. "Remember this for next time," he said, the words thick and slurred. "I like a little resistance, but that screaming works on my nerves." He fumbled with his belt and fly, his eyes locked on her, ready to attack the moment she would bolt.

She gagged as she read his intent, no longer able to deny what was happening. She was all alone in the forest with a dangerous lunatic, who could easily snap her in two, doing with her whatever he pleased. With no one nearby to hear her scream, to come to her aide, and rescue her, she relied on herself. But she lacked the strength to fight him off any longer, the world around her one big daze, the trees swaying back and forth. She was going to faint.

With a quick move, he closed the distance between them and slid his arm around her waist, his fingers digging deep into her ribs. At the same time, his other hand moved down to the button of her pants, searching and groping. "What are you thinking, sweetheart?" he hissed in her face, his breath coming in shallow gasps, the stench of rotting teeth, garlic, and cigarette smoke making her gag. "Are you afraid I'll drag you into the bushes and fuck you? Well, I might just give you exactly what you want."

Repulsion washed over her when he forced his hungry, seeking mouth onto hers, his tongue hard against hers, slithering around. Losing patience with her button, his fingers grabbed the waistband of her pants. He yanked and she heard the fabric tear under his brute force. Aware of his arousal, she couldn't be more terrified.

Dear God, was he really going to rape her? "Only an animal could behave like you," she accused him bitterly, tears streaming down her face.

"Maybe, but I'll enjoy every minute," he replied, gripping the back of her neck and holding her in place. "I wanted you from the first moment I laid my eyes on you in that tight pink outfit at the gym. It's about time I get my fill."

She screamed out her fear and frustration. "You filthy pig! Get your filthy paws of me." In a last effort to fight him off, she kicked his shins, wishing she had the reach to kick him in the groin, his erection repulsive.

For a moment he lost his grip and she ran, scrambling to stay on her feet. Branches hit her face when she crashed through the dense brush, her hands reaching out for anything to keep her balance.

"You bitch," he yelled, right behind her. "I'll get you for that." He tackled her and she slammed into the ground. Kicking and screaming, she crawled away, but he grabbed her slender hips, jerked down her slacks, and tore aside her panties. No barrier or protection remained, the frigid air touching her naked skin, his fingernails digging into her bare flesh, hurting her.

"No!" she cried out, her terrified sobs only heard by the trees. "Please, no!"

With one powerful thrust, he nailed her down to the ground. His assault sent pain screaming through every nerve ending in her body, and she screamed as he grunted his pleasure.

In that moment, Skyla died a million deaths.

CHAPTER

17

THE NEXT MORNING, Harold drove to his appointment with Kim Lowe. Clara had run a background check on the private investigator. She'd passed with glowing reviews.

"Her office is on the east side of the city, in that new business development," his wife had said. "I know rent must be expensive, so there's more proof she's doing well."

Clara's findings made Harold feel confident Kim was the right choice.

His G.P.S. directed him through the unfamiliar streets to a modern four-story building, the trees still small, the parking lot recently paved. On his way to the front door, he could smell the sharp fresh odor of asphalt.

He entered the building. Besides someone coming down the stairs, he was the only one there.

"Any idea where I can find Kim Lowe?" he asked when the man passed him.

"There's a directory, next to the elevators," he answered.

Harold thanked him and headed to the elevators. An accountant, insurance agent, stormwater engineer, a physical therapist, and Kim Lowe were listed. He pushed the up button. After a loud ding, the doors opened, and he pressed the button for the fourth floor. Weary, he leaned against the railing, the opposite wall like a mirror. He cringed as he inspected his reflection. He looked haggard with hollow bags under his eyes, his still thick hair in disarray. Sleep had eluded him since Skyla's disappearance, and a steady pressure on his chest kept him from breathing normally. He took a roll of antacid from his pocket and stuck one in his mouth.

On the fourth floor, the elevator door opened to a sterile hallway, a sign posted on the opposite wall directing him to Kim Lowe's office in suite 404. She'd told him to walk in if she didn't respond promptly to his knock. He knocked twice before opening the door. Several desks cluttered with dying plants and stacks of papers, lined the walls. Three cabinets were overflowing with files. The vertical fabric panels in front of the windows filtered the sunlight into an exotic shade of orange. The unremarkable office fulfilled his expectation of a P.I.'s place of business. He watched too much television.

On the Oriental rug, positioned in the middle of the room, sat a woman with short black hair, her legs crossed. She sifted through several papers and seemed lost in whatever she studied, apparently unaware of Harold Overland's presence. A laptop sat next to her, the face of another woman on the screen.

Harold coughed politely to draw her attention.

She glanced up and gave him a brief smile. "Just one second, Mr. Overland," she said. "I'm in an online meeting. I'll be right with you."

If there was one thing Harold Overland wasn't used to, it was being told to wait. He looked around for a chair and saw one near the window. After he sat down, he noticed the newspaper on the desk next to him, the article about Skyla's disappearance folded open. With a pang in his heart, he traced her cheek in the image with his fingertip. Would he ever see her lovely face again?

Where are you, sweetheart? he wondered. *Where are you?* His throat constricted, the persistent pressure on his chest increasing. He changed position to alleviate his discomfort. He couldn't break down in front of a woman he'd never met.

Despite the antacid, his heartburn only increased, and instead of feeling better, he broke out in a cold sweat. He shouldn't have had that last piece of bacon with breakfast this morning. Would she have a bottle of water? He pushed himself up to alleviate the pain when the walls of the room seemed to concave. The floor swayed in a rolling motion, the filing cabinets tilting in the weirdest angle. Was this an earthquake? Gulping for air, he sank back down. The next moment, he disappeared into a black hole of unconsciousness.

Kim worked against the clock. She'd promised her sister in London a detailed answer before the end of her workday. London was eight hours ahead of Portland. She only had five minutes left, her concentration waning since Harold Overland's entrance into her office. It wasn't like her to keep a new potential customer waiting. God knew she needed the income, but he'd shown up at least ten minutes before his appointment, thus jeopardizing her deadline.

"Almost there, Sis," she told the lady on the screen.

In the middle of the last phase of the difficult mathematical problem she tried to solve, the sound of a sharp gasp interrupted her train of thought. She looked up just in time to see Harold Overland's arms flop to his sides and his head drop forward. She immediately jumped to her feet and rushed in his direction.

"Mr. Overland, are you okay?" she asked. She grabbed his shoulder to keep him from falling out of his chair.

He didn't reply. His eyes remained closed and his breathing turned shallow and labored. Kim realized he might be suffering a heart attack. Everything she'd learned during C.P.R. class rushed through her head. Call 911 first thing. But her cell phone was across the room. If she let go of him, he would fall to the floor.

Looking for something to steady him, she noticed the sheer curtains she'd hung to keep out the sun. She yanked on one of the panels, tearing the fabric and wrapping it around his torso to secure him to the back of the chair. She prayed it would hold him in place.

"9-1-1. What's your emergency?"

With the phone between her cheek and shoulder, Kim searched through her desk drawers for a bottle of aspirin. "Send an ambulance to Lincoln's Business Park, building number three, suite 404," she yelled. "Someone's having a heart attack in my office."

"Try to keep him calm," the dispatcher told her.

"He's unconscious, but still breathing. I found a bottle of aspirin. Should I give him some?"

"If you can, yes," the dispatcher replied. "Aspirin slows blood clotting and might prevent him from going into cardiac arrest."

Kim used her letter opener to crush two aspirins on the flat surface of her desk and swept the powder with her finger into the palm of her hand. Harold was still hanging in his chair, and she lifted his head. With her hand against his bottom lip, she tucked the white powder between his lips. How much ended inside his mouth, she didn't know, but hoped for the best.

"What's going on, Kim?" her sister asked from the screen of her laptop.

"Sorry, Sis," she told her. "I don't have time to explain." As fast as she could, she ran out of her office and down the hallway. On each floor of the building, Automatic External Defibrillators occupied an alcove next to the elevators. She opened the small door, pulled out the device, and rushed back to her office.

A door opened and the worried face of Liam appeared. He worked in the office next to her and did something with computers. "What's with all the noise, Kim?" he asked.

"Please, help me, Liam," she said. "A man in my office is having a heart attack."

CHAPTER

18

IN THE STILL OF THE NIGHT, Skyla awakened in her sleeping bag on the floor of the cabin. She began to weep. Shaking uncontrollably, she felt certain she would never be warm again. She curled into a fetal position, anguish consuming her. He'd raped her, taking her on the ground like an animal! She could still feel the leaves under her bare hands and the cold from the wet soil beneath her knees while he'd pinned her down. The burning pain between her legs debilitated her, the humiliation she now felt as raw and consuming as a festering wound.

She pressed her fists against her mouth to keep from crying out in anger and pain. His brutal attack had awakened something in her she'd never known existed or could be part of her being. *Hatred.* A hatred so powerful, she knew she could kill him if he came near her again. Eyes darkly shadowed by shock, she pulled the sleeping bag over her head. Like a child, she wished she could disappear by just wanting it badly enough. Of course, it wouldn't work. She knew that now.

Morning came much too fast. She felt defiled, terrified, and dirty. Dirt that wouldn't come off, not even if she took a thousand showers.

Until her abduction no one had ever deliberately hurt her, not physically and not emotionally. She'd led a protected, trouble-free life, surrounded by people who loved, cherished and respected her. Aside from reading about such things in the newspaper or watching reports on television, she'd never experienced poverty, hunger, despair, or violence, which only heightened the shock of what had just happened to her. Her life would never be the same. *She* would never be the same. She'd come face to face with pure evil.

Bile rose in her throat. She shuddered, fighting not to vomit. Bjorn Rikkerson had taken pleasure in her misery, enjoying every minute of her anguish and humiliation, and the power he had over her. She'd heard it while he'd groaned with pleasure when he spilled his semen inside her, and in his Tarzan-like shout of victory after his assault had finally ended.

Filled with bitterness, wishing him dead and burning in hell, she watched sunlight pierce the cracks of the door and in between the unfinished, wooden boards of the cabin. An odd looking bug came to life and buzzed against the windowpane. He wanted to escape and fly to the light, just like her. Oh, how badly she wanted to run away. She couldn't stay. If she did, she knew she would certainly die...

At the sound of someone moving around in the bedroom,

she felt paralyzed with fear. He was coming! Pulling the sleeping bag over her head, she pressed against the wall to make herself as small as possible. Her pillow clutched against her stomach, her only support to keep from drowning in terror.

Footsteps came closer. Skyla's whole body began to shake uncontrollably.

"Get up," he said, prodding her with his foot.

When she didn't move, he grabbed the bottom of the sleeping bag, lifted it up and shook her out as if she weighed nothing. He'd torn her slacks completely off last night and she had no idea where they were. Still in her parka, she pulled it around her bare legs to hide them from view. Terrified, she glared at him from behind her disheveled hair, her back pressed against the wall of the cabin.

"You look like you just got back from a roll in the hay," he grinned, winking.

At his cruel words, her anxiety transformed into rage. The bastard! How dare he talk about what happened as though it had been something pleasurable? She pushed her disheveled hair from her forehead. "I loathe you for what you did to me, you awful piece of scum."

He gave her a cold stare. "That was nothing, lady. And if you thought I was done, you're absolutely wrong. You're mine, and this is how it'll be from now on."

Hatred and fury boiled up inside her. "You're insane!" she screamed, clenching her fists. "You can't keep me in this horrible place, just because of some imagined grudge you have against me!"

He stood stock-still and his eyes became slits. "Imagined grudge?" he roared before coming at her. "Don't you realize it's your fault we have to live here?" He grabbed her parka and yanked her up until her face was only a few inches away from his. "You set me up that day in court, and you know it! They made me pay back the thirty thousand and everything else they'd given me in disability. I had to sell my house. I lost everything I owned. Just because of you! So don't tell me I have an *imagined grudge* against you. If you hadn't betrayed me, if you hadn't testified against me, none of this would have happened. It's your fault! Yours!"

He shook her vehemently, his face contorted with rage as spittle flew from his mouth. He shoved her away.

Struggling to stay on her feet, Skyla stared at him in complete shock. He wasn't crazy or just plain stupid. He had all this calculated out, maybe for years, her words finally causing his hatred to boil over.

"I saw you and your family on those advertisements plastered to the city buses!" He paced back and forth. "The perfect family. All attractive, beautiful teeth, expensive clothes, and impeccable coiffed hair and make-up! Overland Insurance, we're on your side. Fuck you! You were never on my side."

Randall Advertising and Marketing handled all the marketing of the agency. Edmond had come up with the latest slogan and used the fact that the third generation of Overland's worked in the family business. Her father had loved the idea, but she hadn't. Having her face all over town made her uncomfortable. Now she knew her instincts had been right. It had attracted the wrong attention.

Rikkerson spread his arms. "Until I was six years old, my family lived in this cabin. My father was a logger and made a good living, until the environmentalists claimed the national forest land was fucking prime spotted owl habitat. A court order halted the logging, taking our jobs with it. And what did they accomplish? Nothing, with wildfires scorching millions of acres across Washington, Oregon, Idaho, and Montana. It's costing taxpayers billions to fight them, and more trees and fucking owls are lost than ever before."

Deep down, Skyla had to agree with him. The nearby Columbia River Gorge National Scenic Area was devastated by the Eagle Creek Fire several years ago. It was the first time a wildfire had come so close, covering the Portland metropolitan area for days in thick smoke, blotting out the sun, and forcing people with asthma and other lung problems to stay inside. If logging would have made a difference, she didn't know, but at least they would have saved the lumber and provided jobs.

"After your family stole everything from me, I took my wife and kids out here. At least we had a roof over our heads, a place to call home, instead of having to live on the streets, in a shelter, or in one of the homeless camps. That's not a place to raise your children."

Still standing with her back against the wall, her bare feet frozen, her legs all goose bumped, her vision blurred with tears. Was it true what he said? Was it her fault he had to live here with his family, under these appalling conditions, without any modern conveniences? Memories of the court case in which she'd testified against him flashed through her mind, her breathing shallow, her hand against her throat.

For years, Rikkerson had collected disability after a job injury, claiming excruciating back pains. The case was partly handled by Overland Insurance. She was very familiar with it, and she'd recognized him at the gym. She'd secretly taken pictures of him with her cell phone while he worked out and immediately informed her father.

Without hesitation, she'd stepped up to testify in court, telling the judge she'd seen him lifting weights, showing off his hamstrings, and easily knocking off two sets of fifty push-ups followed by fifty sit-ups. Other people had come forward as well, testifying he'd worked on the side during all that time. As a tree faller, landscaper, and roofer.

Rikkerson hadn't been able to defend himself. He simply stood there, his expression withdrawn, his jaw clenched. Obviously, he realized he was caught red-handed, his con-game over.

Afterwards, Skyla had been pleased with the outcome and relieved the case was finally closed. Bjorn Rikkerson would not be able to take advantage of the system anymore. What had never crossed her mind was that denying his benefits would impact his family. She'd known about his wife and two children, the young boy so cute when they shared a few grapes in the supermarket. Instead, she'd gone home and hadn't thought once about the consequences. Like where they would live if they lost their house, or how he would be able to provide for his family. Instead of making the blue-eyed boy's life better, she'd only made matters worse. And now she faced the ugly reality that, by testifying against him, she had helped to shatter the life of an entire family, and she had sealed her own fate as well.

CHAPTER

19

BJORN OBSERVED SKYLA.

She was beautiful with her long black hair, flawless skin, and nice rack. He liked tall, trim, and spirited women. She personified everything he'd ever wanted in a wife. He could watch her for hours, months, maybe years, and was in fact planning to do just that. She belonged to him now and was completely at his mercy.

His skin began to burn, and his sex stirred. She'd felt good around him, tight as a virgin. Taming her would give him a huge amount of pleasure. Women could be fantastic and very useful at times, especially after the months of abstinence since his wife died.

But first he had to make sure she wouldn't try to run away again any time soon. He'd enjoyed hunting and catching her, and the sex. But he'd hated the long walk through the woods, worrying if she was still alive. He knew bears and cougars roamed the area. He wasn't about to lose her to an animal. Oh, no! He wanted her just for himself!

"You were a brainless bitch to try to run away," he told her. "Don't you know you could've died thanks to your own stupidity? I have to make sure you won't try that again."

He opened the bedroom door and returned a few moments later, dragging the two sleepy children with him, their faces pallid with fear.

"You know what to do," Bjorn said and pushed them forward.

"What are you doing?" Skyla demanded.

The look in Bjorn's mean, deep-set eyes made her blood run cold. Whatever he was intending to do would be bad.

"I'll teach you a lesson you won't ever forget." He unbuckled his belt. "Grab the table with both hands, kids, and remember, for every cry I hear, you get one more."

When his intentions became clear, Skyla's body began to tremble with terror and rage. "Don't you dare hurt them, you savage!" she hissed.

"You want some of this too?" he said, raising his arm, the belt whipping around.

"You can't do this!" she cried out, lunging at him in blind fury as she tried to snatch the belt from his grip.

With one powerful swing of his arm, he hit her with his fist right above her eye, slamming her hard against the wall. Her knees buckled. With nothing to grab hold of to break her fall, she hit the floor, which sent a crushing pain through every muscle.

In complete horror, she saw him lift his arm, striking Tom

with the belt on his back. The little boy cringed under the hard blow, struggling to keep from crying out. Pure terror paralyzed her. All she could do was cover her ears and turn her back on the horrible scene. She couldn't watch.

For the second time, the belt cracked. A red mist of rage formed in front of her eyes. He would suffer for what he did to those poor children. An animal like him didn't deserve to live.

Waiting for a third lash, an eerie silence filled the room. She looked up as Rikkerson put his belt back around his pants. Both children still held on to the table, their heads down.

"This is what'll happen if you try to escape again," he told her. "The only difference will be that I will beat them ten times as hard and as long. And who knows, maybe by then the baby won't be so lucky to escape without a single scratch."

"You bastard!" Tears of frustration and hatred streamed down her face. "How could you hurt them like that over something I did?"

He gave her a cold stare. "Don't forget this is all your fault, bitch. Going after me. Making me lose everything. You did all this to us and had it coming." He kept on raging, pointing with his finger, waving with his arms, until he grabbed his coat and headed to the door. "Let this be a warning," he said, raising his fist in her direction. "No more running away."

As soon as he left the cabin, she struggled back on her feet. Her head spun, her shoulder and forehead throbbed, and her clothes were soaked with her own perspiration. But she didn't care about her own discomfort. All she cared about was the well-being of the helpless children. She rushed over to them.

"It's all right," she told them, taking them both by the hand. "It's okay to cry. Now that he's gone outside, he can't hear you."

She helped them curl up together in her sleeping bag and sat down next to them, stroking their hair for a long time until their crying stopped and their shaking subsided.

"Let me see if I can sooth your pain a little," she said.

She helped them out of their clothes. They were even scrawnier than she'd suspected, their pale white arms like toothpicks, their chests skeletal. They kept their heads down and avoided eye contact, still too frightened to speak.

With a wet towel, Skyla carefully blotted the angry welts on their backs, suppressing her own tears. There was so little she could do. All she had was diaper rash cream. She almost broke down when she noticed other scars on Tom's back, probably from previous beatings.

"I'll do everything I can to keep him from hurting you like this ever again," she promised them between clenched teeth.

Apathetic, the children let themselves be helped back into their clothes, the look in their eyes vacant. She kissed their blond heads and rubbed their arms. "I'll try to make your lives better and won't leave," she vowed. "Trust me. I'll do the best I can."

She added wood to the stove and started the percolator. The smell of coffee almost made her throw up, but he would demand breakfast when he came back. Swallowing hard in an attempt to keep it together, she washed her hands and face and downed two ibuprofens with a cup of water. It was time to get Julia from the bedroom. She found the baby lying on her back in the middle of the bed, her eyes wide open. As soon as she saw Skyla, a big smile spread over her lovely, little face.

"You recognize me?" Skyla cried.

Grateful the baby hadn't witnessed the terrible scene, she picked her up and held her close.

"I love you," she said, rocking her back and forth and kissing her head. "You're so sweet, and I'm so glad I can make you smile."

In the midst of so much misery, she'd found a source of joy, the sweet bundle in her arms warming her heart and making her feel a little bit human again.

CHAPTER

20

WHEN SKYLA RETURNED to the room, she found Tom and Lexi seated at the table, holding hands and comforting each other. They were so brave, their love for each other undeniable. Had the circumstances in which they were raised created their strong bond? Skyla and her sister had fought constantly. Taylor was four years older and lacked the patience for a younger sister. She'd been too busy with her appearance, always wanting to be a princess. Later she'd dreamed of becoming a model. Skyla never understood her fascination with make-up, hair styles, and clothes. She wanted to play tennis, shoot hoops in the driveway, or go to the swimming pool.

"Dad brought more supplies," Tom said, interrupting her thoughts. He pointed to the pile of plastic bags filled with groceries in the corner.

Had it only been twenty-four hours since he'd left with her shopping list in hand? So much had happened since then. So many terrible things. She peeked into the first bag. "Look, peanut butter and jelly, and bread," she said, trying to sound as cheerful as possible. "Your father brought all kinds of wonderful things for us. Isn't that fantastic?"

Calling that monster "father" ate at her, but he was their only parent. Their feelings for him had to be very complex.

Skyla prepared sandwiches for all of them and fed the baby. After they'd eaten a little, Tom and Lexi sat listlessly at the table. Only Julia cooed happily, blissfully unaware of what was happening around her.

The door opened and Rikkerson came in, carrying more bags. "I bought you some clothes," he said.

She couldn't bring herself to answer, her hatred for him too strong.

Appreciatively, he looked at her bare legs. "On second thought. Maybe I shouldn't give you those new pants. You look pretty good right now."

She bit her lip to keep from spitting at him.

"I'm glad to see you still have some spirit left," he said, dumping the bags on the table. "I like my women obedient, but spunky."

As soon as the door shut behind him, she hurried over to examine his purchases. He'd bought her a six pack of cotton panties, four pair of wool socks, two pair of blue jeans, several T-shirts, a purple sweatshirt and a light grey hoodie with a zipper. After making sure he wasn't in close proximity, she cleaned herself with a warm cloth, unable to stand the sticky feeling between her legs for one second longer, and slipped into her new clothes. In the last bag, she found a pair of rugged hiking boots. She'd given him her sizes and just like the blue jeans, they fit perfectly.

He'd also bought children's books, two dolls, one for each girl, and a plastic train set. How could he beat his children and then shower them with gifts?

Heavy footsteps outside announced his arrival. "Time for breakfast, Darling," he said.

She pulled out a plate and prepared a peanut butter and jelly sandwich, wishing he would quit staring at her.

"I want to start another shopping list," she said to distract him. "I need more pots and pans, seasonings, dish soap, laundry detergent, towels, antibiotic cream, band-aides, and much more."

"That's my woman!" he said with a grin and patted her behind. "I knew we would get along after the first week."

She flinched, detesting his touch. "Dream on," she replied with a grim expression.

He laughed out loud and after throwing his jacket over the back of a chair, he straddled it, eyeing her with curiosity.

"Sorry I never asked, but are you married?"

Not willing to talk to him about her private life, the life he'd taken away from her, she shook her head.

"Boyfriend, then?" he pressed on.

"Why would you care?" she answered stiffly.

"Come on," he grinned. "A beautiful girl like you must have hordes of men lusting after her. Tell me."

"I have nothing to say."

He slammed his hand on the table, scaring the two children out of their wits. They looked up from their new toys, their small faces blank with terror.

"Answer me when I ask you a question!" His voice became

dangerously low. "You better be nice, Skyla. You know what will happen when you're not nice."

"I have a boyfriend," she admitted with a deep sigh.

"What's his name?"

"Edmond."

"Edmond? Yak! A typical name for a yuppie," he said with scorn. "Am I right? Is that what he is?"

She thought about Edmond's good looks, his car, his extensive education, and his good paying job. "I guess you might call him that," she admitted.

"I want you to forget about him," Rikkerson snarled, taking out a pocket knife to clean the dirt from beneath his fingernails. "You got me now."

"Of course," she whispered. She'd seen the insane look in his eyes. It scared the living daylights out of her. Especially while he had that mean looking knife in his hands.

"I'm a good-looking guy," he went on. "Well equipped. Women always liked me. I never had complaints. I know how they want it. You'll find out."

Skyla shivered.

"Don't worry. Once you get to know me a little better, it'll get easier. By the way, I like your new clothes much better than that old-fashioned office suit. I love the color purple."

Why wouldn't he shut up? she thought. In the last ten minutes he'd talked more than in all the days she'd been here.

"I'm sure you didn't mind sleeping with Edmond. I know you ain't a virgin," he continued, glaring at her.

She only half listened to him going on about Edmond, her thoughts on her parents and how frantic they must be right now. From them, her thoughts shifted to Troy. Always Troy, his image etched into her brain since their kiss.

"Hey," Rikkerson yelled, grabbing her arm. "Are you thinking about that boyfriend of yours, you slut! Don't believe for one second, I'll put up with any other man ever touching you again. You're mine!"

Yanking herself free, she grabbed the peanut butter and jelly covered knife she'd used for the sandwiches. "Don't you dare mistreat me in front of these children!" she said, threatening to stab him. "I don't know what ticked you off, but you were asking the questions, not me! Now back off!" She had no idea where her courage came from, but she needed to make sure the children weren't forced to witness another ugly scene today. They'd seen enough. Actually, they'd seen enough for their lifetimes. And so had she.

"We have to come to an agreement," she told him in a low voice. "I promise I won't try to escape, but I need to keep my dignity. If you ever hurt me in front of those kids, I'll kill you."

"I was right about you," he said, sinking back in his chair. "We'll have a lot of fun together. I promise you, sweetheart. Within no time you'll be used to me and your new household, and Edward or Edgar will be in the history books. I'll make sure of that."

"I'm not your darling!" she shot back to him.

"Yes, you are. You just don't want to admit it yet. But you will. Just wait."

Oh, dear God, help me keep my sanity, Skyla screamed silently. *This man is totally insane and so dangerous. Please, let someone come and rescue me.*

CHAPTER

21

"YOU SAVED MY LIFE, KIM," Harold told her two days later when she came to see him in the hospital. The nurses and doctors had told him to take it easy, to relax. How could he when his daughter was missing, and his health had already caused more delay than he could stomach. Steps needed to be taken. He couldn't wait another day.

Kim Lowe sat down in a plastic chair next to his bed, holding a small bouquet of sunflowers and a briefcase. She was sharply dressed in a dark blue skirt suit and a white blouse. Her hair was cut into a bowl-shaped bob, the ends trimmed to frame her face. She looked very professional.

"I'm so grateful," Harold went on in earnest. "The doctor told me if you hadn't performed CPR on me and used that defibrillator, I probably wouldn't have made it."

"You give me too much credit, Mr. Overland," she answered, grinning. "Lots of people get heart attacks around me. It's all part of my job. I'm used to it."

At her joke, they shared a smile.

"Is there a vase around for my flowers?" Kim asked.

"One of the nurses will take care of it," he said. "Thank you for bringing them."

She put them on the stand next to his bed and sat down. "How are you feeling, Mr. Overland?"

"I'm in tip-top condition for a man who almost died. Everyone is wonderful. I don't need surgery, and if it wasn't for my daughter being missing, I couldn't be better." He smiled, strain showing on his face.

"Considering the difficult circumstances you're under, I admire your sense of humor." Kim opened her briefcase. "As you know, I started on Skyla's case the moment you called me. By the way, you have a beautiful daughter."

"I know it," he said. "I'm so glad you decided to meet me here in the hospital. The docs plan to keep me here for at least another week, and I'm bored out of my mind already. I want to get back to work, back to my wife, but most of all, back home. No, I take that back. What I really want to do is find my daughter."

"There's not much you can accomplish right now," she told him. "But fortunately, I have good news. Skyla's credit card was used again, and I want to show you the copy of the receipt." She handed him a sheet of paper. "As you can see, I highlighted the most important items."

"Jeans, a sweatshirt, a bra, and panties," he read. "I don't get it? What's so important about those items?"

"Let me explain," she said. "The list is from a department store. I went over there yesterday to get more details about the purchases. They told me the jeans with this SKU number are a women's size 6 which, I understand, is your daughter's size."

"That must mean her kidnapper is buying her clothes, and that she's alive!" Harold exclaimed.

"That's my conclusion, too," Kim agreed. "I don't think we could've gotten better news than this."

"If I weren't married and confined to this bed, I'd kiss you," Harold said, sinking back against his pillow. Closing his eyes for a moment, he laced his fingers together and said a silent prayer. He'd told himself over and over again that Skyla was still alive, but in a hidden, dark spot in his heart, he'd been afraid she might not be. Now his hope flared.

"Does Troy already know about the receipt?" he asked, turning to look at her.

Kim raised her eyebrows. "I thought her boyfriend's name is Edmond?"

Harold stared at her, temporarily confused. Why had he completely forgotten about Edmond? "Troy is a very good friend and a colleague."

"I see, just a friend," she replied.

Harold realized not much got past her. "Kim, I would like you to go to my house. Clara, my wife, will give you the key to Skyla's apartment. I'd like you to see what you can find in there. Anything at all that might give us a clue. Of course, the police have been there already and before you go, you may want to inform Captain MacMillen. He's in charge of the case."

"I'll do that," she assured him, gathering her papers. "Now, try not to worry too much. I'll keep you posted on anything I discover."

He took a deep breath. "Thank you for coming and

renewing my hope. I have the feeling I might be able to relax a bit now."

"I hope so, Mr. Overland," she said, smiling down at him. "I'll call you later this afternoon. Oh, and one more thing. At my request, there'll be a forensic artist at the police station today. She'll meet with the store clerks to draw a composite sketch of our camo-man."

"Camo-man?" Harold asked, suppressing a yawn.

"Yes, we named him that because both times he was caught on surveillance tape, he wore camouflage clothing. Luckily on the second one, his features show slightly better than on the first, although we still don't have much to go on because of the cap and beard," Kim chattered on."

Harold had never heard anyone talk so fast.

Kim shrugged. "I only wish they had a camera in the parking lot of the store, so we could've seen what kind of vehicle he drives. At any rate, I look forward to going over the tapes myself. Who knows what else I might discover?"

Harold nodded. "I hope we can get that sketch in tomorrow's paper. Contact Troy at Overland Insurance to set it up. He's in charge since I'm laid up."

"I will," she promised, taking her departure as briskly as she did everything else.

After facing yet another drug bust, this one with young children involved, George MacMillen was in a bad mood and needed time to recuperate, mentally and physically. Watching toddlers in diapers crawling on a dirt caked floor, then seeing them drink milk from a bottle that had been used to make methamphetamine made him sick. The Child Protective Services Division would be busy again today.

He rushed past the reception desk. "Hold on, Captain," the officer working behind the counter yelled after him.

"I'm not in the mood," he replied and waved him off. "I need at least half an hour. Hold my calls." In passing he nodded at the officers in the bullpen and came to a screeching halt when he entered his office. "What the hell?" he thundered.

Two women had invaded his office. They sat behind his desk, heads bent over a drawing, completely ignoring his presence. He didn't recognize either of them.

"Pardon me?" he said, barely able to remain civil. "I was under the assumption this was my office, but it looks like I'm mistaken."

The petite one of the two, with short black hair, a slim face, and gorgeous brown eyes looked up. "My name is Kim Lowe," she said. "I'm the private investigator in the Overland case."

Great, just what I need, MacMillen thought, *a stranger interfering in my investigation.*

A frown line appeared on the bridge of his nose. "What are you doing here?" he demanded, taking off his wet grey overcoat. There had been no escaping the rain today. "This happens to be my office, and I don't recall inviting anyone in here."

"I was told to use this office for the forensic artist," Kim explained, flashing him an angry look. "Her name is Clair Fougant. She's drawing a sketch of the suspect, using the videos from the stores and descriptions from the store clerks. "

"I need to concentrate," Clair grumbled. "Can you two be

quiet, please?"

Impatience flickered in MacMillen's dark eyes. "I'm not fond of people who poke their nose in my business and make a nuisance of themselves. Do you realize I'm the Police Captain? I have important casefiles on my desk which require my immediate attention."

"It's not my habit to make a nuisance of myself, as you put it, Captain," Kim said with a hint of irony in her voice, "I'd appreciate it if you'd allow us to finish our work. We won't be long, I promise."

Gritting his teeth, MacMillen found a hanger. He hung his coat on the hook behind the door to dry out. What imbecile had allowed these two women to occupy his territory without his consent? He would get to the bottom of it, and he would make sure this never happened again. "I'll give you five more minutes. Then I want you out!"

Kim shuffled the papers in front of her. "We'll be as fast as we can," she said, flashing an apologetic smile in his direction.

He ignored Kim and her smile. Turning his back to them, he approached the window. It overlooked the parking lot in the rear, reserved for police cruisers and employees of the Rosehurst Police, the pavement and cars wet from the last downpour. Some days were just plain tough and took too much out of him. Knowing from experience what it was to be abandoned, children were his weakness, his Achilles' heel. He could never turn his back on a child in need. Whenever they were involved, he tended to lose control. That bunch of lowlifes needed to be locked up for good, allowing their kids to live in filth, unnourished and mistreated. What was wrong with people?

The Overland case weighed heavily on his mind, too. Besides the credit card activity, they had nothing to go on. He raked both his hands through his thinning hair. What he needed was a good workout in the gym, followed by a juicy bacon cheeseburger and fries. Something to make him feel human again.

"What's up with him?" he heard Clair whisper behind him.

"I have no clue," Kim replied. "I'm not experienced in soothing raging bulls. It's probably best to try to avoid him. Patience has never been one of my strong characteristics, either."

MacMillen was sure Kim didn't care at all he could hear her exact words. She didn't even try to lower her voice. That feisty private investigator would be tough to deal with. Very tough.

CHAPTER

22

WITH HAROLD IN THE HOSPITAL, all Overland Insurance responsibilities landed on Troy's desk. He didn't mind. Staying busy kept his mind from wandering and giving in to his distress about Skyla's disappearance. He'd also become the contact person for the investigation, all the decisions and latest news going through him. Being on the forefront gave him the feeling he was at least doing *something* to rescue Skyla, although the uncertainty ate away at him.

He exhaled, the sound ragged, as he remembered the afternoon of her disappearance. One third of the employees hadn't been there for the party, but Skyla was pleased with the quality of the catering and the overall joyous mood from the attendees. He also recalled her comment that she looked forward to the Thanksgiving break. That she felt apprehensive and needed a couple of days off.

It wasn't like her to be anxious or fearful, but he hadn't

asked her for more details. A lot of people fought the flu this time of year, and he hadn't second guessed her when she said she might be coming down with something, too. In hindsight he wondered if something had happened, or if there had been another reason for her unease.

His heart ached. He'd loved her for years. There was absolutely no denying that. But somehow, he'd managed to keep his feelings under control, safe beneath the surface, until his mask slipped, and he had kissed her. Not knowing where she was or what had happened to her, he realized the depth of his feelings. For him, there would never be another woman. His biggest wish was to see her come home safe. Even if that safety meant she would end up in the arms of another man.

The ringing of his phone brought him back to the present.

"Troy, there's a lady to see you," his secretary said. "She doesn't have an appointment, but she's the private investigator Mr. Overland just hired."

"Bring her in," he replied and stood to welcome her when the door opened.

She took his extended hand. "Pleasure to meet you, Mr. Summerton. My name is Kim Lowe."

After hearing how the private investigator had saved Harold Overland's life, he'd assumed she was an older, sturdy woman. Kim Lowe was the opposite, youthful and fine-boned. He gentled his grip as he shook her hand.

"Please, take a seat, M.s Lowe. Do you care for coffee or tea?"

"Neither," she replied. "I would rather get straight to the point. And please, call me Kim."

Troy liked her business-like approach and sat back down.

When their eyes met across his desk, they both smiled. The ice between them was broken.

"All right, Kim, what can I do for you?" he said, knowing he wasn't the first one she'd interrogated. She'd met with Skyla's parents and sister, as well as with her roommate Pauline, who told her all the details about their circle of friends. It surprised him, though, that she'd decided to speak with him last.

"The main reason for my visit is to meet you," Kim said, settled into the chair across from his desk. "You've been involved in this case from the start. I understand you're in charge since Mr. Overland was taken to the hospital."

In many criminal cases, the perpetrator emerged him or herself during the investigation. He'd seen enough forensic and detective investigations to realize Kim considered him a suspect. He didn't take offense. She was doing her job.

"Unfortunately, there doesn't seem to be anything left for me to do except wait for another development," Troy said. "In the meantime, there's plenty to keep me busy here at the office, with Skyla and Harold's work backlog, not to mention my own."

"You haven't tried to find someone to replace Skyla, yet?" she asked.

He stiffened. "No one can replace Skyla!"

"I'm sorry," she hurried to apologize. "I shouldn't have said that. Mr. Overland told me how close you and his daughter are... As friends, I mean."

Friends? Did she really think that? Troy wondered. No, she was shrewd and only wanted to know how he would react.

"I talked to Edmond," she added. "His alibi is solid. So is

yours, but I particularly wanted to talk to you, because you were the last one to see her."

Her intelligent brown eyes pierced his soul, and he flushed. "I know my alibi means squat. That I could've killed her and disposed of her body on my way back from the airport, after dropping off my mother. I also realize I'm a likely suspect because I love her, and she doesn't love me in return. But on everything I hold dear, I swear I have nothing to do with her disappearance and continued absence. So please, all I ask is that you focus your attention on our only real suspect."

"Your love-life is none of my business, and I certainly don't want to offend you in any way. I'm here to help and to do as much as I can to bring her home," Kim replied.

Troy nodded. "Thank you."

"Let me sum it up," Kim said. "As far as we know, no one has seen her since five o'clock on Wednesday, and no one has seen her vehicle either. She's been missing now for two weeks. Statistically, not a good sign. Most people who disappear are found within the first two or three days. The only good news we have is that Camo-Man was buying underwear and other clothes in the size Skyla wears, and using her credit card to pay for them."

"I know about that," Troy replied, getting up to pour himself a glass of water. He was too restless to stay in his chair.

"The composite sketch of the man doesn't reveal very much either, I'm afraid," Kim continued, waving with her hand to decline the glass of water he offered. "The guy's wearing a baseball cap pulled over his eyebrows and most of his face is obscured by his facial hair. He's tall. You can see that. Broad shouldered. Ugly nose. I know if you'd met him before, you would probably recognize him. But I wondered if there isn't anyone, work-related or otherwise, who resembles him just a tiny bit?"

"I studied that composite for hours and even tried to picture him clean shaven. He really doesn't resemble anyone I've ever met." Heaviness pushed on his chest, and he swallowed hard to vanquish the lump in his throat. "I have a hard time digesting he might have her. He looks frightening and unstable."

"I agree," Kim admitted. "But you have to remember this is only a sketch. You have to keep an open mind. Now, isn't there anyone who recently had a claim denied? Was someone fired, who may have been upset about that? Did she have any bad run-ins lately? Was anyone angry with her or being mean? Please, think really hard about this, Troy."

"I wracked my brain over it, but can't come up with anyone." Troy emptied his glass. "Skyla is kind, interested in everyone's welfare, and honest. She's nondiscriminatory, has a wonderful sense of humor, is well-liked, and always ready to smile."

"Which is what I've been told by everyone so far," she said, her voice clipped in an effort to hide her exasperation *There had to be somebody who had a grudge against her, right? Nobody could be so flawless.* "Please, give it some time. Who knows, you might remember something insignificant that could be important."

"All I can say is that something bothered Skyla that day. She claimed she was under the weather, but I thought it might be something else. What it could've been, I don't know."

"That's exactly what I mean. We have to pursue every

option, even the ones that seem remote or non-specific. Ask everyone else if they noticed anything unusual about her that day or in the days leading up to her disappearance." Kim made several notes on her yellow pad before looking back up. "How long does the agency save all of its files?"

"I'm not sure," Troy answered. He'd only worked at Overland Insurance for four years. During that time, every piece of paper was scanned and would probably be saved on the computer for the next hundred years. "Nowadays, everything is scanned, but I believe all of the files from previous years went to the basement for storage. They're generally kept for at least ten years before being destroyed."

"I'll check with Harold," Kim replied, making another note.

Troy grimaced. "Wouldn't it be wonderful if you could scan a face, like you can scan a piece of paper, an entire file, or a fingerprint?" he asked. "If that would be possible, we might be able to find him in no time."

"Technology can do so much already." Kim smiled. "Facial recognition software is becoming widespread. But keep in mind people can change drastically over time. In some cases, people change in a matter of days, courtesy of an accident or severe stress."

Troy thought about Harold Overland and knew exactly what she meant. Skyla's father had aged dramatically since her disappearance and his subsequent heart attack. He was still in the hospital and not recovering as quickly as the doctors had hoped. They'd said he might be able to come home just before the weekend, but that he wouldn't be able to return to work for at least another week, possibly two or three.

"I'll ask my secretary to print out a list with all the names, addresses, and case information from clients who had a claim denied in the last five years," Troy promised. "I'll take that list to Harold in the hospital as well. He'll be eager to go over it."

Kim stood and picked up the briefcase she'd placed next to her chair. "I've taken up enough of your time. It was very nice meeting you, Troy." She headed to the door.

Troy walked her out. "Please, keep me informed."

Before he could close the door behind her, she suddenly turned around. "I almost forgot something," she apologized and walked back in. "Mr. Overland asked me to check Skyla's apartment, so I spent several hours there, going through everything in the hopes of finding any clues the police might have missed. I also checked her mailbox and decided to bring the mail here for you to sift through." She opened her briefcase and handed him the small stack.

"I'll check it out," Troy replied. "Thank you."

Left alone, he went through her mail. The magazines and advertisements were of no interest at all, and he tossed them in the garbage. With a letter opener, he opened her electric bill. The bill was for two months. Nowadays, most people paid their bills online or with an automatic withdrawal. He assumed Skyla did the same, but he made a mental note to double check with the electric company.

The second letter was an offer for a credit card. He considered it junk and dropped it in the box underneath his desk that contained all the papers going to the shredder. The third envelope came from her credit card company. This was more personal. He felt slightly uncomfortable opening it. To his relief it didn't contain anything worth hiding, the charges from Skyla's abductor the only ones standing out between a purchase at an online vitamin store, and a payment to her dentist.

He picked up his phone and called Harold. "Skyla's credit card bill was in the mail. Should we cancel it?" he asked. "If we do, the next charge will be declined when they run it. That might be a chance to catch him."

"That's true," Harold agreed, thinking it over. "But when it's declined, he won't try to use the card again, so it will be impossible to continue to keep track of him or his whereabouts."

"Yes, and Skyla might not get what he wanted to buy," Troy added.

Next, they discussed the agency's file policy.

"It's been at least ten years or more since everything is scanned," Harold said. "Anything before that will be of no use. Unless her abductor has a grudge against me or my father, but I highly doubt that. Yes, get me that list with names as soon as you have it."

"I'll get right on it," Troy promised.

CHAPTER

23

NOTHING HAD HAPPENED during the previous week. Rikkerson hadn't touched her or the children and her wounds had started to heal. Skyla was grateful for that, but she constantly caught him ogling her. Sometimes he made kissing sounds when she was near him. He terrified her, making her feel she lived with a time bomb that could explode at any moment.

The welts on the children's backs faded. Every time she thought about the damage he was doing to them, she fought back tears. She couldn't let them know how horrified she was, and how she loathed the man who'd done this to them. It would only upset them more. He was a filthy animal! How in God's name could a father treat his children this way?

She spent long hours each day teaching the children better table manners, reminding them to sit up straight in their chairs, and to use a fork or a spoon instead of their hands. She also continued their writing and reading lessons. They enjoyed the children's books Rikkerson had bought for them. One of them contained a variety of fairy tales. The children wanted to hear the short stories over and over again.

Every day, she prepared them the most nourishing meal possible with the meager supplies she had, in the hope their gaunt little bodies would start to fill in. Her shopping list began to grow. She added chewable multi-vitamin tablets. Fresh fruits and vegetables were impossible to keep, and the children needed more vitamins and minerals. Especially since it had gotten so cold, the sun barely visible behind the dense grey cloud cover. They wanted to stay inside.

Lexi adored her doll. She carried it around wherever she went. Even Julia held onto her loveable plush dolly, bubbling and gurgling in her own baby language. As for Tom, he couldn't get enough of his train set. It came with a lot of tracks he could set up in multiple ways, and several little houses and trees. His only disappointment had been when the batteries died. Now he just pushed it around and imitated the sound of the whistle. Batteries were on Skyla's shopping list, too. She knew Rikkerson wouldn't object, no matter how long the list grew, since she paid for everything.

That morning, he'd left in his truck. She'd found out he often left to check his traps, to scour for firewood, or to hunt. She was always happy to see him leave. Only today, he returned a few short hours later, bulldozing through the door with a newspaper.

"Open it and look on page two," he ordered, throwing it on the table in front of her.

Her heart sang. How she'd longed to find out news from

the outside world. She glanced over the headlines, but Rikkerson didn't give her a chance and opened it to the second page. On the top were two pictures, one of herself and the other of what had to be a sketch of Rikkerson, wearing his camouflage clothing and baseball cap. Reading the article brought tears to her eyes. They were on the right track. They knew what he looked like. They would find her!

"Do you know what this means?" he snorted. "It means I can't go shopping anymore, because I'll be recognized. Do you get it?"

"But you have to go out, Bjorn," she protested, her heart dropping. "We're running out of supplies."

"Well, then help me come up with a solution, smart ass," he growled.

She knew he was right. In the article, they called him the Camo-Man and everyone would look with suspicion at any man wearing camouflage, especially one with a lot of facial hair and a baseball cap pulled down over his eyes. "Put on different clothes, or shave off your beard," she suggested.

"I don't have different clothes!" he yelled at her. "What do you think? That I can go into my walk-in closet and pick out one of my twenty suits, like your boyfriend, Ed-something?"

"There's a big, navy sweatshirt in the closet in the bedroom," she told him firmly. "As long as you don't wear any more camouflage clothes, you should be fine."

From across the room, he stared at her with distrust, his fingers fumbling with his beard. "You want me to get caught. I won't listen to you." Taking a step closer, he balled his fist, shaking it in her direction. "I intend to keep you here for a long time. You're a real cash cow, lady. And you deserve whatever I decide to do to you. Don't forget you asked for it when you turned me in."

Although she trembled inside, afraid of what he could do to her, for some reason she felt less terrified of his threatening demeanor. The worst that could possibly happen to her already had happened. He'd raped her, and she knew that threat remained. But she'd toughened up over the last several weeks.

"Come on," she said, hoping he would buy into her solution. "All you need to do is change your appearance with different clothes and a different hat. And buy a razor!"

"I have to think this over." He walked out the door.

As soon as he was gone, Skyla began to read the entire article about her disappearance. How she missed her parents, her sister, Pauline, Edmond and *Troy*...

The children had watched the scene from a safe distance. Skyla wondered if they had any idea what was going on, if they understood the situation, that their father had kidnapped her and held her against her will. Probably not.

"What's in that paper?" Tom asked. With his father gone, he stood to join her at the table.

"It says that my parents hired a private investigator to find me," she explained, pointing to her picture. "They're looking for me and want to bring me home."

He took a step away from her, his eyes accusing. "But we don't want them to find you. We want you to stay here with us!"

Lexi looked up at the shrill sound of her brother's voice. She immediately rushed to his side.

"You promised you wouldn't leave us!" Tom continued, pain and fear underscoring his accusation.

"Listen, you two!" she said, reaching out to both of them. "I promise, like I did before, that I won't try to escape. But you can't blame me for hoping they might come and find me, can you?"

"We don't want you to leave us," Lexi cried. "We don't!"

"Both of you listen to me," she said, drawing them into her arms. "When the authorities find me, I promise I'll take you with me. We'll go back to the city, and I will do everything in my power to make life better for you."

"You would?" Tom asked. Sudden tears appeared in his eyes. "Would you really take us to the city, so I can see the real trains?"

"I promise," she vowed, realizing yet again how young and innocent they were.

CHAPTER

24

FIVE DAYS LATER, Rikkerson made a decision. "On this trip, I plan to max out your credit card. It'll be the last time I use it. I don't know what they can do these days. They might be able to inform the police as soon as they run it. I don't trust you. You're too willing to help."

They were dangerously low on supplies, so relief washed over her. "You can also use my bankcard to get cash from an ATM-machine." She thought of the cameras that recorded all ATM activities. "I'll give you my pin code."

"Save it for next time," he replied as he left.

This time, he stayed away for four full days. She almost began to believe he might never come back. That he'd landed in jail or had decided to run for it, leaving them to fend for themselves. She scraped by with the food. The last of the potatoes were gone, the final can of baby formula almost empty. Without the occasional hare, raccoon, or coyote he caught in his traps, their meals consisted of grains, starches and sugar. It had also turned bitterly cold over the last couple of days. A thick layer of snow covered the ground, much to the delight of the children. Bundled up in layers and in coats that were too small, they went outside to build a snowman. With the stove burning around the clock, their supply of firewood had dwindled down fast. She didn't know how they would survive if he didn't come back. When his truck pulled up in front of the cabin at the end of the fourth day, she was actually relieved.

He walked in, still wearing the same baseball cap and hunting clothes. She shot him an inquisitive look.

"Instead of changing my appearance, I decided to do my shopping in a different city," he explained. "Here, Tom! I brought you a baseball cap."

"Thanks, Dad," the boy smiled, catching the cap in mid-air.

Skyla's stomach dropped. She'd counted on him shopping in the same area, but she'd underestimated him once again.

Rikkerson carried in a big bag of oranges and apples. Besides six trays of eggs and a huge bag of carrots, it was the only fresh food he'd bought. The rest of the bags contained canned foods, formula, candles, oatmeal, diapers, laundry detergent, and towels.

"This will help us through the dead of winter," he said, carrying in four more bags with dried brown beans, flour, rice, and potatoes.

"Help us through the winter?" she replied, almost choking on the words.

"They're expecting heavy snow in the mountains," he said. "Even though my truck has four-wheel-drive, this was my last time through until the snow begins to melt."

Skyla's heart fell. Could it be possible she would be here until spring? Could that really be her immediate future? No, this couldn't be happening! She didn't know how she would survive, being cut off from the outside world - both by snow and invisible chains.

The children helped put everything away, excited the cabin was packed with food. Skyla started dinner on autopilot. Although it was impossible to regulate the heat from one moment to the next, she'd gotten used to cooking on the woodstove. The only way to make sure the food didn't burn was by lifting it up or by pushing it to the left side, where the heat was less intense.

After dinner, she fed Julia her bottle and put her down for the night, urging Tom and Julia to play quietly so the baby could sleep. Rikkerson had bought new batteries. They were totally absorbed in the train set, playing happily, but making a lot of noise.

"The food was great," Rikkerson remarked and belched loudly before he went outside to relieve himself. He'd been in high spirits since his return, stirring up a sense of foreboding in Skyla that he was up to something. She knew she wouldn't like it. The minute he returned, the back of her neck began to prickle. All her carefully built up bravery washed away.

"Turn around and look at me," he ordered.

His arrogance infuriated her. Wishing he would drop dead on the spot, she did what he asked.

"Now smile and toss that lovely hair around, the way I like

it."

Cold glinted in her eyes when she stared at him.

He scowled at her reaction. "I have something for you in the truck that'll make you happy."

"It's too cold," she protested. "I don't want to go outside."

"Aren't you curious about what I got for you?" he said, taking hold of her arm.

She yanked herself free from his grip. "No, I'm not."

Suppressed rage rolled off of him in waves. When she backed away, he started for her, dragging her outside with brute force.

"Let me go!" She clawed at his hands around her arms. The door slammed closed behind them.

Pellets of freezing rain, mixed in with snow, stung her face, the ice-cold wind slicing through her thin layer of clothes. Within seconds, her hands became numb from the cold.

In the faint light cast from the windows of the shack, his eyes raked over her body and the swell of her breasts underneath the purple sweatshirt. Alarmed, she turned away from him in the direction of the door. He whirled her around, lust glittering in his eyes.

"Time for some fun," he said, pressing her back up against the wall.

Repulsed, she tried to shove him away. The wad of chew tucked in his bottom lip stank as he forced his seeking mouth onto hers. She pressed her lips closed, shaking her head as she tried to escape, his arousal evident as he thrust his pelvis against her abdomen, stimulating himself like an animal.

"See, I knew you wanted it, little bitch," he said, the words thick and slurred, his long facial hair rasping against her skin.

"Let me go!" she shouted, shoving him forcefully enough to break free of him. She didn't get far. His fingers dug savagely into the flesh of her shoulders as he whipped her around.

"This is where I want you," he growled, pushing her against the back of the truck. "You'll enjoy what I got for you. Take a good look." With his hand on her neck, he forced her to look inside the empty truck bed. His weight held her in place, crushing the air out of her lungs as she tried to squirm away from him.

"Did you miss me while I was gone?" He breathed heavily in her ear, his fingers crawling up in her hair.

"No!" she screamed. "Don't do this."

"I've been patient enough, keeping to myself for as long as I did. I'm a man, you know. So, did you miss me? Answer my question, damn you!"

"I hate you!" Skyla screamed.

CHAPTER

25

"ONLY TWO DAYS until Christmas and still nothing," Troy said to Harold.

The two men sat in Harold's office, going over the latest news. Both struggled hour by hour to hang on to hope. They looked at each other, a heavy silence falling in the room.

After several minutes, Harold exhaled and tiredly rubbed his eyes. "I'll be back full time after the New Year," he said.

He hadn't fully recovered from his heart attack. He only spent a couple of hours a day behind his desk, although he claimed to feel better and wanted to take back some of his old workload.

"Go slowly," Troy warned him. "There's no rush. You and I both know it's never busy this time of the year. With the holidays, people have things on their minds besides taking out insurance."

"Yes, I'm glad about that. It's hard to concentrate

sometimes."

"Any plans for the holidays?" Troy asked.

Harold gave him a sad smile. "Clara and I will spend most of our time at home. We cancelled all our plans, and we'll spend Christmas day with Taylor, her husband and their kids. That way I'll be available at any time if something about Skyla comes up. Then, nobody will complain about us being in a depressed mood, ruining the holiday for them. What are you going to do?"

"I don't know yet," Troy answered. "My mother invited me for dinner. My brother and his family will be there, too. I might do that."

"You should accept her invitation," Harold replied. "It's important to spend the holiday with family."

Troy shrugged, uncertain if he would go. He didn't feel like visiting anyone. Just like Harold, he knew he would be lousy company.

"I haven't heard much from Kim. Have you?" Harold asked.

"Yes, I called her last night," Troy replied. "She's frustrated. Since Camo-Man used the credit card in Seattle, there hasn't been any activity, and nothing else to report. Unfortunately, that guy is smarter than we hoped. The clerk at the store told Kim he bought tons of food. Again, mostly canned and dry goods, and baby formula. We both have the feeling he read the article in the paper and is trying to avoid recognition. The other reason might be that he's traveling with her through the entire Northwest, but somehow I don't think that's the case."

"What do you think, Troy?" Harold asked.

Troy rubbed his thumb from left to right over his bottom

lip.

"I have the feeling he's hiding her in a rural area. That he was stocking up for the winter and shopping that far north so he wouldn't be recognized. We need to widen the search parameters to include the entire states of Washington, Oregon, and Idaho. George MacMillen said Skyla's case is starting to attract nationwide attention. He's been called several times by reporters. We should take advantage of that as soon as possible."

"I agree one hundred percent," Harold replied with a tired look. "The local news channels did a wonderful job, but their reach hasn't been widespread enough. And that list of names, of people who had a claim denied, didn't amount to anything either. It's been too hard to remember most of the cases, some of them so insignificant they weren't even worth the paper they were written on. I also couldn't have done it without the help from all the employees. Expanding the time frame further than five years seems impossible, unless it's the Rikkerson case. I'll never forget that one."

"The Rikkerson case?" Troy asked, immediately interested.

"Yes, Skyla was just out of college and had only worked here for several weeks when that case landed on her desk. Rikkerson claimed disability from his employer. Something about a back injury. But Skyla had seen him working out in the gym and testified against him in court."

"That must've been very stressful for her," Troy said. "What else can you tell me about it?"

"I don't think we ever had a case that dragged on as long as that one. We celebrated after he was convicted and the case was closed," Harold continued. Then he stopped talking for a moment, rubbing his chin. "Now that I think about it; Rikkerson was a tall guy, broad shouldered, and all muscles, attracting a lot of attention with his good looks. He must have been in his early thirties during the case. I can't believe I didn't think about him sooner."

He looked upset with himself.

"There's nothing handsome about that Camo-Man, with that crooked nose and all that hair," Troy assured him. "Instead of a womanizer, he looks more like a crass backwoodsman, carrying a gun and sporting unsightly tattoos, ready for a fistfight at the turn of a dime. Or a homeless man, living in one of those camps. I'm fairly certain we're not talking about the same guy, so don't be so hard on yourself."

Harold nodded his agreement. "It might be a long shot, but we shouldn't rule him out."

~~~

The next day, Kim stopped by the office to talk about the Rikkerson-case. Troy had printed out all the paperwork. There were two full boxes.

Kim carried one down while Troy took the other, following her outside and across the parking lot.

"You don't have to ask how I'll spend my Christmas," Kim joked, unlocking her car doors with the remote.

"Don't hesitate to call me if you have any questions," Troy told her. "I have my cell phone with me all the time."

He opened the trunk, placing both boxes inside. The scene reminded him of the last time he saw Skyla. His heart cringed. Just like that day, it was cold and raining, the only difference that it was broad daylight now.

Kim gave him a warm smile. Although she was suspicious of him at first, she didn't consider him a suspect any longer and shared all the details about her investigation with him. "Are you going somewhere for the holiday?"

With difficulty, he pulled himself together. "I'm still contemplating if I should go and have dinner with my family, but I think I'd rather stay home by myself," he said with a half-smile. "I'm not in the mood to celebrate."

"Don't give up hope, Troy," she replied, stepping in the car. "Once I stick my nose in a case, I don't stop until I've found my missing person. No matter how long it takes."

Throughout the holiday and in the days after, Troy found himself anxiously waiting for a call from Kim. It wasn't until the New Year before she got back to him in his office. She brought in two paper cups with coffee, one of them smelling like pumpkin spice.

"I spent four days in bed with a nasty flu bug," she apologized, handing him the one without added flavor.

Troy liked to drink his coffee black and took the cup, realizing it was part of her apology.

Kim settled into a chair and opened her coffee to blow inside and cool the hot liquid. "That Rikkerson fellow really got nailed by Skyla in court, don't you agree? He had to pay back the lump sum he'd received from his employer and everything he collected in disability. To be able to do that, he had to sell his house and ended up on the street with his wife and two small children."

"I didn't know he had children before I read the entire file myself," Troy said, the thought of any family having to live on the streets disturbing. With a somber look on his face, he listened as Kim continued.

"I found out that the sale of his house didn't come close to covering what he owed, so he filed for bankruptcy. I also learned that afterwards, he did odd jobs here and there. Most of those, he wasn't able to keep longer than a couple of weeks, mainly due to what was referred to as 'excessive aggression'."

"Sounds more and more like our man," Troy said, the hope that they were finally on to something lifting his spirits.

"I agree with you there," Kim said. "But there's no known recent address, only a PO box." Her silky short black hair fell across her forehead and she pushed it back with an agitated gesture. "All I could think of was going all over town looking for this asshole. I ended up at the Social Security office. Since Rikkerson has a wife and children, I expected he might be on welfare."

"Smart thinking," Troy replied, nodding his approval. "What did they say?"

"They directed me to the Rosehurst Social and Health Services. I talked to one of the secretaries and showed her the sketch from the newspaper. Guess what she said? *'Oh, yeah, that could be Rikkerson'.*"

"Are you serious?" Troy asked with growing excitement.

Kim's hair fell back over her forehead. This time she ignored it. "I was ready to celebrate and asked, "Why didn't you notify the police?"

"Wow, what was her answer to that?"

"She said the guy on the sketch could be Rikkerson, but that it just as well could be Smith, Fraser, Cooper, or Kelley."

"I don't get it?" Troy said from the edge of his seat.

Kim threw both arms up in the air.

"Portland's homeless population is huge, and so many men resembled the sketch. Unshaven, gruff looking, ..."

"I get the picture." Troy couldn't hide his disappointment. He got up from his chair and walked to the window. Red-hued evening clouds floated on the horizon, letting rays of sunlight peek through and giving the buildings around him an eerie orange glow.

Kim joined him at the window. She barely reached his shoulder.

"I knew you would be disappointed, but remember, no matter how bleak the outlook, you must keep your hopes up." She gave his arm a reassuring squeeze. "Tell you what, I think I'll go back to the DSHS office and ask if they can make Rikkerson come in for a meeting." She snapped with her fingers. "Yes, I'll ask them if they can tell him his case needs to be evaluated. That he could receive more money if he complies. I'm sure that'll bring him in. And if he does, I'll make sure I'm there to interrogate him."

"How soon do you think a meeting like that could be arranged?" Troy asked. It sounded like a good idea, but it might take weeks.

Her smile wavered. "I'll get the ball rolling. In the meantime, I'll try to find out if he has a vehicle registered in his name. Who knows what might show up there?"

"Shouldn't you inform the police about all of this first?" he asked.

He knew Captain MacMillen and Kim didn't see eye to eye. They both used him as an intermediary, most of the news going through him. "They might be able to help, especially with a potential car registration."

"I will," Kim promised. "But given their attitude so far, I might as well save my breath."

CHAPTER

26

EMOTIONALLY NUMB, the days crept by for Skyla. Something inside her had died, and nothing seemed to matter any longer. The only thing she still cared about was the welfare of the children, innocent victims in the ugly world that this demon had created. Even at night there was no reprieve, as frightening images troubled her dreams and kept her awake.

It was still early in the morning and there was no movement in the house. Restless, she got up and sat in a chair in front of the woodstove, hugging her pillow for comfort, and listening to the crackling of the wood and Julia's even breathing, who slept in the sleeping bag they shared.

The weather had been bitter cold for a long time, with endless grey clouds. The wind penetrated the cracks between the walls. Snow lay thick around the cabin and there was no place to go. They were completely stuck. Each day dragged on and seemed to last forever, giving her the feeling she'd been here for an eternity. She hadn't kept track of the days, and no longer had any sense of time. It could be Christmas or maybe New Year's. She had no idea. And the not knowing robbed her of the smallest spark of joy she might have felt, thinking about the people around the world, welcoming the New Year with champagne and fireworks. A spark she so desperately needed to feel human again.

For hours, she sat in abject misery. In the cabin, each day went by exactly the same as the previous one. Every morning while she prepared breakfast and cleaned up, Tom got water and Rikkerson brought in firewood. After that he left on foot, checking his traps or running his chainsaw, and she would teach Tom and Lexi a few more letters and help them with their reading. When she was in the mood, she taught them a few songs she remembered from her years in grade school, until it was time to prepare dinner, followed by another long, miserable night. That was about it. Of course, the children had no idea how impoverished and monotonous their life was, and how much excitement they missed. They were used to living here, day in and day out, and they couldn't even visualize a different life. When she'd asked them about it, Tom had told her he remembered a little about the time he'd lived in the city, but Lexi, who was a toddler when they moved to the cabin, retained no memories of it at all.

They'll have to do a lot of catching up if they ever get away from here, she thought, hugging herself to fight off the desolation which made her feel hollow, cold, and terrified to the bone. *Was there nothing she could do?* If only she knew where the son of a bitch hid his car-keys. She'd tried to find them everywhere. In the truck, in the pockets of his coat, in the storage shed and the outhouse, in the bed, and even under the floorboards. They were nowhere to be found, and despite seeing dozens of car-thieves hotwiring a car on TV, she had no idea how to do it.

Thinking about cars reminded her of her beloved Jeep. Rikkerson had threatened that her vehicle would end up on the bottom of the pond. *Had he actually carried out his threat?* If not, it might be still parked somewhere in the woods. Would the police be able to find it? Or was that hope as insubstantial as a helicopter landing next to the cabin to rescue her?

Getting up, she stretched and looked outside. The morning dawned bitter cold and grey. She could tell more snow was on its way and escaping on foot was out of the question. She wouldn't last one day. Shuddering, she turned her back on the discouraging sight and returned to the chair in front of the woodstove. How she wished she'd never gone through those files and seen Rikkerson's photograph. If she'd known what would come of it, she would never have reported him. There wouldn't have been a trial, and she wouldn't be here.

Julia made a sucking sound in her sleep. Skyla looked at her, the baby's cheeks rosy, her pink lips adorably pouty.

Fortunately, she had the children. They were the only reason she hadn't lost her mind.

CHAPTER

27

KIM DROVE TO the police station, dreading her meeting with Captain George MacMillen. Since their very first encounter, he'd been arrogant and intolerant of her ideas. She didn't understand why. Yes, their first meeting hadn't gone well, but she'd tried to make up for it by being as considerate as possible and watching her words to avoid a confrontation. *What else could she do?*

She turned into the parking lot of the police station, checking her reflection in the rearview mirror before getting out. If it wasn't for Troy pressuring her to include the police, she wouldn't have been there. But Troy was right. A meeting was long overdue, and Captain MacMillen's help could be very useful.

She stopped at the reception desk in the hallway.

"I've a two o'clock meeting with the Captain," she told the officer behind the counter after he opened the glass partition.

She glanced at the clock on the wall behind him. Five minutes after. She was late.

The officer checked his computer. "Go right in, Ms. Lowe."

Kim opened the door to the hallway leading to the bullpen and MacMillen's office, hoping he wouldn't be in a bad mood. When she arrived, she found the door ajar and the office empty. Plopping down into one of the uncomfortable wood chairs in front of his desk, she decided to wait and looked around. Within a few minutes, she was already bored. This was a waste of her time. She took out her cell phone to check her email just as MacMillen made his appearance. He hung his coat and sat down without acknowledging her presence or apologizing for being late.

That came as no surprise to Kim. Taking his dismissive attitude in stride, she threw Rikkerson's picture on his desk.

"We have a suspect."

He glanced at the picture. "On what grounds?"

Realizing they were again off to a bad start, she took a deep breath. "Skyla testified against him in court. The case forced him into bankruptcy."

"That's it?"

He was such a prick. "It's more than you have."

MacMillen narrowed his eyes. "Maybe." He pushed the picture back in her direction. "But you better change your haughty attitude and come up with something useful if you want us to take you seriously."

Kim stood and snatched the photograph from his desk. "This isn't a game or a competition, Sir." With a disdainful scowl, she turned and walked out of the office.

"You all right, Kim?" one of the officers asked as she

stormed by him.

"That boss of yours is trying my patience in a way no one has ever done before, Brian," Kim fumed.

Brian followed her to the exit. "You just happen to catch him on a bad day," he said, defending his boss.

"Does he ever have a good day?" Kim replied, leaving Brian stare after her. She hopped into her car, thumped her fist against the steering wheel, and stared straight ahead, the light coat of fresh snow covering her windshield blocking her view. *My instinct is right*, she thought, *I know it*.

A knock on the window interrupted her inner tirade. It was Brian. He looked at her with concern, his boyish features in contrast to his imposing patrol uniform. He couldn't be older than twenty-one.

She started the engine and rolled down the window.

"Do you want me to talk to MacMillen?" Brian asked. "With the case becoming high profile in the media and public pressure mounting, I want to do whatever I can to help."

"I appreciate that, Brian," Kim replied. "But I can handle it myself."

A week later, Kim regretted walking out of MacMillen's office instead of pressuring him more. The letter from Rosehurst Social Services had gone out to Rikkerson's PO Box. For four days straight, she'd sat in her car, parked along the curb in front of their office, waiting for her suspect to show up. She wondered if he even collected his mail and if it'd been better to set up surveillance at the post office. There was no way she could cover both places, and sitting here, watching the constant raindrops fall on her windshield, was more miserable than undergoing a root canal.

Sharon, her contact at Social Services, was her only supporter. Sharon worked as one of the case workers in the front office and had met Rikkerson several times throughout the years. She was convinced his welfare check was his only income, aside from food stamps, and that he eventually would show up.

Despite believing Rikkerson was involved in Skyla's disappearance, doubts had begun to assail her in the long hours of waiting. She tugged on her bottom lip. Hanging around the office, dodging pedestrians on the city's busy sidewalk, and watching every stocky guy in a baseball cap with mistrust and apprehension, might have been a complete waste of time. She glanced at her laptop on the passenger seat, the browser still open to multiple websites, and the thick file beneath it.

Come on, Kim, don't lose confidence and allow your mind to spiral down, she told herself. Rikkerson is your guy and you found out so much about him while waiting. She went over the facts in her head.

Rikkerson had no known siblings and both his parents were dead. For most of his life, he'd worked in construction, never able to hold onto a job for more than a couple of months. The longest stint was at a local concrete company across the river. A phone call to the manager confirmed Rikkerson's often aggressive and bizarre behavior, his employment ending after a fistfight on the job four years ago. Rikkerson had landed in the hospital with a severely broken nose and a fractured eye socket, changing his appearance forever. For Kim, this had felt like evidence she was on the right track.

After informing MacMillen, he had grunted his first approval, but warned it was only circumstantial. They would need proof.

At her request, he'd checked out vehicle records without protesting or giving snide remarks. Communication between them was definitely improving, her calls put through immediately instead of him letting her wait on hold for five minutes or more.

It turned out Rikkerson didn't have a car, truck, boat, or motorcycle registered in his name. Neither did his wife, a sickly woman suffering from gastrointestinal problems, possibly irritable bowel syndrome, Crohn's disease, or another undetermined disorder. She'd quit going to the doctor before getting officially diagnosed.

How Rikkerson and his family had gotten around without a car was anyone's guess. They'd fallen off the grid. Aside from the checks being cashed, there wasn't any proof they were still around.

"Mental issues bring a special set of challenges to the table, Kim," Sharon told her after another fruitless day of waiting had gone by. "They're difficult to assess, often because of a reluctance to counseling. Bjorn Rikkerson is a good example of that. He wasn't willing to talk about anything, and he categorically refused to discuss his anger and impulse control issues. He considered himself too macho for that, always blaming others for his problems and never admitting it could be his fault that he'd gotten fired or had no money."

Kim knew the type. In her line of work, she'd met several others just like him.

"It's tough, Kim," Sharon continued. "A welfare caseworker

has to decide when an individual is ready for work and should be cut off from assistance. But when you know a guy isn't able to hold a job and is living on the streets, with two children and a wife with health problems, how can you tell him he can't get his check or food stamps any longer? That he has to get his ass back to work, even though you already know he'll be fired again?"

CHAPTER

28

JANUARY TURNED to February. Snow still covered the surrounding hills. People were grateful with the heavy snowpack in the mountains. It secured the water supply for the coming year, and the ski resorts would enjoy a full season.

Kim longed to go skiing. She pulled out her phone to check the condition on the slopes. Partly sunny skies, highs in the mid-twenties, and a dusting of fresh snow. Being confined in her car drove her crazy and hitting the slopes would be just what she needed. "You should call it quits, Kim," she spoke to herself. If she only told herself that every five minutes, maybe she could ultimately convince herself to take a break. She made a funny face. There was no way she could leave the case and enjoy herself with Skyla Overland still missing after more than ten weeks.

Kim stepped out of her car to stretch her legs when her phone rang. The caller ID told her it was Edmond. Skyla's boyfriend reached out so now and then for an update, adding to her feelings of incompetence and guilt.

"Still nothing?" Edmond accused her. "What are we paying you for?"

Over the last six weeks, no new leads had come in, and no one had used Skyla's credit card. It troubled her deeply, one of the biggest fears that Skyla might no longer be alive. She sighed. Edmond was right. It was about time something happened, so she could pursue another direction, because hanging out here was going nowhere.

"I haven't seen any money from you, Edmond," she snarled and bit her lip so hard it started bleeding. "I'm sorry. I shouldn't have said that."

"I knew Harold should have hired a professional instead of a woman," Edmond replied and disconnected.

That arrogant, good for nothing man Kim raged, venting her frustration by pounding her fist on the roof of her car.

"Good morning, Ma'am," a passerby greeted her. "Is everything all right?"

Kim slipped her phone in her pocket and put on her professional face.

"I'm fine. Thanks for asking," she replied, recognizing the man she'd seen walking his dog several times a day. He wasn't the only one who'd started to look at her oddly, many pedestrians beginning to recognize her. This was getting ridiculous. She'd never had a case that lingered for so long without any results. She felt guilty. She got paid for all her wasted hours and all she did was ... nothing.

From the corner of her eye, she caught a woman waving at her. It was Sharon.

"Kim!" Sharon cried out, running in her direction. "You're missing him!" She pointed with her finger into the crowd. "Over there! At the crossing!"

"Oh, shit!" Kim gasped, trying to see who it could be. "What's he wearing? Camouflage?"

Sharon shook her head. "A dark blue coat!"

With her heart beating in her throat, Kim started running. She'd been daydreaming and if it hadn't been for Sharon, he might have disappeared with her none the wiser. How could she have been so unobservant at such a crucial moment?

"Mr. Rikkerson!" she yelled when she caught sight of him. He just started to cross the street, looked up, and stopped.

Gasping for breath, she reached him. "Can I ask you a few questions?"

"What do you want?" he growled, glaring down at her.

At least six feet tall, his broad shoulders stretched the material of his dark blue coat, his long hair hung around his face in greasy strands.

"I'm a private investigator handling the case of a missing person. Your name came up in the investigation. I was hoping to talk to you about that."

"I don't have time," he barked and turned away.

It was obvious he had no intention of talking to her.

"There's a reward for her safe return," she pressed, following him as he sped down the sidewalk. It was difficult to determine if he was the Camo-Man they were looking for. He did resemble the composite sketch, with his crooked nose and deep-set eyes, but he only had a mustache, and no beard, baseball cap, or camo clothes.

"Can't help you," he said. "Leave me alone."

Keeping up with his fast pace, she continued. "I know you're familiar with this missing person. I would greatly appreciate your cooperation."

"Come on, lady!" he growled, stopping at a side street to let cars pass by. "I'm just a homeless person. I live on the streets. I can't be of any help to you."

"But you do know the Overland Insurance Agency, don't you?"

Giving her a sneering once-over, his hands formed fists, the expression in his eyes warning her to be careful. She was glad they were surrounded by people.

"We know you must have a grudge against them, because you lost your house, your income...."

He looked at her, eyes blazing. "What are you implying here?"

Kim swallowed. The guy scared her to death. "I'm talking about Skyla Overland. She's missing for over two months now. So far, we don't have any suspects, but if you refuse to cooperate, we might look further into your background."

"Are you out of your mind?" He hit his forehead with his hand. "I'm homeless, with no place to go. Do you think I keep her hidden under my jacket?" He turned and crossed the busy street, ignoring traffic, horns blaring as he dodged between cars.

Kim lost sight of him when he turned a corner.

"Damn it!" she cursed, angrily stamping her foot. He was gone. What was she supposed to do now?

Within five minutes, Kim was back at Social Services.

Sharon immediately got up from behind her desk. "Were you able to talk to him?" she asked.

"Only briefly," Kim admitted. "Did you?"

Sharon gave her a sad smile. "Nicole called in sick today and Allison had gone for lunch, so I was alone when he walked in. I was so unprepared and all I could manage was to make an appointment for him to come back at a later time. I know I should have been more assertive. What if he's got her, Kim?"

"You were smart to tell him to come back," Kim complimented her. "Thank you for going out of your way for me in this case. I really appreciate it." She knew she'd asked too much of Sharon as it was, but she still had a few more questions.

"When was the last time you saw Rikkerson's wife and children?"

"Wow, you got me there," Sharon sighed. "I believe the last time I saw his wife was about three years ago. She looked unhealthy and troubled, like she always did, but the children weren't with her." Sharon's sharp blue eyes glittered in anger. "If I'd seen bruises on her face, or if she'd just come forward to tell me she needed help, we would have been able to do something for her. But she never said a word."

"You think he abused her?"

"More than likely. I tried to talk to her several times, but even when he wasn't able to listen in, she wouldn't say a word against him."

"I'm sure you did your best," Kim replied, feeling hollowed out and upset. She came from a disadvantaged neighborhood herself, rife with drugs and abuse in the streets and neighboring apartments. Some of the abuse was accompanied by door slamming, running footsteps, and violent screaming and yelling. A lot of the men were just like Bjorn Rikkerson, and the women sad individuals, trying to keep it together.

Kim's mother had always wanted to shield her daughter from what was going on around them. She'd kept the door deadbolted at all times and put on background music the moment they came home. But there was no escaping, the walls too thin, the hallways littered with junk, and the smell of marijuana infiltrating through the tiniest cracks.

Sharon cleared her throat, her eyes holding a deep sadness. "There are women out there who live through their spouse and who'll never say anything bad about him, even though they're physically and mentally abusive."

They fell into a gloomy silence, knowing that if the women didn't seek out help, hands were tied and nothing could be done to aid them.

"I have another question for you, Sharon," Kim said. "You said Rikkerson went to work across the river. That means he must've had a vehicle, but DMV records show he hasn't registered one for years."

"That's strange," Sharon replied, looking surprised. "Because he always showed up in a white pickup truck with four-wheel drive."

Before going home, Kim stopped by at Overland Insurance to tell the two men about her latest findings. Harold Overland had already gone home, but Troy was still in the office.

"You look overheated," Troy said when she walked in. "I just talked to Edmond. He's home with the flu. I hope you're not getting sick, too."

"Oh, did you hear from Edmond?" she asked with a smirk. "How long has it been since he last called you?"

"He's such a busy man." Troy winked. "But let's not talk about him. Tell me, were you finally able to track down Rikkerson?"

Kim told him of the encounter. "Even though I tried to prepare myself for every possible scenario in my head, asking nonthreatening questions and acting professional, it all went wrong." She felt her cheeks flush with embarrassment.

"I'm sure there was nothing you could've done to prevent him from walking away, Kim. We certainly don't want you to put yourself in a dangerous situation."

Kim shrugged. "All I did was sit there and wait, and that's not the way I usually make my money. When I finally could do something, I failed, and I'm sorry."

Troy studied her with concern. "The police should've been there with you. That would have changed the outcome."

"I'm not so sure about that," Kim grimaced and stood.

Troy walked her to the door. "Since Rikkerson claims to be homeless, he and his family must be known in one of the shelters and in the homeless circuit. I'll call MacMillen to check it out, while you go home and rest, Kim. You deserve it."

Relieved her surveillance was over, Kim treated herself to a visit at her favorite sandwich shop where she compiled a list of homeless shelters and food banks nearby. There was no way she was going to lay low, her battery already fully recharged.

Without booking any results, she headed to the Rosehurst police station the next day. It would be fun to harass MacMillen and see what he was up to. Maybe even tease him a bit.

"He's in his office, Kim," Brian said, working the counter in the lobby.

Kim knocked on the door and feigning nonchalance, she sat down in the uninviting hardback chair.

MacMillen closed the file on his desk and looked up. "If it isn't my favorite PI," he said with a tired smile.

Kim noticed he looked worn-out, the worry lines around his eyes pronounced. Despite their strained relationship, she couldn't help but feel sorry for him. Even though law enforcement personnel were supposed to keep their distance, and not make a case personal, some of them just wore you out, grating at your insides.

"So far, all we know is that Rikkerson is a frequent visitor of the soup kitchen in Belmont, but we don't have a clue about his whereabouts," he said, stretching his back.

"How about his wife and children?"

"No one has seen his wife and children in years." MacMillen yawned, his mouth wide open. "Sorry, I'm exhausted from cracking my brain over this case. The press doesn't leave me alone, and even the mayor is getting involved." He sighed and ran his hand through his thinning short-cropped hair. "The lack of results is keeping me up at night, but it's not like I can work it twenty-four-seven. Other cases require my attention, too."

Success in high profile cases required a tight relationship between law enforcement agencies and involvement from the community. To communicate effectively between all parties was not a skill everyone possessed, and Kim knew MacMillen and everyone involved were being pushed to their limit. She felt the pressure herself.

"I don't get it, Kim. They must be some place close to Portland." MacMillen sighed, letting his hand slide down his tired face.

He wasn't his hostile self, she noticed. He even used her first name. Could it be possible he wanted to work as equal partners, or was he just too exhausted to care?

"I know this isn't such a big city that an entire family can simply disappear into thin air," Kim said. "I believe they probably live somewhere out of town. Maybe with her parents? Or a sibling? What do we know about them?" Discouraged she wasn't any closer to a solution than the day Skyla disappeared, she was willing to grab at straws. Anything was better than giving up.

"Kate Rikkerson's parents live in Arizona," MacMillen said. "Her sister Nora is a flight attendant. I don't see them living with either one."

Another dead end, Kim realized. Nevertheless, she intended to verify the information.

"The chance of ever finding Skyla Overland alive has diminished so drastically, we're considering changing the case from a missing person to a possible homicide," MacMillen said, breaking the silence.

CHAPTER

29

AFTER TWO MONTHS, the confinement of their small world and the isolation were too much to bear another day. Skyla fought to stay afloat, a hopeless downward spiral sucking her in, the cabin walls suffocating, the harsh winter conditions keeping her locked up.

"We'll starve if you don't go to town," she begged Rikkerson. The children clung to her sides, the watered-down oatmeal not enough to sustain them through the day. They shivered underneath their thick layer of clothes. "I have nothing left to make for dinner, other than rice and beans."

Rikkerson opened the cabinets, finding them empty. "Did you ever hear about rationing provisions?" he yelled. "Where's all the food?"

Skyla couldn't believe his narcissistic behavior, blaming her for his inability to provide. His lack of empathy and compassion was repulsive. "I've told you for days," she snapped, gnashing her teeth.

"Damn you!" he cursed. On his way out, he grabbed his coat from the hook. "You better pray I make it through the snow and back."

Through the window, she watched him get in his truck, start the engine and plow his way out.

In the late afternoon, she stared out of the same window, anxiously awaiting his return. What if his truck got stuck? What if he decided to stay away for days, as he often did? Hunger increased the leaden fear in her stomach, her frame thinned to the point of boniness.

The loud roar of his engine made her jump up in anticipation. She rushed to the door and flung it open. She could almost taste the food, a cold cheeseburger from a fast food chain sounding delicious.

Instead of bringing in the expected bags, he walked in empty handed.

"Where's the food?" she cried out.

He shrugged and walked past her.

She slammed the door shut behind them, bitterness fueling her disappointment.

"What the hell happened?" she demanded; hands firmly planted on her hips.

At the sound of her shrill voice, the children immediately disappeared into the bedroom to hide, like they did with every confrontation.

Instead of hitting her or grabbing her hair, he seemed distraught, his fingers searching his pockets for a pack of smokes. He'd been out for weeks. The realization he didn't have any threw him into a demonic fit. "Shut your fucking mouth!" He grabbed one of the chairs and smashed it into the wall. Pieces of wood went flying through the room.

"You better fix that, or it'll be your ass sitting on the floor," she yelled, too distraught to watch her words.

"It's a conspiracy against me," he ranted, his heavy boots hammering the floor, making the walls vibrate. "They're after me, those people. Fuck'em all!"

"How dare you come home empty handed, you jerk!" she screamed, her hands closing into tight fists as she restrained herself from attacking him. "We're starving right in front of your eyes."

He shot her a warning glare, taking a combative pose.

Skyla swallowed hard. She could hardly believe her own hysterical behavior. *Had she turned into a raging madwoman? Had it really come to that?* Mortified, she forced herself to breathe, her reflection in the window revealing an unfamiliar hardening around her mouth. New lines had formed underneath her eyes, making her look much older.

He relaxed his stance. "I went in for more money, but there's some woman tailing my ass. I ain't going back," he growled, gathering the splintered pieces of wood. The chair looked like a total loss.

"What woman?"

"How the fuck would I know?"

She squeezed her mouth tightly shut, battling anger, fear, and desperation. This time, she'd lucked out not to get beaten for speaking up, the chair his only victim. But if she tested him more, he might explode. Her jaw still hurt from the last time he'd punched her. "This is bullshit," she muttered and donned her parka. She needed fresh air.

Skyla walked around the clearing, breathing in and out. It had finally warmed up a little and the snow started to melt. She raised her head to look at the beautiful sapphire-blue sky and feel the warmth of the sun on her face.

Thankfully, her period had come again, an unwanted pregnancy her biggest fear. It gave her renewed hope. Just like the snowstorms and frigid temperatures, her ordeal would end someday. With warmer weather coming and the feel of spring already noticeable in the air, she felt she might survive.

Today was a setback, but it wouldn't be long before Rikkerson would go out again. He had no other choice. Soon, they would have plenty to eat again. With the weather improving, the possibility of being found would increase, too.

Skyla left the clearing and started walking down the dirt road. It ran between the old growth forest of Douglas-firs, Hemlock and Ponderosa trees, blocking her view. The snow lay thick between the trees. She walked on the tracks Rikkerson's truck had left to a split in the road about half a mile away. He'd taken a left, towards the south, giving her the first indication of where she was. She scratched the back of her head. Since she'd been kidnapped, she hadn't had a shower. Her hair was a dry, tangled mess and her wrinkled clothes smelled musty. She didn't care. Her soul was wounded past bearing. With every dreadful day that passed, it seemed harder and harder to remember what her life used to be like. Was she really in a relationship with Edmond? Even when she tried really hard, she couldn't remember his features. Instead of Edmond's image, Troy's face appeared. Troy... How she longed to see him. He'd kissed her, hadn't he? Yes, he'd kissed her in the parking lot just before that piece of scum, that *bastard*, had abducted her.

Hunger gnawing in the pit of her stomach prompted her return to the cabin. She'd been rationing their meager supplies and had lost weight. She held up her jeans with a length of rope. How she hated her captor. He was repulsive, sneaking up on her when she least expected it, treating her like she was his whore and servant. She wanted to hurt him, destroy him, kill him, even though she and the children were totally dependent on him for their survival. If it wasn't for the traps he set out, they would have run out of food weeks ago. But eating oatmeal and beans, and the occasional rabbit or turkey, wasn't enough. Her shopping-list seemed a mile long. He needed to go into town again, or else they might not make it through the winter at all.

CHAPTER

30

GEORGE MACMILLEN went through the evidence of his latest case, the door of his office closed and the blinds in front of the windows drawn. He enjoyed working on a Sunday, with hardly anyone at the station to disturb him. It was the only day of the week he was able to sit down and get something done. He frowned when his desk phone rang, breaking his concentration. Was it his ex-wife again? She was the only one who knew his habits, calling him for no other reason than to be a pest.

"I know you said no calls," the officer working the reception desk said. "But somebody's asking for you specifically."

"Don't worry, I'll take it," he said.

A woman came on the line. "Hello?" she said, "Is this Captain MacMillen?"

"Yes, it is. How can I help you?"

"My name is Connie Peterson. I'm calling about a shoe my son found this afternoon."

"A shoe?" he asked, regretting that he'd answered the call.

"Yes," the woman said. "It's a dress shoe. Finding a shoe like that in the middle of the woods is so strange, it made me think of Skyla Overland, the young woman who was abducted."

He'd had many strange calls in regard to the Overland case. This one topped them all, but it was a tip and he couldn't ignore it. "Can you tell me a bit more about it?" he asked, pulling out Skyla's file.

"It's a black pump with narrow straps and about a two-inch heel."

The details about Skyla's shoe hadn't been released to the public and the woman described it in detail. He straightened his back. Cases had been solved with smaller clues. "Can I get your address? I would like to come by to pick it up and see where you found it."

MacMillen called Harold Overland four hours later, the shoe next to him on the passenger seat. The woman who'd called lived across the river in a wooded area quite a distance from Portland. It had taken him forever to get there, to see the location where the shoe was found, and then drive back.

"A couple of teenagers went scouring in the National Forest and found a shoe," he told Harold. "It looks very similar to Skyla's, and I wanted to follow up with you."

"I wish I could help, but I don't know anything about shoes," Harold said. "Troy was the one who knew exactly what she was wearing and provided the details."

Feeling in his gut that he was onto something, he called Troy. The case needed a break. Maybe this was it.

Early the next morning, MacMillen contacted the sheriff across the river and joined him with two other officers in the forest. Troy had seemed certain the shoe was Skyla's – a certainty that may have been exaggerated by his excitement. MacMillen didn't care. He'd take what he could get.

At the end of a dirt road was a clearing, the snow almost all melted with only a few patches lingering between the thick vegetation and tall trees. There was evidence of numerous abandoned campfires, the location a spot for locals to camp out; the murky water of the nearby lake a fun place to swim in the summer.

The four men roamed along the dirt road and into the woods surrounding it, in search of other evidence that Skyla might have been there. They found nothing. In the late afternoon, after having searched for hours, they were about to give up when MacMillen caught an unusual reflection of sunlight coming from the lake in his peripheral vision. He walked to the edge of the water, narrowing his eyes, willing them to look beneath the surface. He went down on his knees on the wet ground. The water was freezing.

"You're going in?" the Sheriff asked, watching him take off his shoes and pants.

"It's my case and somebody has to do it," he replied, the freezing water numbing his feet the moment he got in.

"You're a brave man," the Sheriff said, holding him by the sleeve of his coat to help him keep his balance.

After only a few steps, MacMillen bumped against a hard surface. He reached down and felt what could be the hood of a car, his fingers following the outline.

"I think I found a car," he yelled. "We need a tow truck."

MacMillen sat shivering in the front seat of his car, the heat at full blast, when the tow truck arrived. Two men in waders stepped into the lake to hook the vehicle up on its hitch. He got out and watched closely as they pulled out a grey Jeep Compass. It was the same kind of car Skyla Overland owned. And the license plate matched the one registered to Skyla. Expecting to find a body inside, he braced himself.

With several curious spectators looking on from a distance, he opened the driver side door. Water poured out of the vehicle, but otherwise it was empty.

"We need divers to check the entire pond and additional officers to search the surrounding forest," MacMillen told the sheriff. "She has to be here somewhere."

CHAPTER

31

SKYLA PREPARED LUNCH out of nothing while Julia looked on. Her nurturing had transformed the pale, scrawny infant into a chubby baby- the only joy in Skyla's life. She was so precious in her innocence, returning her love without reservation. Tom and Lexi had worked their way into her heart, too. She'd become their mother.

They were starting to read and write, long hours of work at the kitchen table beginning to pay off. Skyla wished she could teach them more about the world. They knew nothing about computers, the interstate, a washing machine, a microwave, or even the ocean. Airplanes were just small moving dots in the sky that made noise, electricity a concept they couldn't grasp. How could she explain any of this to them without being able to show them pictures?

When the door banged open, she didn't have to look up to know who it was.

"I need your bankcard." Rikkerson opened her purse to grab her wallet.

"What happened in town the other day?" she asked, not able to hide her curiosity any longer.

Throwing her purse back into the corner, his gaze bore into her. "There's a weird woman hanging out at the welfare office, causing trouble. Trying to frame me. What's your pincode?"

Skyla gave him the code, her mind racing. Was this a good development, or was it only causing more trouble?

He looked down in the pot with watery soup. "Is that all you have to eat?"

"Don't blame me," Skyla shot back at him. "This is all that's left."

"I'm not eating pee," he replied with disgust and waved the bankcard in front of her face. "With this ... with this I'll find something much better in town."

Knowing he would be gone for a while made her feel better. After they finished the soup, she told the children to put on their coats. "I want to go for a walk, maybe climb the hill over there," she suggested. "Would you like that?"

"Sure," Tom said, picking up on her upbeat mood. "I've been there before and know the way."

She ruffled his hair. "Then you'll be our guide."

With Julia on her hip, she followed Tom into the dark forest. The children's boots were too tight, but they didn't complain and laughed while they chased each other.

Water dripped from the branches of the trees and the occasional clump of melting snow landed on the ground, proof that spring was coming. They began to climb the hill. Skyla hoped that when they reached the top, she might see some signs of civilization. Instead, all she could see were trees covered in snow, stretching over the mountains to the horizon. Only the valley in between the mountains showed signs of green.

Although disappointing, she felt more alive than she had in a long time. She sank down onto a snow-covered log, relieved to rest for a moment or two. Without a trail, the hike up the mountain had been challenging, the brush so dense in places, they'd had to fight their way through it. Carrying Julia, and holding Lexi's hand, made it almost impossible.

"We should do this more often," she said, her gaze traveling over the rugged terrain.

She knew instinctively that Rikkerson would never let her go. If she wanted to make it out of here alive, she needed to build up her strength and endurance.

Although Skyla's body was still tired from their hike the previous day, she encouraged the children to go outside again. Usually, Rikkerson stayed away for several days or more and she had no idea when her next opportunity would arise to leave the cabin and explore.

After another meager breakfast, they headed out. From a burlap bag Skyla had found in the shed, she'd devised a sling to strap in Julia on her hip. This would leave her hands free in case needed. She wanted to explore as much of her surroundings as possible, hoping one of the other hilltops close by would give her a view on a landmark, like a river, a road, or the top of a volcano. The weather continued to cooperate. The sun shone brightly in the clear morning sky with only a few white clouds, and there was no wind. It promised to be another gorgeous day.

"This time, I want to walk in the opposite direction from yesterday," she said. "Have you been that way before, Tom?"

"That's the way Dad usually goes to set his traps," the boy told her, making Skyla change her mind. She didn't want to accidentally step in one of them and get injured. She also didn't want to walk over the dirt road, afraid to run into Rikkerson. This made going into the dense forest in front of them the only option. It didn't look promising, and they might get lost.

She walked back into the cabin and started to cut up one of the tattered towels in long strips. "We have to tie these onto the branches along the way," she explained.

"What are we going to look for?" Tom asked.

"It will be like a treasure hunt, where you have to follow the signs," she replied, knowing she had to make it fun for the children.

His eyes grew big. "Like gold, buried in a big treasure chest?"

Skyla laughed. "This forest seems the perfect place to hide one, don't you think?"

The children got caught up in the spell she'd created and hung the little flags. They moved so fast, Skyla had trouble keeping up and quickly ran out of steam. Although the carrying device worked, Julia was still heavy and the weight strained her back.

"I think it's time to take a break," she said, acknowledging they wouldn't get very far today. "Let's have a picnic."

Feeling betrayed by her own body, she sank down onto the ground. She pulled the oatmeal bars she'd made the previous night from her pocket, and leaned her back against the trunk of a ponderosa pine, exhaling in exhaustion.

"Are you tired?" Lexi asked, sitting down next to her.

Julia smiled, her hands reaching for her older sister's oatmeal bar. She already had six teeth and had eaten solid foods for quite a while. Lexi gave her a small piece.

"Yes, I don't think we can go any further than this today," Skyla admitted.

Accustomed to doing what they were told, the children nodded. It didn't even occur to them to argue.

"I hear running water," Skyla said.

"Can we go and see where it is?" Tom asked.

"Sure, but don't go too far," she warned them.

Within a minute they'd found a creek, the rapids cascading over an ancient lava flow. Closing her eyes, she could hear them splashing and laughing. A headache threatened at her temples, and she tried to relax the tense muscles in her neck. If she could only fly high above the treetops, to the safety of her home, far away from the dangerous man, who dominated every waking moment of her days and nights. He terrified her. Now that the snow had begun to melt, she silently vowed to figure something out.

"Skyla," Tom yelled. "Come over here to see what we found."

She scrambled to her feet, picked up Julia, and walked over to the creek. Tom had discovered a small cave, brush hiding part of the opening.

"I think I found the perfect hiding place for the treasure." Tom jumped up and down, excitement written all over his face. "Next time we come here, we should bring a shovel and do some digging."

"Did you go in there?" she asked, worried.

He nodded. "It's empty and small, with dry leaves and loose rocks. It really is a perfect hiding spot. Why don't you go see for yourself?"

A hiding spot? Her heart contracted as her imagination shot into high gear, filling her mind with promising ideas. Could this cave, formed by lava many years ago, be an unforeseen blessing? She sank down to her knees and crawled inside. The air was damp, but not unwelcoming, the ceiling was low and the leaves covering the ground were dry. Although small, the rock walls sharp, there was room enough for all of them inside.

"This is a very nice cave, guys," she said. "What do you think? Should we make this our secret hide-away?"

"I won't say anything," Tom said.

"I won't either," Lexi echoed.

Wondering if it was wise to hide something from their father, she hugged them close to her chest.

When they made it back to the cabin, Skyla cried out in relief that Rikkerson wasn't there yet.

By the next morning, he still hadn't returned. Deciding to stay close, Skyla and the children walked into the woods that surrounded the cabin. Going too far away was a risk she wouldn't take. They also needed to conceal their footsteps that revealed their foray deep into the woods. On their way back, they hadn't needed the little flags on the branches at all. All they had to do was follow their footsteps in the snow, raising concern that Rikkerson would find their cave. She'd come up with the idea of making as many trails as possible, just in case he decided to check where they'd been.

After an hour they went back inside for lunch. Skyla cleaned up after them and warmed up water to do laundry, hanging it to dry over a sisal rope Rikkerson had attached between the two walls in the cabin, close to the woodstove. It was good to stay busy, to occupy her mind.

"Sometimes I miss my mom," Tom said, interrupting her. "I want to go and see her grave."

The children hardly ever talked about their mother and his request startled her. "I understand, sweetheart," she replied. "I'm sure you miss her, but you really have to ask your father to take you to her grave."

"Why?" he wanted to know. "It's only a five minutes' walk from here."

Completely taken aback, she looked at him. "Is your mother buried around here? In the woods?" She couldn't believe it.

"I don't want to go," Lexi protested. She held Julia's hands, helping her to walk around the cabin. Nothing was safe around the baby anymore. Everything disappeared into her mouth and they had to keep a constant eye on her.

"Lala," Julia smiled, showing her six baby teeth. Julia had started to talk a few words. Lala was her word for Skyla.

Skyla held out her hands, encouraging Julia to walk in her direction. Lexi let go of her hands and Julia took her first steps by herself.

"Did you see that, Tom?" Skyla grinned, catching Julia when she fell forward.

Tom sat in his chair, his arms folded. He wasn't interested.

"Can't we do it another day?" Skyla asked. She didn't feel

like leaving the cabin either. Rikkerson could appear any moment, and the sky had turned a deeper shade of gray. It seemed they would get more snow before nightfall.

"Please," Tom begged.

Despite her reluctance, Skyla had to admit she was curious. Tom never asked her for anything. Deciding to give in, she told Lexi to put on her coat while she dressed Julia. She wouldn't leave the two young girls by themselves. They needed to come with her.

When they set out, Julia on her hip and Lexi's hand warm in hers, the wind picked up. A few spring snowflakes brushed against her cheeks. She shivered. It was terribly cold in the shade of the towering firs. Too cold to make an escape, especially since she had to take the children with her.

"How long ago did your mother pass away, Tom?" she asked along the way.

"I don't know," Tom replied. "A long time."

"Julia was a baby," Lexi said.

Skyla grinned. That didn't get her anywhere. Julia was still a baby. "You probably mean a newborn," she said.

After a few minutes they reached a small clearing. Tom dropped to his knees in the snow, in front of a simple wooden cross. The name Kate Rikkerson was burned in the wood, along with her birth year and the year she passed away.

Skyla recalled the young woman in the grocery store with Rikkerson. Her heart ached for the poor mother and her children. She'd only been thirty-one and far too young to die. Skyla knelt next to Tom and wrapped her arm around his shoulders, pulling him close. "What happened to your mom? Was she sick?"

Tom stayed silent for a moment. "She was always sick." He raised his hand to brush away a tear.

Lexi tugged on Skyla's hand. "Can we go home now?"

The knot in Skyla's stomach tightened. Lately, she felt weak and dizzy, and tired fast. The lack of nutrition in her diet had started to take its toll. Was that how it had started for Kate Rikkerson, before she got so sick that she never wanted to leave the cabin anymore? Could that be her destiny, too? Would she be the next woman to be buried here in these woods, a small wooden cross the only reminder of her existence? No! That would not happen to her. She would never give up. She was strong, and would fight to the end.

CHAPTER

32

FEBRUARY HAD TURNED well into March. With it, the Overland case had gone cold again. Kim started to give up hope. For a few days it had looked promising. They'd found her car, but her body was never recovered.

MacMillen was convinced Skyla had made it out of the car in time, before it was submerged. He believed it had been an accident, that she'd been wounded and had tried to find her way out of the forest, succumbing to her injuries somewhere in the woods. Her remains were probably scattered by animals. He felt it was time for him to move on to the next open case needing attention.

Kim couldn't do that. Not just yet. Troy and Mister Overland had told her Skyla never drove out by herself into the woods and neither could imagine a single reason why she'd been out there.

All of MacMillen's arguments were based on speculation

and Kim still wanted hard evidence. She wracked her brain, even though she had no idea what her next step should be. Her gut still told her it was Rikkerson. He hadn't shown back up at the welfare office, and she wondered if he'd moved away or was too worried about another confrontation.

MacMillen had tried to convince her that Rikkerson, or whoever the suspect was, had found Skyla's purse in the woods, and that the fact he'd bought clothes in Skyla's size was only a coincidence. She didn't believe that either. She'd seen Rikkerson up close, the dark and dangerous rage in his eyes. He had seemed more than capable of violence.

Several new cases had begun to distract Kim. Bills needed to be paid, and she needed the income. She limited herself to weekly phone calls to Troy, Mister Overland and Sharon at the Rosehurst Social Services. Until she received a phone call from MacMillen.

"Late last night, somebody withdrew $500 from Skyla's bank account," he said. "This morning they did the same, both withdrawals the bank's limit on an ATM. We don't want to jump to conclusions, but it means someone has her pin-code..."

"... and he must have gotten it from Skyla," she interrupted him in mid-sentence. "That means she's probably still alive."

"Exactly," MacMillen said. "The bank handed over the tape from the ATM's security camera. I've seen the footage. Even though his facial hair is less heavy and he's wearing a black stocking cap, I believe it's the same guy who used her credit card. Harold Overland wants his picture in the newspaper tomorrow morning. It'll be a huge improvement from that composite sketch."

Kim appreciated the phone call. MacMillen had definitely warmed up to her over the last several months.

"Can I stop by to look at it?" she asked.

"I was hoping you would," he replied.

By now a familiar face at the bureau, Kim headed straight through to MacMillen's office. He looked up when she walked in, a steaming cup of coffee next to his keyboard.

"Look at this," he said, getting up from his chair, gesturing for her to take his place.

She couldn't believe he allowed her to sit behind his desk.

Standing next to her, he clicked his computer mouse several times until the black and white security tape started.

"Oh, yes, it's him!" Kim hooted, immediately recognizing him the moment his face appeared. "It's Rikkerson."

She flew up from the chair and danced around the room, knowing her gut had been right all along and that all the weeks of waiting in front of the welfare office hadn't been a waste of time. This was a high-five moment and she couldn't be happier.

"Well done, Kim," MacMillen said. His voice was all business, but his eyes betrayed he was just relieved and excited as her.

"Thanks," she replied, smoothing her hair in the brief awkward silence that ensued. Since their ceasefire, their relationship had improved, but he'd never praised her. It felt odd, but good. Real good.

MacMillen took his seat behind his desk. "We have to inform Overland."

"Of course," she said and walked to the window, listening

to him while he spoke to Harold over the phone.

"Overland hopes to get it on the news tonight and in the papers tomorrow, telling the public that Rikkerson is a person of interest," MacMillen said after disconnecting.

"Great, will you keep me posted?"

When he nodded, she gave him another smile and left his office. She couldn't wait to find out how many tips would come in after Rikkerson's face appeared on the air.

Back in her car, she called Mr. Overland.

"I've been thinking about Rikkerson's white pickup truck," she said after he answered the phone. "It might be worth mentioning the details, too

CHAPTER

33

AFTER COMING HOME late last night, Rikkerson slept in for hours and seemed in a good mood when he finally emerged.

His trip must have gone well, Skyla thought, but kept her mouth shut. She was used to tiptoeing around him, his moods changing in the blink of an eye. She could never figure out what set him off. It could be something as insignificant as a spoon falling on the floor, or an airplane flying overhead.

"Time for breakfast, woman," he said, bringing in one bag filled with groceries after the other.

Within minutes, the cabin was filled with the mouthwatering smell of crisp bacon and fried eggs. It had been so long since they'd had anything decent to eat, the children couldn't wait until she was done.

Lighting a cigarette, Rikkerson smoked, his stare never leaving her. After clearing the table, she filled the cast iron pot with water from one of the buckets to do the dishes. Rikkerson lit his second cigarette, still eyeing her.

"You're acting like someone died or something," he said. "Anything happen I should know about while I was gone?"

Skyla shivered at his words. Like the Devil himself, it seemed he could look straight into her soul and read her thoughts.

"The weather was nice while you were gone," she said, her voice quavering. "Maybe I should grow a garden this summer so we can have fresh vegetables."

He gave her a sharp look and stood, stopping right in front of her. "A bit complacent, aren't we?" he said, his breath hissing through his lips.

She looked away from him. "It was just an idea."

He let out a short laugh before wrapping his arm around her neck, almost choking her. "I have an idea, too," he whispered in her ear.

She cringed under his touch; his intentions clear.

Before letting her go, he emitted a harsh bark of laughter. "But it has to wait 'til tonight." He took a long drag off his cigarette and threw it on the floor. "I have to check my traps." He crushed the still burning tip with his boot as he walked out the door.

To make sure he was gone, Skyla waited five minutes after watching him disappear into the woods and ran outside to his pickup truck. Maybe for once, he'd left the key in the ignition, and she would be able to drive away. No such luck. Frantically she searched in every possible place where he could have hidden it. Again, nothing. Through unshed tears, she searched the glove compartment for the second time, throwing the maps and other paperwork onto the seat. Nothing. She began to stuff everything back inside the glovebox when one of the maps fell on the floor. It was the map of the Gifford Pinchot National Forest. Tom had told her they lived in the Clifford Forest, named after a big red dog. This was it. She knew now where she was, and that when she made her escape, she would need to go south to get home. The same direction as the cave.

After making sure everything was exactly as she'd found it, she went back inside to organize the groceries. Rikkerson could return at any moment. Tom and Lexi were already busy emptying the bags and putting everything out on the table. The beef jerky and candy bars he'd bought would be great to hide inside the cave. He'd also bought a backpack. That would be useful, but if she snuck that out, he would miss it right away.

The door flew open and slammed against the wall with a loud bang. "What have you guys been doing while I was gone?" Rikkerson thundered. His angry gaze riveted on her.

Skyla dropped the candle in her hand. It rolled across the floor.

"There are footsteps leading in and out of the woods everywhere," he ranted on, spittle flying out his mouth. "Don't bullshit me about not being out. Somebody better speak up."

He took several threatening steps forward, a low growling sound in his throat.

Dread settled heavily in her stomach, her pulse beating rapidly, her mind a total blank.

"That's it!" he yelled, lunging forward.

She took several steps back to get away from him.

"The weather was nice," she managed to say as he caught

her between himself and the woodstove. Steam from the boiling water rose from the cast iron pot.

"Don't bullshit me, damn you!" He dug his fingers into the flesh of her arm, shaking her. "Where have you been?"

"We went to see mom's grave," Tom said, his gaunt face pale with fear.

"You had no business going there, boy!" Rikkerson roared, releasing Skyla as he turned on his son. "But that's not the only place you guys went. I warn you, don't jerk me around."

"We didn't go anywhere else," Tom said, fighting back tears. "We only walked around the cabin and played in the snow."

"Don't give me that crap!" his father shouted. "I want the truth!"

Skyla watched him reach for his belt and immediate rage replaced her fear. "Don't you dare strike him, Bjorn!" she burst out, her heart thundering in her chest. "He's telling the truth!"

"No, he's not, bitch!" he screamed, his eyes wild and bloodshot. "And I'll get the truth out of one of you before this morning is over."

She didn't want to succumb to the terror raging through her, but she'd never seen him like this. He was insane, totally insane. Like a crazed animal.

Despite her desire to stand up to him, she found herself cowering in the face of his deranged behavior, both her hands covering her mouth and nose.

"Afraid of me, aren't you?" he sneered. "Maybe I should beat the living daylights out of you first. Let the kids see who's boss. Ha! After they realize what a gutless wonder you really are, it won't be 'Skyla this', and 'Skyla that' anymore."

"Don't hurt her, Daddy, please!" Lexi cried as she ran to Skyla, clinging to her leg. Tom joined her, defiantly eyeing his father.

With both his children taking her side, the confrontation spelled nothing but disaster.

When he reached out to Skyla, she screamed. "Leave us alone, you bastard!"

"What did you call me?" he said, his voice hard as steel.

Holding her ground, tears of anger blinding her, she raised herself up. "Don't you dare hurt us!"

"I don't allow my women to speak back to me," he spat. He shoved Tom and Lexi away from her with a powerful swing, knocking them into the wall.

Skyla grabbed the handle of the pot on the stove and swung it around, knocking him in the head. Boiling water splashed out and streamed down his face and neck.

"You bitch!" he roared, reaching for his face, which contorted with rage and pain. "You crazy bitch! I'll kill you for this..." Before he could finish his sentence, she swung at him a second time, the pot connecting with his temple.

He swayed back and forth for a moment, a bizarre expression on his face, until he fell forward onto the floor and writhed briefly. Then, he lay completely still.

Skyla stared down at his motionless body, stunned by what had happened.

Tom tugged at her arm, crying hysterically. "Come on, Skyla," he cried out. "We have to leave before he wakes up. If we don't, he'll kill you."

His words didn't register until she heard Lexi sobbing. A frightened Julia joined in, their wailing like a siren going off in her head. She snapped into action, ready to fight for her life once again.

"We have to tie him down so that he can't follow us," she said. "Get the sisal rope from the shed, Tom. Hurry!"

Lexi still sobbed uncontrollably, while little Julia screamed at the top of her lungs. "Lala! Lala!"

Ignoring both girls, Skyla hurried over to the backpack and threw in a few diapers and as much food as it would hold. She didn't have time to hug and soothe them or assure them that it would all be fine. They would have to wait.

As soon as Tom came back with the roll of sisal, she bound Rikkerson's wrists together behind his back, going around several times until she was certain he wouldn't be able to free himself. After that, she searched through his pockets, almost throwing up from fear that he might wake up. "Tom, do you know where your father might hide his truck keys?" she asked.

He shook his head, his mouth quivering.

"It's okay," she said. "Now try to calm down your sisters. We all have to put on an extra t-shirt, two sweatshirts, and grab our coats and hats. We're leaving."

Dressed in several layers of clothes, she picked up Julia and placed her in the sling, at the last moment topping off the backpack with the two dolls. After that, she grabbed the sleeping bag and wrapped it around her neck. They needed to take something to keep them warm.

The two children joined her, their worn little faces pale, their eyes terrified. The horrible event that had enfolded was taking its toll. Skyla sensed they were both in shock.

"I love you very much," she told them. "But we can't waste any time, and we have to make it to the cave. Understand?"

Their breathing was shallow, and their shoulders shook from trying to suppress their anguish and fear. Skyla's heart broke for them. With tears streaming down her face, she led them into the woods.

It took them two hours to reach the cave. Exhausted, they crawled inside. Skyla couldn't take another step, the weight of the baby and the backpack too heavy for her emaciated frame.

She took off the sling. Julia smiled, happy to be released from its tight grip. Tom helped her remove the backpack from her shoulders. Her muscles ached with the weight of their lives literally on her back. Lexi spread out the sleeping bag, so they didn't have to sit on the cold dirt floor.

These kids are amazing, Skyla thought not for the first time. Their mother must have been an admirable woman. She opened a box of cheese crackers and gave them all a candy bar. They ate in complete silence, too wrung out to talk.

"Let's try to sleep here for a little while," she said, trying to make it as comfortable for them as possible. The four of them curled up together in the sleeping bag, seeking warmth from each other's bodies. She stroked the children's hair and began to sing a lullaby. Would they ever heal from what had taken place, their father throwing them against the wall as if they were nothing? Would she?

The children slept restlessly, waking up several times. Skyla assumed they were having nightmares, just like her. At the end of the day, they ate a little. Tom slipped out of the cave to get water from the creek in the plastic bottle he'd carried along.

"What direction do we go, Skyla?" he asked.

"Don't worry," she answered. "I know which way, but we

can't leave now. It's getting dark and we must wait until daybreak before we can get going again."

Feeling safe in the cave, the narrow opening covered with branches, they snuggled up together for a cold night. The temperature felt like the low forties, and their breaths showed in the cold air.

CHAPTER

34

EARLY THE NEXT MORNING, cold to the bone and teeth chattering, Skyla braced herself for another grim and challenging day. Unless they came across a road, she didn't believe they would find a way out of the endless wilderness anytime soon.

"We have to hurry," she said, encouraging the children to get ready. "Let's go." She hoisted the backpack up and threw the sling over her head, paranoid to see Rikkerson appear any moment.

Julia crawled away, making herself small against the back of the cave, sulking. "Please, Julia," she coaxed the toddler. "Come here." When that didn't work, she offered her a piece of candy, too worried to hang around any longer.

When they departed, the first rays of sunshine crept over the hills to her left, the sky partly cloudy with a thin layer of fog hanging between the trees. Stiff limbed, they followed the meandering creek downstream. Without a path through the dense forest, their progress was slow, the terrain uneven and the ground cover thick. Ferns and moss grew in abundance close to the stream, the clear water tumbling swiftly over the rock bottom, making the soil wet and slippery.

"What's that?" Tom asked, when they heard rustling between the shrubs.

Despite the cold penetrating deep into her bones, Skyla felt drops of perspiration between her breasts. "Probably just a small animal," she replied, one hand clutching her throat in fear it could be Rikkerson, prowling them.

If it was him, all hope was lost, the weight of Julia and the backpack too heavy for her to carry much longer. Every muscle hurt, as if they'd walked for days instead of hours.

Ten minutes farther, her labored breathing burned in her lungs. What if they couldn't find their way out? What would happen if she got injured? Close to a panic attack, she shivered and wiped the cold drops of perspiration off her forehead.

"We have to stay optimistic and brave," she encouraged the children and herself. "Every step will bring us closer to home."

Gradually it warmed up as they struggled their way downstream, around massive boulders and tall fir and pine trees, and through the heavy undergrowth, the snowpack on the ground getting thinner and thinner.

"We'll take a break soon," she told the children, her back screaming to be relieved from its burden. "Do you see that clearing through the trees, just ahead of us? That's where we'll have a picnic."

They left the creek and were rewarded by warm sunlight

bathing the meadow, the snow already melted. With a moan of relief, Skyla sank down on her knees and put Julia on the ground before lowering her backpack. Excited to be free, Julia immediately walked away on her wobbly legs, falling after making it only a few feet. Skyla forced herself back up, afraid she would start to wail. The sound would travel for miles in the stillness around them. Instead, Julia rolled over, smiled, and worked her way back up.

"You want some candy?" Skyla handed the children a candy bar, sharing her own with Julia, who'd wobbled back at the prospect of food.

Tom had carried the sleeping bag and spread it over the tall grass next to a log that must have fallen over years before, most of the bark already gone. They sat down next to each other, leaning up against it.

Skyla pulled out two apples and shared them. Who knew how long they had to be out here? They needed to be conservative with their meager supplies. After changing Julia's diaper, the baby fell sound asleep without a care in the world, thumb in her mouth. Tom and Julia lay down, too. With the children snuggled up against her, she slipped her arms around them and looked at the clearing. There were tree stumps everywhere, cut off straight with the use of a chainsaw. New trees had started to grow around them, most of them not taller than three or four feet. It was evident they had been logging here years ago. An access road had to be nearby. Giving her tired body a bit more rest, she closed her eyes for a while and then forced herself up.

"Tom," she whispered, gently shaking the arm of the dozing boy. "I want to walk around the clearing, to see if I can find a road. You have to stay here with the girls. You understand?"

He looked up, immediately alarmed.

"I won't be long," she promised.

CHAPTER

35

TIPS CAME IN all day after Rikkerson's name, photo, and the description of his car were published in various newspapers and on their websites. Harold Overland had increased his reward for the tip leading to Skyla's safe return. He hoped to persuade people to come forward with information, especially the people who might know Rikkerson personally and who would be the least inclined to give him up.

Most tips came in through the police hotline. They were mainly from callers interested in the reward, people who'd seen Rikkerson around town, in a homeless shelter or soup kitchen, or from people who'd worked with him at various job sites in the past. Other tips came in through the police's website, most of them from people who wanted to stay anonymous. One of them was from a man claiming he was Rikkerson's stepbrother, others from a bank clerk, a social worker, and a former employer, none of them leaving their name.

Kim lingered around the police station all day, too nervous to do anything else. Her phone rang every hour. It was either Troy Summerton or Harold Overland, asking for an update since Chief MacMillen didn't answer his phone, too busy following up on leads.

MacMillen worked his way through all the tips that came in. He'd been at it non-stop since six in the morning, another cup of black coffee keeping him alert. So far it had been disappointing, the most promising tip coming from Kate Rikkerson's sister. She was extremely worried over her sister's whereabouts. She hadn't seen or spoken to her in more than three years.

"That truck you're talking about belonged to our parents," she said. "They gave it to my sister, but kept the registration in their name, paying for the tags and insurance. It was the only way they could help her and the grandchildren."

With the license plate number and accurate description of the make and model of the truck at hand, MacMillen updated the all-points bulletin.

"Where does he keep them hidden, if even her family hasn't seen her for so long?" he muttered to himself.

His desk was covered in notes, his eyes roaming over them as he pieced them together in chronological order, making it possible for him to find what he wanted to find or to see what he wanted to see.

A knock on his door made him look up. "I've someone on the line who claims to know where Rikkerson lives," a police officer said, excitement written all over his face. "Can I patch him through?"

"Of course," MacMillen said, picking up the phone.

"Is this the detective who's working the Overland case?" a man said, the connection cutting in and out.

"Yes, it is. Can you state your name, please?"

"My name is Peter Santiago, sir," the man said.

MacMillen pulled out his notepad and wrote it down.

"Sorry about the bad connection," the man continued, "But I'm calling from a remote area and cell service is limited out here."

"Go ahead, Mr. Santiago." MacMillen took a sip from his cold coffee and then pushed it away.

"I'm a park ranger's aide in the forest. The guy looks really familiar to me. I also believe I've seen that white pickup out here numerous times."

MacMillen narrowed his eyes, trying to decipher what the man said. "Out in the forest, you say?"

He slid forward to the edge of his seat. Skyla's car had been found in a remote part of the National Forest and this guy might be onto something.

"There's an old cabin out here, just outside the forest's boundary. I believe that's where he hunkers down sometimes."

"Can you take us to this cabin you're talking about?" MacMillen said, the air he breathed suddenly filled with urgency and expectation. This was the call he'd been waiting for. He knew it for certain.

"How far are you from the city?" He checked the time on his cell phone. It was already getting dark.

"I'm not sure," Peter replied. "I believe it's at least an hour and a half to the ranger station. From there, probably another forty-five minutes to the cabin."

MacMillen opened Google Maps on his computer and typed in the location of the ranger station. Peter was right. By the time they would make it out to the cabin, it would already be dark for hours.

"The last part of the way may not be accessible yet because of snow," Peter continued. "Those roads don't get plowed in the winter and four-wheel drive will be required."

MacMillen wanted nothing more than to solve the case, but trying to find his way in the dark to follow up on a lead that might not pan out would be irresponsible and foolhardy. "Why don't we meet tomorrow morning at the ranger station. Does nine AM sound all right to you? I definitely want to check it out."

"I'll be there waiting for you," the young man said and disconnected.

Brian, the officer who'd taken Peter Santiago's call, stood waiting in the doorway. "Sorry I'm hanging around," he said. "I couldn't wait to find out what he said."

MacMillen repeated what he was told. "I don't want to get stuck somewhere in the middle of nowhere," he explained his reasoning. "Besides, confronting Rikkerson on his own turf without visibility could be dangerous. He more than likely carries a gun and might use it. We can't take that risk."

Brian nodded. "Can I join you tomorrow morning?"

"Yes, I want to take you and Larry along."

MacMillen called the ranger station to double check Peter Santiago's story. He waved Brian into a chair. The young officer had worked the case closely with him and been a great help.

"With all the hunting and fishing out here in the forest, we see people wearing camouflage all the time," the ranger said after he got him on the phone. "But Peter's right about the white truck. I believe it's worth checking out, and I plan to join you."

MacMillen's stomach began to growl, and he stood. He'd worked long hours today and had to get up early again tomorrow morning. Time to grab a burger and get some much-needed sleep.

"Aren't you going to inform Mr. Overland?" Brian asked, watching his boss grab his coat on the way out the door. "I'm sure he's waiting to hear from you."

MacMillen shook his head. "No, I don't want to get his hopes up. It's already hard enough on the guy and it might be a dead-end."

"How about Kim? She's been hanging around all day, pacing the hallway and emptying the coffee pot."

Brian's words stopped him in his tracks. Kim had been pestering him continuously for the latest news, but if they encountered Rikkerson tomorrow, the case might escalate, and the situation could become volatile. He didn't want her around. This was police business.

"Don't tell her anything. She may want to come along."

In the hope to evade Kim, MacMillen tried to sneak out of the police station. No such luck.

"What's up, Sherlock?" Kim joked when she caught sight of him in the hallway, giving him a big smile.

"You're still hanging around here?" he asked, heat creeping up his collar.

"No, I just came to see how you're doing, Georgy," she

replied.

He knew she was teasing him, trying to get under his skin. She was good at that.

"Bull!" he growled, trying to make his way around her. If he ignored her, she might get the message he didn't want to talk.

"Don't you remember we're working on the same case here?" she said, taking a step to the side to block his way.

She moved so unexpectedly, he stepped on her toes and almost knocked her over.

He reflexively grabbed her shoulders to steady her.

"Ouch, you clutz!" she exclaimed, her cheeks a bright red. "What did you do that for?"

"Sorry," he mumbled. He felt like a clumsy ox. "I don't have time for this." He ducked his head in embarrassment, taking off before she could delay him again.

~~⌇~~

Instead of leaving, Kim walked into the bullpen. Brian, who sat behind his desk, was the only one there. She liked him, the look in his eyes still eager and unspoiled from all the gruesome realities police officers often faced, his enthusiasm to help unexpected in the hard world around him.

"Hi, Brian," she said in her most cheerful voice. "Anything happen I should know about?" She stopped behind him and looked at the computer screen. His browser displayed a map of the national forest across the river, the same forest where they'd found Skyla's shoe. That couldn't be a coincidence.

Brian clicked the site away. "Just checking for a weekend getaway," he said, blushing like a child.

She knew he was lying. "What? Don't tell me you didn't get any useful tips today."

Brian's face now turned beet red. "We did, but nothing panned out," he said and began messing around with some of the papers on his desk.

"Come on, Brian. I know you're hiding something. Please, tell me. You know how hard I work on this case."

"The Chief wants to keep this under wraps, Kim." He glanced around to see if anyone was listening to their exchange. But they were alone.

"I wouldn't do anything to interfere in his investigation. You know that, right?"

Brian still hesitated.

Kim heaved a sigh. "Mr. Overland hired me to help with the case, but I haven't been able to earn my wages. I'm frustrated and need something to tell him. Besides, we're all in it for the same goal."

Brian's shoulders slumped; his eyes trained on the floor. "As you know, we've had a ton of phone calls, but nothing about the guy's whereabouts until late this afternoon."

He spoke so softly, Kim needed to bend forward to hear him.

"A guy who works in the Gifford Pinchot National Forest says he's seen him out there. Tomorrow morning, we're driving out to the ranger station to meet him at nine."

Kim smiled warmly in the hope he didn't sense her guilt for pressing him.

"I owe you, Brian," she said, vowing to herself to make it up to him if he got into trouble because of her. "Thank you."

On her way out of the station, she called Harold Overland.

"Tomorrow morning at eight-thirty, I have a meeting at the ranger station in Trout Lake with a guy who claims to know where Rikkerson lives," she said. "Do you want to join me?"

CHAPTER

36

WITH HER COAT knotted around her waist, Skyla walked around the meadow. She almost dropped to her knees in gratitude when she noticed what had once been a logging road. It was heavily overgrown, but a potential way out and the only glimmer of hope she'd felt in days. She immediately ran back to the children.

"Don't ever leave us alone again," Lexi said, crashing into her the moment she appeared. "I was so scared." Tears rolled down her cheeks.

Even Tom looked angry. "You promised you would never leave us, but you did," he accused.

She'd only been gone for twenty minutes, but for the children it had been far too long. "I'm so sorry, sweethearts," she said, almost in tears herself. They depended on her and had been terrified she wouldn't come back. "I tried to figure out in what direction to go, and found an old road we can follow. Are you ready to walk a bit farther?"

It was much easier to walk on the dirt road than through the dense vegetation of the forest as it curved its way down the mountain slope. Skyla was optimistic. This was exactly what she'd hoped for.

After walking for several minutes, Tom pointed into the forest. "What's that?" He left the road to take a closer look.

Skyla followed him several yards until she detected an abandoned vehicle among the dense shrubs and bushes. It was completely rusted out and overgrown with moss. One of the doors was missing and the tires were gone.

"Why would somebody leave a car here?" Tom asked.

"It was probably old and broke down," she said. "Let's go, Tom."

The car was of no use to them and she wanted to take advantage of the daylight, the sun already starting its descent behind the Cascades Mountains.

A sudden distant rumble made her stop. She glanced up, the sky now a dark grey instead of blue. It looked like a thunderstorm was headed their way. Uncertain of what to do, she glanced around. Besides the old junker a few hundred yards back, there was no place to take shelter. A lighting flash, followed by a second deep rumbling, decided for her.

"Let's head back to the car to ride out the storm," she said, hitching Julia up higher on her hip.

Closer to the car, she noticed it was an old station wagon. The front window was broken, and the driver seat door was missing, but the trunk was spacious and pretty much intact. It smelled moldy and damp, but the leaves piled up inside were dry and it wasn't unpleasant. Lexi and Tom spread out the sleeping bag and the moment they huddled inside, the first raindrops fell. They'd made it just in time.

The storm intensified almost instantly. The sky cracked wide open above them, the branches of the trees thrashing wildly back and forth by the force of the strong wind gusts. For hours, they listened to the heavy rain beating down on the metal roof and the crashes of thunder, followed by lightning that splintered the darkened sky. Skyla didn't even want to consider what would have happened to them if they hadn't found the abandoned vehicle.

"They're taking pictures of us," Skyla told the children, remembering what her father used to say to her when, as a little girl, she'd been afraid of a thunderstorm. But the children had no idea what she meant. They'd never seen a camera before.

Slowly the rain began to ease and soon the thunder dissipated.

"Perhaps the worst is over," she said, knowing they wouldn't be able to go any farther today. It was completely dark outside, and they would have to spend another night in the forest.

Skyla woke up at first light. The night had been like all others, with endless hours of insomnia as anxiety took over. Even during the day, her mind was a mess of jumbled thoughts, and her apprehension churned in her stomach.

After waking the children, she went outside to empty her bladder. Overnight, the rain and wind had stopped and the weather looked promising, but it was still early and bone-chillingly cold. She hoped that as the sun climbed up higher in the sky, it would gain strength and warm everything up. Her survival instincts prickled. She wanted to get moving.

Inside the car, Lexi rolled away from her. "I don't want to," she moaned. "I have a headache."

"Come on, sweetie," she encouraged the child. "We have to eat something and then head out."

"It's too cold," Lexi whined, slowly pushing herself up.

The girl's face was flushed. She looked feverish. Skyla reached out to touch her forehead. She was burning up.

Overcome with despair, Skyla's features crumpled, her shoulders shaking from suppressed sobs. She was close to collapsing and felt like pounding her fists against the sides of the trunk, so hard that it would hurt. She'd been a fool to attempt an escape with three vulnerable children. She'd put them and herself at an intolerable risk.

Julia reached into the backpack, pulling out a pack of saltine crackers. She blew a few bubbles and smiled. Tom went for the bag of jerky. Skyla tore open the plastic wrapper of the pack of saltines with her teeth.

"Here," she said and handed the baby a cracker. Then she turned toward Lexi. Her cheeks were bright red and her long black hair a tangled mess. "Let's just give it a few minutes and see how you're feeling then," she said, hoping it was only a temporary bout of whatever that caused the girl's sudden spike in temperature.

Lexi obediently took the saltine Skyla handed her and took a small bite. Her eyes glazed over.

Overnight, they'd put the water bottle outside to fill it with fresh, rainwater. Skyla encouraged the children to drink.

"What do we do now?" Tom asked.

Skyla closed her eyes to think. She'd had no other choice than to escape from that crazed man. They wouldn't have come out of it unscathed, and the children would have been subjected to additional horrors. But what could she possibly do now with a sick child on her hands? She couldn't drag her through the forest. Leaving her or the children behind was not an option, either. Neither was sending out Tom. He was far too young and would be petrified on his own.

"I don't know, sweetheart. I really don't know," she whispered, desperate tears streaming down her face. "Let's just pray for a miracle."

CHAPTER

37

REGAINING CONSCIOUSNESS, Rikkerson found himself in such intense pain he could barely breathe, let alone raise his head. With his eyes closed, he lay still for several minutes. He didn't know what had happened, but he did feel the unbearable pain that encompassed his head, face, and hands.

It was dark. Pitch black. And cold. He tried to move, but he couldn't. His shoulder. His hands. He drifted in and out of consciousness. Minutes could have gone by, or hours. He didn't know.

What the hell was going on?

Forcing himself to remember, images of Skyla and his screaming children gradually started to take shape in his mind.

That crazy bitch! She'd thrown boiling water in his face and hit him with that iron pot, knocking him out. White-hot anger flared up within him. He forced open his eyes but could open only one of them enough to peer through his lashes. He tried to move, his body stiff from lying on his shoulder in the freezing cabin.

When he realized he couldn't move his hands either, his fury exploded. She'd bound his wrists together behind his back and they'd made a run for it, leaving him here to die.

In a blind rage, ignoring the excruciating pain of his burned skin, he struggled up into a sitting position. She would face the consequences for what she'd done to him. He would see to it.

The moon cast pale shadows throughout the cabin and the door stood wide open.

He moved in the direction of the stove. Cold. He knew that meant he'd been unconscious for hours.

Quaking with rage, he forced himself to his feet, beads of sweat drenching him. Skyla had a lot to answer for. He couldn't wait to wrap his hands around her neck, to see the terror in her eyes when he choked her. All he had to do was get his hands free, and he would track them down.

A wave of dizziness overcame him, and bile rose up in the back of his throat. He leaned against the doorjamb to keep himself from toppling over. When the nausea subsided and the shadowy world around him came back into focus, he stepped outside and staggered half-blind to his shed. He would find something there to cut the ropes. A pair of scissors, a utility knife, a wire cutter, or maybe his brand-new tree saw. It was foldable and easily capable of cutting through two-inch branches. The thick rope would be no match for its sharp teeth.

He groped around in the dark until he found the saw. He

folded it open and moved it around in his hands to get the blade in the right angle behind his back. Twice, the saw fell on the ground and he started over. It took forever. As he continued his efforts, first daylight began to replace the darkness inside the shed. It helped him get his bearings and stave off the worst of his vertigo. Trying to concentrate on his movements, his fingers numb from the tight restraints, he cursed and muttered, his demonic bloodthirst making it increasingly difficult to control his movements.

Cutting deep into his skin, blood welled up from his wrist and dripped down his hands. He almost lost his grip for the third time, the handle slick from the oozing blood and almost impossible to hold. Fucking hell. Unable to keep his rage under control, he yanked hard. The sisal rope gave out under the sharp-edged teeth and blood spattered in every direction. He rubbed his wrists and staggered toward the cabin in search of a towel, leaving a blood trail in the snow. Half blind, he roamed around until he found one and wrapped it around his wrist. His body twisted against the grueling pain on his face as he pulled on one end with his teeth to tighten the knot.

Back outside, he feverishly gazed around through his eyelashes, trying to make sense out of the many footsteps. They were freaking everywhere. It was probably just a smoke screen. They must have gone down the road. That's what he would have done. All he needed to do was make sure not to drive too fast, so they wouldn't hear his engine from miles away and hide in the woods as he approached.

He opened his truck and reached below the seat for the key, hanging on one of the loose springs. His head nearly exploded when he bent over. Gasping for air, he straightened, his heartbeat pounding through his entire body. He hurt everywhere.

After a few misses, he managed to get the key in the ignition and start the engine. He gazed ahead. Everything looked murky, the trees contorting, the road in front of him going up and down like the waves in the ocean. At a crawling speed, he drove off, the copper smell of blood, warm and fresh, hovering around him. Disoriented, he tried to focus, the world around him one big blur as he faded in and out of consciousness.

What am I doing here? he wondered.

Trying to wrap his mind around it, he touched his right eye. It was closed shut from the swelling of his head wound and the burn blisters covering seventy-five percent of his face. He winced. *Had somebody hit him over the head?*

The image of long black hair and a purple sweatshirt surfaced between the haziness. A woman. Of course. With his one good eye, he stared down at the red towel and his blood-soaked jeans.

Weak from blood loss, his head bobbed until the truck began to jolt. Bewildered, he looked back up. The front tires had gone over the shoulder of the road and the truck tilted to one side. With all the energy he could muster, he jerked on the steering wheel. His efforts proved futile when the truck began to bounce down the slope.

Gripped by panic, he pushed the brake with both feet at the same time, a scream rising in his throat. With everything he had in him, he tried to regain control, but the truck continued its descent until the right tire hit a boulder. The truck rolled over, turning him into a rag doll inside the cabin.

His body slammed against the steering wheel, knocking the wind out of him.

Then his head hit the ceiling, then the window, until the truck came to an abrupt stop against the trunk of a ponderosa pine.

CHAPTER

38

IT WAS QUIET on the road this early in the morning and they'd driven a steady sixty-five miles per hour on Interstate 84. After crossing the bridge over the Columbia River into Washington State, Troy turned onto a scenic highway that took them through a few small towns, with several whitewater rafting companies right along the road.

"Look at the water of that raging river," Troy said, trying to make conversation.

Harold Overland, who sat in the passenger seat, trembled with tension.

"I have," Kim replied from the backseat, but she said nothing more.

They drove on until they pulled into the empty parking lot of the ranger station. Troy parked his SUV and got out. Everything was still wet from last night's thunderstorm, drops falling from the trees, the pavement glistening in the watery sunlight. Raising the collar of his coat, he looked at the one-story building, the siding a dark brown. No light shone from the windows. It looked like nobody was there.

"We're a little early," Kim said, joining him.

Harold stepped out of the car, too, a strained expression on his face. "I hope we don't have to wait too long before someone shows up." Skyla's father had barely spoken the entire trip.

Troy didn't reply. Before they'd left, Harold had shown him the small handgun he carried in his pocket. An argument had ensued between them. Troy didn't want Harold to take it with him, but he refused to leave it behind.

"We're heading into unfamiliar territory, and you never know what we might encounter," Harold had reasoned.

Aware that Rikkerson might be armed, Troy had given in, but he wasn't happy about it. He rubbed the back of his neck, his muscles tight with tension. "I'll check if someone's there." He crossed the parking lot, taking the two concrete steps leading up to the front door.

After finding it locked, Troy looked in through one of the windows. "I don't see anyone," he said over his shoulder to Kim and Harold. "I'll check around back."

Just before he disappeared around the corner of the building, he heard a car approaching. A white four-wheel drive pickup truck with the logo of the forest service on its doors pulled in and stopped. A young man, dressed in Carhartt pants and a camouflage coat, with a baseball cap covering his curly brown hair, climbed out.

"I'm Peter Santiago," he said. "Are you from the police?"

"You bet," Kim answered without hesitation. "I know we're a little early, but could you take us to the cabin right away?

We're anxious to find this guy."

"No problem." Peter smiled. He looked at Troy's car and nodded approvingly. "Nice rig. That should make it out there no problem."

"You think we'll hit snow?" Troy asked.

Peter raised his eyebrows and appeared confused. "You're not detective MacMillen."

"The chief's in the front seat," Kim said, pointing toward Mr. Overland who'd stepped back into the car. "It can't go fast enough for him."

Peter shrugged. "Follow me."

Back in the car, Troy looked over his shoulder at Kim. "Why did he assume I was MacMillen?"

Seeing her smile, he understood. "He had a meeting with the chief, and we beat him to it, didn't we?"

"Maybe," Kim replied.

Troy started the car and followed Peter's truck. He knew of the strained relationship between the chief and the private investigator. It'd been interesting to see the two of them dance around each other. They reminded him of his older brother and his wife who were constantly in each other's hair, but were inseparable, their bond strong, their love undeniable.

They drove twenty long miles over a winding but well-maintained paved highway around Mt. Adams, its snow cap glittering in the morning sun.

"This forest is huge," Harold commented, concern evident in his voice. They'd driven for almost an hour and hadn't seen a single car. "Where is this guy taking us?"

The white pickup in front of them blinked to the left, slowed down, and turned off the main highway onto a dirt road, the tires immediately hitting a deep pothole filled with water.

"Here we go," Harold said, holding onto the grab handle above the door.

Troy steered around it, only to bounce into the next pothole with his right front tire.

"This is rugged terrain," he agreed after driving through a thin layer of snow for several miles. He'd become increasingly concerned himself, and was almost happy that Harold insisted on carrying a gun. This cabin's location was quite remote.

The dirt road narrowed, and they took a few turns, branches of trees and shrubs scraping the sides of his car. After another fifteen minutes, the car bounced along a road covered in deep snow. He felt increasingly worried.

"I'm beginning to wonder if this trail will actually lead us somewhere. Can you call Peter and find out if he's lost?"

"We're out of cell service," Kim replied. "But these are all old logging roads, and I'm sure Peter knows what he's doing."

Her words didn't ease his mind. It meant they were on their own, not able to call for help in the event it was needed.

They drove on for a few more minutes until they took another turn. Peter stopped his vehicle. They'd driven onto a small clearing that contained a dingy looking cabin and two other smaller outbuildings. All three shacks looked like a strong wind gust could blow them over, the siding dilapidated, the metal roofs completely rusted. It was a miracle they still stood after last night's thunderstorm. They'd even lost power in the city for several hours.

"Looks like we're here." Harold still clutched the grab handle, his knuckles white.

Troy regretted bringing him along. The stress might just be too much for him.

"Stay in the car, Harold," he said, uncertain of what they would find. "Think about your heart."

Peter's truck was parked to the side, as far away from the cabin as possible. Troy parked next to him and got out, followed by Kim.

"Let me go first," she said and pulled out a handgun.

"What are you doing, Kim?" Troy exclaimed, watching her stealthily approach the cabin, the gun raised in front of her. He had no idea she was carrying, too. "Put that thing away!"

"I need to be able to protect myself in case he gets violent. Now shut up, we don't want to alert him," she said in a low voice, as if the noise from their vehicles hadn't been enough evidence of their arrival.

"If he's home, I'm sure he knows we're here," Troy said. "But I don't think he is, because his truck is gone."

A sigh of relief escaped from Kim's lips. "You're right," she said. With a few determined steps she covered the last few yards to the cabin and pushed open the door with her gun, ready to defend herself if the need arose.

Nothing happened.

Troy joined her in the doorway and followed her inside. The room was empty.

"There's another door," Kim whispered, creeping further into the cabin, still on high alert.

"Kick it in." Troy rolled up his sleeves. He'd never handled a gun, but he wasn't afraid to use his fists if it came down to it.

Instead of kicking, Kim pushed open the door. "It's a bedroom, and it's clear," she shouted.

Troy placed his hand on the woodstove. Cold. Shit. Skyla wasn't here. Nobody was.

"Come, let's check the outbuildings," Kim said, elbowing Troy in his side. Outside, they found Harold and Peter talking.

"Cabin's empty," Troy said.

"I was just telling Mr. MacMillen I noticed tire tracks leading away from the cabin," Peter said. "Rikkerson must have left not too long ago."

"At least we don't have to worry about dealing with him." Troy looked over his shoulder when he heard Kim yell at them from one of the outbuildings. "There's blood in here. A lot of it."

Harold moaned, leaned over, and clutched his arms.

"Peter, stay with him," Troy said, dread so heavy in his limbs that he was barely able to put one foot in front of the other. If Rikkerson had hurt Skyla, he would...he would....

Inside the shed, Kim waited for him and pointed at a handsaw. "It's completely covered in blood."

Troy's face paled visibly at the sight of it. That couldn't be good.

"I also found this long piece of rope on the floor," Kim continued. "It's covered in blood, too. Looks like someone cut themselves free and may have done a lot of damage in the process." She placed her hand on Troy's sleeve. "Just make sure you don't touch anything, Troy. You might ruin evidence."

Having seen enough, Troy made his way out of the shed, the leaden fear in his stomach almost making him lose his breakfast. He bent over. With a hand on each knee, he breathed in the cold morning air until he recovered enough to tell Skyla's father what they'd found.

"She's not dead until we find her body," Harold replied, drawing in a couple of shaking breaths. The man was on the edge of breaking down.

Kim joined them. "Let's go back into the cabin and see what else we can find," she suggested.

Peter roamed around the clearing at the edge of the forest and waved at them. "I see all these footsteps over here. I want to check it out," he said.

"I don't know if that's a good idea," Kim said. "It's too dangerous and you might get lost."

"Don't worry. I'm an outdoorsman at heart and was born and raised here, my passions hunting, fishing, and mushrooming," Peter grinned. "These woods are my backyard." The next moment, he was gone.

"It seems he know what he's doing," Troy commented. "Come, let's go back into that ramshackle of a cabin and see what else we can find."

Still on high alert, they wandered back inside.

"I can tell people live here," Kim commented. "And from how tidy it is, I assume someone other than Rikkerson lived there. He just doesn't seem the type to pick up a broom."

Troy had to agree with her. The floor was swept, the pots and pans all clean, the dishes neatly stacked in a cupboard. He walked around the table a few times. Nothing caught his interest. Everything was old, the floorboards sinking down under each step, the clothes scattered around threadbare. He picked up a small t-shirt. It was pink with white flowers and had to belong to a young girl. Several other pieces of clothing were in a young boy's size. He had no idea why they were strewn around the room. Had there been a fight?

"We already suspected he had a baby. This is the proof of that," Kim said, holding up a pack of opened diapers.

They fell silent, the idea of raising a baby under such abominable, primitive conditions seemed impossible.

"Did you find anything of interest?" Harold asked, joining them.

"Not really," Kim said.

They walked around the cabin a few more minutes, absorbing all the horrid details.

"With a man, a woman and three children living here, the bed is way too small. I suspect some of them slept here on these blankets in the corner of the room," Kim said. She went down on her knees to rummage through them, her hands coming in contact with a piece of leather. She pulled out a purse.

Could this be Skyla's? she wondered and opened it. The next moment she let out a jubilant shriek, jarring both men.

"What the hell, Kim?" Troy roared.

Kim had found Skyla's wallet inside the purse, along with her driver's license. She held it in front of his face. "It's Skyla's! Look!"

Finding her purse didn't surprise Troy. They'd known Rikkerson had it. He sank down on a chair and hid his face behind his hands. The image of Skyla living here, held captive in this horrible place for so many months tore him apart inside. Hanging onto hope was becoming near impossible.

CHAPTER

39

AT NINE, Chief MacMillen, Brian, and Larry arrived at the ranger station. The lights were on, the door unlocked. They walked inside and found a woman behind the counter. She stood up from her chair the moment they entered.

"What can I do for you so early in the morning?" she asked, looking them over.

"We're here to meet Peter Santiago and the ranger," MacMillen said.

"I don't think they've arrived as yet," the woman replied. "Do you want me to page them for you?"

The door opened and a man walked in. Looking at his thick green parka with the emblem of the forest service on his shoulder, he had to be the ranger.

"You must be from the Rosehurst Police," the ranger said, lifting his green cap in greeting. "Glad you made it."

MacMillen made a few short introductions and the men

chatted for a little while about Rikkerson and the cabin.

"I don't understand what's keeping Peter," the ranger said, looking at his watch. "He's usually very punctual. If you want to get going, I can take you there."

"Sounds great," MacMillen replied.

The ranger opened the door, and they followed him outside.

"Is this what you're driving?" the ranger asked, looking at MacMillen's inconspicuous unmarked car.

"It is," MacMillen answered. He drove the car so he wouldn't be easily pegged as a cop. It was five years old and had front wheel drive.

"Let's take my truck," the ranger suggested. "Once we get off the main road, bad road conditions and snow can make it rough. There's no reason to get your car stuck."

The ranger's four-door SUV was white, with a green stripe down the middle, and a heavy-duty push bar on the front.

MacMillen agreed and climbed in the passenger seat. Larry and Brian stepped into the back.

"How far out is this cabin?" MacMillen asked after they'd driven for forty-five minutes at high speed. Snow and ice covered the road, but the truck's tires had plenty of traction and grip.

"We're not the first ones out here this morning," the ranger said after they veered off the main road. "I see at least two different car tracks."

"Is that unusual?" MacMillen said.

The ranger laughed, making him feel naïve. He was a city cop at heart, his duty to maintain public order, apprehend criminals, and to protect and assist the general public. Park rangers were the keepers of natural resources and public lands. MacMillen was out of his league in the rugged terrain.

"We're in a very remote area of the forest," the ranger explained. "Cars hardly ever make it out here, unless it's hunting season. The only roads are old logging roads, most of them leading nowhere."

The ranger maneuvered the truck around potholes, the tires having no trouble plowing through the snow.

In the backseat, Brian and Larry appeared awed by the seemingly endless expanse of wilderness surrounding them.

"Wouldn't you love to work out here?" Larry asked. "To breathe in the fresh air every day, and only having to battle bears and poachers instead of drug dealers and traffic violators?"

"Not me," Brian replied. "I love the city's conveniences way too much."

The car traveled further up the winding narrow road. After taking another turn, the ranger pulled to a stop. "It looks like there are fresh tire tracks going down over the side of the road here." He opened his door to get a better look.

The other three men immediately followed, their boots sinking ankle deep in the snow. The ranger pulled a pair of black gloves from the pocket of his parka and started to make his way down the steep slope. His heavy boots and clothes seemed warm and waterproof.

"There's a car down there," Brian said to MacMillen. "You think we should follow him?"

MacMillen looked at his own attire. He wasn't dressed as suitably for the conditions as the ranger, but could tell the car tracks were fresh. He had to go down. Someone might be hurt.

"Brian, follow me," he ordered, the first snow already penetrating his socks. "Larry, stay with the car." He put on his gloves and started down the hill, past one of the car's tires. From what he could tell, the vehicle had crashed against a boulder, losing its tire before rolling over several times and skidding further down the steep incline. Holding on to overhanging branches to keep from sliding down, he carefully continued his descent, followed by Brian.

"Someone's inside!" the ranger shouted from below. He'd already reached the vehicle and stood on top of its side, trying to pull open the door.

Brian and MacMillen soon joined him. It was a white pickup truck. Just like the one described as Rikkerson's.

"Is it a man or a woman?" MacMillen asked, not sure what answer he was hoping for, because whoever was inside had to be seriously injured.

"It's a man," the ranger replied. "Let's see if the three of us can open that door."

Brian climbed on top of the truck and the two of them were able to lift the passenger door, holding it open so MacMillen could climb inside.

The man's body lay curled up on the bottom, mangled between the door and the steering wheel. MacMillen pulled off his glove and placed his fingers in his neck. The skin felt cold, and he detected no pulse. "We're too late. He's gone," he reported.

"You think it's Rikkerson, boss?" Brian asked.

MacMillen looked at the man. He seemed badly burned. Both the left and right side of his face were covered in blood. It was too difficult to tell.

"Can you radio in for forensics, an ambulance, and a tow truck?" MacMillen said, taking the ranger's extended hand to help him back out. "I want to get all possible evidence from the scene"

"No problem," the ranger replied.

The three men scrambled back up the hill where Larry waited for them.

"I want you to stay here on the scene, Larry," MacMillen said. "We'll continue on to the cabin."

For MacMillen, working a case was like a complex puzzle. Solving one gave him the satisfaction he thrived on, and if that dead man in the truck was his suspect, they would more than likely find Skyla Overland soon. This was a good day.

"It should be less than a mile from here," the ranger said.

Within a few minutes, they pulled into a clearing. Two cars were parked along the dirt road.

"That's Peter Santiago's truck," the ranger said. "What's he doing here?"

"I think I know why," MacMillen said. He'd recognized Troy Summerton's SUV and there could only be one explanation how it got there. He turned around in his seat to look at Brian. "Did you talk to Kim yesterday?"

A guilty expression appeared on Brian's face, his cheeks turning red.

MacMillen snorted loudly to suppress his anger. "Don't bother answering. I already know."

"I'm sorry," Brian said, following his boss out of the car. "You know she's working on the same case. I didn't see any harm in it."

"We'll talk about this later," the Chief said. The idea that Kim was out here, putting herself in harm's way by looking for an erratic kidnapper in the middle of nowhere, bothered him. He picked up his pace. He needed to find her and make sure she was okay.

At the sound of their approaching footsteps, Harold Overland appeared in the doorway of the cabin, pointing a gun at them.

"Shit! Put that down, Overland," MacMillen yelled, reaching for his sidearm.

Harold lowered his arm. "Sorry, I thought you were Rikkerson." He sobbed and started to shake.

MacMillen wrapped his arm around the man to steady him and help him back inside, guiding him onto one of the chairs.

"She was here," Harold said. "Skyla was here. We found her purse. She was here." He kept on repeating himself.

"That's great news," MacMillen said, taking in his surroundings.

"But we found blood. In the shed," Harold continued. His voice quivered with fear, and he blinked rapidly as though to clear his vision. The man had lost a lot of weight over the last four months and looked like a wreck. MacMillen felt sorry for him.

"Did you see Kim Lowe?" he asked.

"Peter found tracks leading into the forest in various places. They all left to check it out."

"Is everything all right in there, boss?" Brian asked. He'd appeared in the doorway, holding his cap in both hands, his manner apologetic. "The ranger is talking to Kim. She found something in the woods and seems upset."

Harold immediately got up from his chair and hurried past MacMillen and Brian. "Did you find Skyla?" he asked, reaching for Kim's arm to steady himself.

She put her gloved hand on his, trying to comfort him. "No, I didn't. I found a grave and it isn't hers."

The four men followed Kim down a short trail and stopped in front of a wooden cross.

"Rikkerson buried his wife Kate out here." Kim looked up at MacMillen. It seemed she was ready to burst into tears. Instead, she clenched her teeth and hissed. "That asshole. He just stuck her in the ground without letting anyone know."

MacMillen laid a comforting hand on her slender shoulder. Instead of pulling away, she moved a little closer to him.

"I spoke to Kate's parents over the phone. They hadn't heard from her in years," he said. "I'm glad we can give them closure."

CHAPTER

40

MACMILLEN AND KIM reentered the clearing, noticing Peter Santiago and Troy as they emerged from the forest on the other side.

"Where's MacMillen?" Peter asked Kim.

"I'm MacMillen," the chief said.

Kim burst into a nervous laugh.

"He's right, Peter. The older man is Skyla's father, and I'm Kim Lowe, a private investigator. Sorry we lied to you, but we wanted to find her so badly."

Instead of being upset, Peter started laughing. "I already thought something wasn't right. The older man seemed so emotional and he didn't look like a police captain at all. Now it all makes sense."

Troy shook MacMillen's hand. "Glad you're here," he said. "We followed the footsteps going in and out of the forest.

Most are small, some bigger. Then I noticed a piece of cloth wrapped around a low hanging tree branch. Not much later, I found a second and a third. Skyla isn't here, and I want to follow the trail further into the woods with Peter."

"Sounds good," MacMillen said. "I have to secure the scene, and Kim will stay here with Mr. Overland. Let us know as soon as you find anything."

Peter pulled a two-way radio from his pocket.

"With this, I can stay in touch with the ranger," he said and walked to his truck to grab his backpack. It contained a knife, rope, and rope clamps, a headlamp, several energy bars, and two bottles of water.

Before heading out, he retied the laces of his ankle-high leather boots and put on his sunglasses, to protect his eyes while whacking his way through heavy brush, the lenses able to adjust to the low light in the thick forests. Next to him, Troy looked like a city guy going out on a Sunday hike.

"You're ready, Troy?" he asked.

The two men left the clearing and headed into the woods, the footsteps in the snow easy to follow until the vegetation became denser. "From what I can tell, we're following the footprints of an adult, probably a woman, and two young children," Peter said.

Troy was impressed with the young man's tracking skills.

"This is easy." Peter laughed. "My father started to take me hunting in these woods when I was barely six years old. He taught me all the valuable old-school skills, like identifying tracks, figuring out which way they went, and how to stalk wild game to within fifteen yards." He stopped and pointed at a few small indentations in the snow. "Look at these footprints.

They're so small. I think the woman is carrying a baby or toddler, occasionally letting them take several steps on their own."

After a solid two hours, they reached a swift running creek, and Peter came to a halt, taking in all the details.

"They spent quite some time here," he said and jumped over the creek to the other side where the terrain was less challenging. After following it downstream a few hundred feet, Peter detected a cave. With all the volcanoes, the Cascade Mountain Range was home to many caves, including volcanic lava tubes and glacier ice caves. They had traversed over several lava beds and to find it didn't surprise him. He pushed the vegetation that partly covered the entrance away and crawled in.

"Not much to see," he reported. "It's small, but I can tell they slept here by the imprints of heels."

When he came outside, he held up a candy wrapper before tucking it into his pocket.

"How long ago do you think they were here, Peter?" he asked.

"From what I can tell, no more than a day. All the prints are fresh, but last night's storm might make it more difficult further down. You can already tell the snow on the ground is much thinner. They're going downhill. I hope they kept following the creek. That'll help."

After two more hours of brisk hiking, the tracks meandered away from the creek. Troy started to feel it in his knees, the constant uphill and downhill and uneven terrain making it challenging.

They'd also faced several downpours along the way, and his "waterproof" raincoat was saturated.

"Looks like they headed to that meadow over there," Peter said, pointing in the direction of an opening between the trees.

When they reached the clearing, the snow was gone, and the tracks ended."

CHAPTER

41

LEXI HUDDLED underneath the sleeping bag until she was seized in a coughing fit and began to cry.

For lack of a handkerchief, Skyla pressed one of her gloves against Lexi's mouth, holding her in a caring embrace. With her other hand, she pushed the tangled hair away from the girl's burning forehead.

"Oh, sweetie, don't cry," she whispered.

They'd spent three days and two nights outside. Although they'd been relatively protected in the cave and inside the trunk of the car, Skyla couldn't endure anymore. She was completely exhausted from lack of sleep, and incapable of dragging her mind up from the depths of her despair. She'd lived under its pressure for too long, the constant threat to her life and sanity unbearable.

Humming to herself, she stroked Lexi's hair. Tom had gone out. The water bottles were empty. He wanted to fill them with snow. She worried about him. He kept up a tough front, but she knew how scared he was his father might appear. At the thought, her throat constricted with renewed horror. She was completely defenseless against Rikkerson's brutal strength, the knife she carried dull and not even able to cut a slice of bread. Was he hunting for them, like a wounded animal out for blood? Was he already close by?

She looked up when Tom appeared out of nowhere. He crawled inside the trunk and flew up against her, wrapping his arms around her neck. "I hear him. He's coming, Skyla," he cried.

Wild with fear, his eyes darted back and forth, snot running out of his nose. "He's calling your name! He's coming!"

"I don't hear anything," she whispered, urging him to stay quiet. If they wanted to make it out of here alive, they couldn't make a sound.

Julia pulled on her arm, trying to grab her attention. She wanted to play. Skyla opened the backpack and found another pack of saltines in the hope it might distract her. She pulled it out, but Julia shook her head, keeping her mouth shut tight. She wanted something else. Skyla held up an apple and Julia turned away. It wasn't until she gave her a candy bar that Julia smiled. Skyla didn't care, she would give her anything as long as she wouldn't start screaming.

"You hear that?" Tom said.

Holding her breath, Skyla listened and detected the sound of a man's voice calling her name. Powerless terror took ahold of her entire body. "Let's hide under the sleeping bag. All of us. And don't move. Quick."

Barely able to breathe through her closed throat and clenched teeth, the minutes ticked by and panic built up inside her. She wanted to scream, let it all out, the pressure too much to bear. When Lexi started to cough, unable to stop, she almost did. "Stop that, Lexi," she hissed.

"Did you hear that?" a man's voice said.

"Sounded like someone's coughing," another voice answered.

Skyla released the pressure of her hand on Lexi's mouth. "Is that people talking?" she whispered.

Lexi immediately coughed again.

"Skyla, is that you?" a man's voice came again. This time more urgent.

She didn't reply, unable to speak. Even Lexi and Julia stayed mouse quiet, the tension paralyzing them.

"Skyla, it's Troy. Are you out there?"

The scream she'd suppressed rose up in her throat and came out in a whimper. It couldn't be. She was hallucinating. It couldn't be Troy out there.

Tom moved next to her and sat up, taking the sleeping bag with him. "There's people out there, Skyla. It's not my dad."

"How do you know?" Skyla cried out, grabbing his arm to keep him inside the trunk. He was ready to crawl out.

"It's not. I know!" he said and yanked his arm free.

Still too afraid to believe him, Skyla stayed where she was, watching in horror when he climbed over the backseat and went outside. "Tom, stay here!" The next moment, he was gone.

Holding her head between her hands, she waited until the terror induced wave of nausea subsided. Then she wrapped the blanket back around Lexi and Julia and crawled out. She couldn't let the young boy go out by himself. She had to protect him.

Lexi and Julia both immediately started to wail. "Don't leave us, Skyla!"

Torn between staying and leaving, Skyla stopped in her tracks until she noticed sudden movement. From between the trees and the shrubs a man appeared, and he made his way toward her.

First, she froze, until recognition slammed into her and then she started to shake all over her body. Within seconds, Troy closed the distance between them, almost crashing into her as he cried out,

"Skyla, I found you. I found you. You're alive."

His arms closed around her waist and he lifted her off the ground.

Skyla felt like she had stepped into a warm ray of sunshine. All around her, she saw white puffs of clouds, the bright light blinding her. She felt like she was in heaven.

When he let her down, he took hold of her shoulders and looked into her eyes. Tears streamed down his face.

"I can't believe we found you," he said, his voice breaking. Then he pulled her back up against his chest, almost crushing her in his tight embrace. With his mouth against her ear, he whispered, "Skyla, I love you. I love you so much."

His words glided down into her heart, the anxious cries of the children the only sound keeping her from floating away. The miracle she'd prayed for had come true. They were found and she was safe, at last.

After standing like that for several minutes, she reluctantly freed herself from his arms. "I have to find Tom," she explained.

Through the woods, a young man in a ranger uniform appeared behind Troy. He held Tom by the hand. The moment Tom saw Skyla, he immediately let go and wrapped his arms around her waist, sobbing.

"You were so brave to go out there, sweetheart," she said, stroking his hair. "You're my little hero."

Troy placed his arm around her shoulders, and she looked up. She'd never seen a more handsome face, his presence still surreal. Her eyes filled with tears and everything blurred. "I have to go to the children," she said. "They're crying so hard."

"I'm not letting you go alone," he replied, taking her hand.

Together, they reached the station wagon and looked inside. The girls stared back at them, wide-eyed, their faces wet from their tears.

"It's alright, girls," Skyla said. She climbed into the trunk to reassure and comfort them. Julia immediately wrapped her arms around her neck and hid her face against her shoulder. Besides her father, she'd never seen another man. Lexi clutched the sleeping bag, her body stiff, the look she gave Troy hostile and defiant.

"We're safe, Lexi," she said. "They found us. You don't have to be afraid anymore."

When all the children were out of the car, Troy looked at Peter, fully aware there was no way Skyla and the children would be able to hike out of the forest and back to the cabin. Skyla looked exhausted and haggard from prolonged torment and anxiety. He felt her suffering as if it was his own. With effort, he kept his face calm and reassuring.

Peter pulled the push to talk two-way radio from his pocket.

"With this, dispatch can locate our exact GPS location and the ranger will figure out a rescue plan. If he can't get a truck out here, he will request a helicopter. That clearing looks big enough to land."

"Tell them to hurry. It's starting to rain again, and it'll be dark in a few hours," Troy said.

At the edge of the clearing, they tried to find shelter underneath the thick canopy of the trees, as Peter talked to the ranger.

"I'm so happy you found me," Skyla whispered against Troy's chest. She sat next to him, finding comfort in his arm around her shoulders. Julia and Lexi sat in her lap, and Tom pressed up against her side. "I can't tell you how much I've prayed for this moment."

"Me too," Troy said, kissing her wet hair. "Thank God, you're alive and safe."

Skyla swallowed the lump in her throat away. "But what about Rikkerson?" He's a raging, uncontrolled, vicious maniac.

She'd seen the murderous look in his eyes before she'd knocked him out. He would be out for revenge.

"He won't come," he assured her. "He left in his truck. If he returns, the police and the ranger will apprehend him. They're at the cabin."

"But he might be looking for us in the woods," Skyla said. "He's lived here for so long, and he could be anywhere."

Troy stroked her hair in the hope to comfort her. "They're all armed, and they won't let him escape. You're safe, sweetheart. You have to believe me."

She soaked up his familiar features, her heart soaring when she saw the love in his eyes. With a shuddering sigh, she rested her head against his shoulder.

CHAPTER

42

AFTER THE HELICOPTER landed in the meadow just before sunset, Skyla climbed on board with the children. With not enough room in the helicopter, Troy stayed behind, trusting she was in good hands with the Life Flight's critical care providers.

"Peter and I will hike back to the cabin and join your father. Together we'll drive to the hospital right away." He kissed her goodbye, their hands touching for as long as they could.

The helicopter flight went by in a blur, the children still too scared to comprehend what had happened. After they arrived, they were immediately rushed into the emergency department. Soon after, they were all moved to a private room on the fourth floor of the hospital.

Even though they'd barely been there for an hour, every time Skyla heard footsteps in the hallway, she hoped to see Troy and her father walk through the door.

"Her cold may have turned into pneumonia if she'd been

exposed to the elements for a longer period of time, but you don't have to worry. She'll feel better soon," the doctor who examined a shivering Lexi assured Skyla. He put away his stethoscope and typed something on the keyboard of the mobile workstation he'd rolled in.

Skyla looked on from the edge of her hospital bed. Her hands moved restlessly over the muslin sheets. They were whiter than white and softer than soft, the fine weave pleasing to the touch. She pulled them up to her nose, the fresh laundered scent in combination with a faint disinfectant smelled heavenly. What a difference from the sleeping bag where she'd slept in for so long, the pillow that didn't have a case, and the wooden, drafty floorboards beneath her. Being here still felt surreal, and hearing the doctor's words brought renewed tears to her eyes.

"Thank you for letting the children stay with me in the same room," she said.

They would have been terrified in this strange, unfamiliar environment. Even with her here, the expression in Lexi's eyes was haunted. Tom did a little better and seemed asleep. He was exhausted, his face still dirty and his hair a greasy mess. He refused to take a shower or let anyone come near him. The children had a long way to go to feel comfortable in their new surroundings.

Only Julia took it all in with a curious look in her big blue baby eyes.

"Based on her teeth, I estimate that Julia is about eighteen months old," he said. "Her first top canine is starting to erupt and that usually doesn't happen until toddlers are at least sixteen months old, but usually later."

"Eighteen months already?" Skyla asked. When she'd first seen Julia, she'd been like a doll, undernourished and sick. Because of her condition, she'd assumed she was much younger.

"Yes, she may be a little behind in her development because of the circumstances," the doctor determined. "But look at her. She's smart, inquisitive, and already starting to talk."

Lexi finally dozed off. The doctor had given her something to calm her nerves. After Skyla was convinced the girl was in a deep sleep, she got up from the bed. She hadn't taken a shower in four months and longed to wash off the built-up grime. Her hair was a tangled, dry mess, and hadn't been brushed in ages. She was afraid a million bottles of hair products and conditioner wouldn't be enough to fix the damage. With a pair of scissors one of the nurses had given her, she disappeared in the bathroom. If needed, she was ready to cut it off.

In the white-tiled bathroom, she turned on the water and started to undress. The devil had bought her those ugly, awful clothes and she never wanted to see them again. She stuffed them in the small waste basket and stepped under the hot spray.

For the first several minutes, all she did was stand there, letting the water splash over her hair and face, and down her body, until it circled around the drain and disappeared. It was hypnotizing, the hot jetting spray stinging her skin like needles, the steam thick.

With vigorous strokes she began to wash her body, the flowery fragrance of the soap comforting and soothing, the heat wrapping itself around her, enfolding her. It was divine.

She reached for the shampoo to wash her hair, but with each pass her fingers got snarled into the twisted, entangled mess.

How he'd admired her long jet-black hair, letting his loathsome fingers twirl around the ends as he sniffed her neck. A tortured-sounding moan escaped her throat, her face flushed, her eyes wild.

She wanted that hair gone, gone, *gone.*

Overcome by a sudden fury, she pushed the shower curtain open and stepped out in front of the mirror. The glass was fogged up, but she didn't need to see. All that mattered was getting rid of that hair. She couldn't stand it. She hated it. She grabbed the scissors and started snipping. Long and short strands of wet hair landed on her shoulders, in the sink, and on the floor. *Snip. Snip. Snip.*

The door of the bathroom opened, but she kept on cutting, venting her fury with curses and tears. "Leave me alone! It has to go!"

An alarmed cry sounded before two soft arms wrapped around her trembling, naked body, forcing her to stop.

"Oh, honey, what are you doing?" her mother cried, pulling her close and rocking her back and forth. "Oh, sweetie, I'm so sorry, so sorry."

Choking sobs echoed off the bathroom wall as Skyla cried uncontrollably in her mother's arms, crumpling against her until she sagged down into a desperate huddle on the tiled floor. Her mother followed her down, still holding her until her deep moans started to subside. When they did, Clara Overland pulled on the alarm and immediately a nurse appeared in the doorway. She quickly turned off the shower and laid a towel around Skyla's shaking shoulders. Together with her mother, they dried her off, dressed her in a hospital gown, and guided her back to her bed.

"I'll inform the doctor," the nurse said and left.

Skyla's mother draped a blanket around her shoulders and sat down next to her on the bed. She clasped her daughter's hands as her eyes brimmed with tears. "I'll call my hairdresser. I'm sure she'll be more than happy to see you here at the hospital and fix your hair, sweetheart."

Skyla's tears spilled onto her cheeks. "I'm so grateful you're here. Is Daddy coming soon, too?"

Clara pulled a tissue from the box next to the bed and dried her daughter's cheeks with gentle hands before drying her own. "He *is*, sweetheart, he's almost here. So is Edmond. He couldn't wait to see you."

For a moment, Skyla had to think. *Edmond?* In all the months she was held captive, she'd given him very little thought. "I don't want him here!" she cried out.

"But, honey," Clara replied. "Why not?"

To hide her confusion, Skyla took another tissue and blew her nose. "He can't see me like this. It's too embarrassing and I'm not ready to face him."

"I'll tell him." Clara patted her hand. "I'm sure he'll understand when I explain."

A moment later, the doctor walked in. "How're you feeling, Skyla?" he asked. He placed his hand on her forehead and smiled. "No fever, that's good."

"I think I kind of lost it for a moment." Skyla grimaced, trying to make a joke, but instead the words came out as a cry for help.

The doctor nodded, his kind brown eyes only reflecting understanding. "I have a mild sedative for you, something very similar to what I gave the children. It'll help you through the night."

Too tired to care, Skyla took the pill with water. She knew she needed something, her mind one clustered mess, her entire nervous system bristling with tension.

"Can you stay with me tonight, Mom?" she whispered with her eyes closed.

"Of course," Clara replied and squeezed her hands.

Every time Skyla became restless throughout the night, she opened her eyes and noticed her father sitting in the chair next to her bed. He'd arrived in the early evening, together with Troy and her sister, Taylor. It had been an emotional reunion, the effort of suppressing her grief and the exhilaration of seeing them and knowing she was safe, leaving her exhausted.

All the excitement had stressed out the children, and when everyone left, except for her father, a nurse had come in administering a mild sedative to help them sleep.

The sound of someone walking past her hospital room woke her up. In the faint light, she noticed her father, slumped in the chair, snoring. Knowing he was there and looking out for her, calmed her. She eased back to sleep.

When morning arrived, Tom was already up, wearing new pajamas. He played on the floor of the hospital room with a box full of Duplo blocks. Her father helped him build a tower. The scene warmed her heart and brought her to immediate tears.

Hearing her muffled sobs, Harold Overland immediately rushed over to her side and took her in his arms, hugging and kissing her. She clung to his shoulders and wept. When he let her go, his eyes were wet, too. He dried them with the cuff of his shirt.

"It's such a miracle you're here and safe," he said, his voice rough with his own tears. He sank down into a chair next to her bed, still holding her hand. "How was your night, sweetheart?"

"That pill the doctor gave me kept the demons and nightmares away, but so did you. Thank you for staying with me all night."

They heard water running in the bathroom and her mother appeared, carrying Julia in her arms. Right away, Julia stretched her arms towards Skyla. "Lala," she said.

Clara placed the toddler next to her on the bed, keeping hold of her arm so she wouldn't fall off.

"Julia woke up in the middle of the night. I made sure she got something to eat and drink, we played a little, and I put these on her. Aren't they darling?"

"You look so pretty in your new pajamas," Skyla cooed, sending her mother a grateful smile. She knew it was her who'd bought the clothes.

"After you fell asleep, Taylor and I went to the department store. We bought all of them several outfits and underwear. I hope that's okay."

"Of course, Mom. That's wonderful."

Not much later, Lexi woke up and immediately jumped into bed next to Skyla, clinging to her side. She didn't want to look up, not even when a nurse brought in a cart full of food.

Tom seemed to deal with his new environment much better. He sat at the foot of her bed, enjoying a cup of pudding, a bagel, and scrambled eggs. Julia sat in Clara's lap. She'd cut up a pancake in small pieces and was feeding it to her, the contents of a small box of Cheerios scattered on the floor.

Over the heads of the children, Skyla looked at her father. "Rikkerson?" she mouthed. She had to know if they'd captured her abductor, but didn't want to ask it out loud, for the children's sake.

Harold immediately understood. "His body is in the morgue," he whispered close to her ear, his voice barely audible.

Skyla straightened abruptly, making Lexi cry out. He was dead? Had she killed him? "How, Dad? How?"

"A car accident. His truck went down a steep slope."

Trying to process the information, she took several deep

breaths. Of course, she'd wanted Rikkerson dead. She'd wanted him to burn in the eternal fires of hell for how he treated his children, and for what he'd done to her. But now that he was actually gone, she didn't know how to deal with that knowledge. His death made the children orphans. What would she tell them? They had to know.

She fell back against her pillow and kissed Julia on her head, her protective, motherly instinct shooting into high gear. She loved them. They were *her* children now, her responsibility. She was going to be there for them all the way. To make sure no one ever hurt them again, that they were well taken care of and loved.

After breakfast, her mother's hairdresser arrived to cut and style her hair. Intrigued by the process, Lexi finally started to relax and asked to have her hair cut short, too, just like Skyla. Staying constantly by her side, the girl allowed herself to be washed under the shower. Tom followed a short while later. The new experience of warm water coming out of a shower head was too intriguing for him to pass up. He cooperated and had his hair cut, too.

Dressed in their new clothes, smelling like shampoo and soap, they sat on the floor next to her bed and played with the Duplo blocks and several of the other toys the hospital employees had dropped off. Skyla looked at the children with pride. It hadn't even been twenty-four hours since Troy had found them in the woods, and they were already adjusting. It gave her hope.

CHAPTER

43

ALL DAY, NURSES AND DOCTORS WALKED IN to check on them and were pleased how well they did, including Lexi, her cold already much better.

"We want to keep you all here for two more nights, just to be sure," the doctor explained.

Skyla was glad. She didn't want to leave the safety of the hospital, to face the outside world. She wasn't hurt physically, but mentally it was a different story. The idea of going out on the street terrified her.

"Your parents requested we try to keep all visitors at bay, but I understand you have a boyfriend, Edmond Randall? Can we let him come up?" asked one of the smiling nurses. "He's quite persistent."

Skyla felt her body stiffen and her heart rate quicken. She looked left and right, hoping to find an answer. She was still too confused, scared and uncertain about everything. About her feelings, the present, her future, anything. And she was in no condition to make any decisions. All she wanted was to make it through the day. Trying to hold on to her sanity in the reassuring presence of her parents and the children, with the help of a sedative. She knew without it, she would probably be lost.

"Do you want to see him, Skyla?" her father asked, breaking the long silence that stretched far too long.

His words sent an icicle down her back, cracking through her numbness. She barely remembered what he looked like and didn't love him. That she knew for certain. "Sure, let him come in," she said.

"There's a vending machine at the end of the hall. We'll take the kids for a snack, to give you some privacy," her mother said.

When Edmond appeared, a large bouquet of roses in his hand, he bent over to kiss her on the cheek. "I missed you so much," he said. He placed the flowers on the table next to her bed and sat down in one of the plastic chairs.

She pulled the sheets up to her chin, to keep him from seeing her in her light blue hospital gown with the little pink flowers, relieved he chose to sit in the chair instead of next to her on the bed.

"Thanks for coming, Edmond," she replied. "And thanks for the flowers."

She didn't know what else to say and swallowed hard.

"I couldn't wait to see you," he said, his eyes revealing genuine concern. "I've been so worried."

Biting her bottom lip, she looked at the handsome man next to her. The bright hospital lights outlined the strong features of his face and reflected off his jet-black hair. It was as if he sat under a spotlight, drawing all the attention to himself. She could barely believe she'd actually dated him, shared her bed with him, and that he loved her. It seemed so long ago, like something that had happened in another lifetime and to a Skyla who no longer existed.

He reached out to brush her hair with his fingers. "It's so short. Why did you cut it off?"

She recoiled at his soft touch.

As if he'd been bitten, Edmond pulled his hand back. The warm smile dropped off his face.

"I'm sorry," she began, feeling her cheeks turn red. Hurting him was the last thing she wanted to do. She didn't want to hurt anyone. "Please, don't take it personally. I've…" Her lips trembled and a single tear slid down her face.

After several long moments, he released a long breath. "I understand. You've been through a lot." His features softened with compassion and understanding. "Let me assure you, I want to be there for you. I want to help."

His understanding was more than she'd expected. She remembered he'd never shown much empathy for people who were sick or disabled, saying most of them were weaklings and abusers of the system. It was nice to see a softer side of him. A man who understood what trauma could do, and the damage it left in its wake.

"They told me you were found in the woods with your kidnapper's children. That he abducted you to take care of them?" Edmond said.

At the sudden vivid memory of her anguish and desperation in the endless forest, she made a choking sound and her shoulders started to shake.

"Oh, Skyla," Edmond said, and stood. "Sweetheart. Don't cry."

He sat down next to her on the bed and took her in his arms.

Despite her fear and reluctance to allow him near her, the smell of his aftershave nauseating, she leaned against him for a few moments. When she managed to regain some part of her composure, she drew away.

Over his shoulder, she saw a man turn and leave her room. A man with blond hair that curled over the collar at the back of his neck. A man who resembled Troy. She tried to get a better look, but he disappeared before she could. She fell back on her pillow, waves of exhaustion crushing over her, swallowing her. She felt on the verge of drowning.

Edmond took her hand. "They also told me those kids are staying with you, here in your room. I hope Social Services are informed, because you couldn't possibly want to keep them here, do you?"

"Edmond, please, stop it," Skyla cried out, putting a hand over each ear, not wanting to hear him. "We shouldn't discuss this right now."

"I'm just concerned you're getting too involved in their lives," he went on. As he spoke, he tried to catch her gaze.

All tiredness forgotten, Skyla pressed her lips together, her eyes blazing, full of resentment and rage. "I *am* already involved!" she yelled. "They are innocent victims! Just like me! And they need my help."

Edmond jumped to his feet. "You're right. You're right." He backed away from the bed.

His pained expression cut through her soul. Edmond didn't mean to be insensitive. He just didn't know how to handle the difficult situation. Nobody did. Neither did she. She had no idea how to move on from here or how long the road would be before her life would have a semblance of normalcy again.

"I'm just worried about you," Edmond said from a safe distance as he inched closer to the door.

Swallowing a sob, Skyla brought her arm up and over her eyes. Just like for her family, these last four months must have been difficult for him too, the uncertainty killing him. And he didn't know her feelings had changed. That she longed for another man. "I'm sorry," she managed to say.

He stood in the middle of the room without movement and then gave her a sad smile. "How about I let you rest. I can see you're tired. I'll be back tomorrow."

Skyla nodded wearily.

Without looking back, Edmond hurried out the door.

At the sound of his fading footsteps, she closed her eyes, wishing he would stay away forever.

CHAPTER

44

IN THE AFTERNOON, Skyla's parents went home. They were both exhausted and so was Skyla. She tried to sleep, but the children kept her awake. So did the constant stream of hospital employees and visitors coming in, and all the activity in the hallway outside their room.

"There are so many people," Lexi complained, her two fingers in her mouth. She was the only one still scared of a new face or an unfamiliar noise, the silence in which she grew up too sharp a contrast.

Skyla's sister visited for the second time, this time with her husband and their two young children. It was fun to see Julia's fascination with Taylor's sixteen-month-old son.

"He already walks," Skyla said, realizing how much she'd missed in the last four months. The tears came again.

After Taylor and her family left, her roommate Pauline stopped by. She brought several outfits from Skyla's closet in the apartment, toiletries, and make-up. Troy arrived at the end of the day. He only stayed half an hour. The room was filled with chatter, giving them no privacy to talk.

The next day proved even busier. In the morning, Kim Lowe had stopped by, expressing her relief about the good outcome. Next came Chief MacMillen with a long list of questions that took several hours to go through.

Two social workers stopped in as well, to check on the welfare of the children and inform Skyla they had contacted Kate Rikkerson's parents. They were taking a flight from Arizona within the next several days, to take care of Rikkerson's funeral arrangements and to see their grandchildren. Decisions needed to be made about their future. They were an important part in that process.

During visitor hours in the afternoon, two reporters gained access to her room and were taking pictures. Skyla completely froze and rang the alarm bell. Personnel showed up in seconds, escorting the invaders out.

"People are interested, sweetheart," Harold explained after he came in later. "Your name and photo have been on the news, in the papers, and on missing- posters all over the Northwest for months. People want to see you. Hear your story."

Skyla had noticed the curiosity from the moment she'd stepped off the helicopter. With many people waiting for her, welcoming her home. Even medical personnel entered her room for no other reason than wanting to say hi and wish her well.

"Edmond called me earlier today. He suggested to organize a press-conference to satisfy the curiosity. I think it's a good plan, because the phone at Overland is ringing off the hook."

"Forget it," Skyla cried out. The idea scared her to death. It had been that darn advertisement for Overland Insurance that had drawn Rikkerson's attention to her in the first place. Who knew what kind of lunatics a live broadcast would bring out of the woodwork? She didn't want any part of it. She didn't want to discuss what had happened to her, not even with her parents, sister, Pauline, or the well-meaning psychologist who'd tried to talk to her several times.

The hospital had released everyone, and Skyla's parents drove her and the children to their home. Returning to the apartment she'd shared with Pauline, and picking up her old life where she'd left it, would be impossible. Skyla lived in a constant state of fear, her mind scattered, her emotions in turmoil. She needed time.

Her parents had plenty of room in their four-bedroom house, especially with the finished daylight basement and an extra bathroom downstairs. The basement still had a ping-pong table in it, as well as board games, children's books, and toys from when Skyla and Taylor were young. Skyla decided it was the perfect place to stay with the children. They were used to living in confined quarters, huddled up together, and the basement was three times the size of the cabin. It would be large enough and much better than separating them. Although they seemed to be adjusting well, they'd grown up in isolation. Even with the help from counselors, they might need years to catch up and heal.

MacMillen stopped by the next day. He had a few more questions and wanted to inform her that Rikkerson's autopsy confirmed he'd died from either blood loss from a severed artery in his wrist, or due to head trauma caused by a single car accident. He also had numerous broken bones. Questions were raised about the burns on his head, but only as a side note.

All of Skyla's misplaced feelings of guilt washed away. She couldn't thank the medical examiner and MacMillen enough. Once the children were older and started to ask questions, she would be able to assure them she wasn't responsible for their father's death. That was a huge relief.

Skyla felt that same relief when the doorbell rang and Kate Rikkerson's parents arrived the next day with Kate's sister, Nora, who'd picked them up at the airport. All three carried bags with gifts for the children.

At first the children shied away, unsure of who the unfamiliar people were, the concept of family foreign to them, and what to do with the wrapped boxes. It didn't take long before they were completely wrapped up in their new toys and the adults could talk.

"We'd love to be part of the children's lives, but reside in a gated retirement community in Arizona," Kate's mother explained over coffee in the living room. "They do allow visits from grandchildren, but only short term. If we need to take care of them, we'd move of course. That won't go overnight."

"My husband and I recently divorced," Kate's sister said. "I moved into a one-bedroom apartment downtown and with my job as a flight attendant, there's no room in my life to take in three children just yet. But I'm dating a man who has sixteen-year-old twins. If needed, I'll do whatever has to be done."

Skyla had already done extensive research on the computer

about becoming a foster parent. She'd reviewed the Foster Parent Orientation manual and talked to the Child Welfare workers who'd come to inspect the house for safety.

With the children playing at her feet, Skyla shared her interest in fostering and possibly adopting them. The relief on the faces of Kate's parents and sister was evident. "We'll do whatever we can to help," they promised.

"Does that mean we can stay here, Skyla?" Tom asked.

It was obvious he understood more than she'd expected. She tousled his hair. "I sure hope so, sweetie."

Clara Overland's voice interrupted the conversation.

"Lunch is ready."

They all sat down around the dining table, enjoying fresh sandwiches, coffee, tea, and glasses of milk.

"I found a tutor for Lexi and Tom who already came to the house for their first private lessons," Skyla told Kate's family. She knew they were far behind in their education, and it was her hope they could go to school after the summer. In what grade they would start depended on the progress they made over the course of the next six months.

"Do you like your new teacher?" Nora asked the children, pouring Tom a second glass of milk. Tom and Lexi had already warmed up to their aunt, the kind woman obviously great with children.

Skyla herself had trouble with each bite, battling against the nausea in the pit of her stomach. After lunch, they would attend the service for Rikkerson, to give the children an opportunity for closure. She was worried about them.

"You know we're going to say goodbye to your father this

afternoon, sweethearts?" she asked them, dressing them in new coats and hats.

Instead of showing sorrow, Tom's eyes lighted up. "Are we taking the train?"

His reaction worried Skyla even more. "No, but we'll be in a big black car together."

The service was held at a funeral home's chapel, the time, date and location kept quiet to avoid curious onlookers. Skyla noticed there were no more than twenty-five people in attendance, most of them there to support her. During the short service, she had trouble to keep from turning around. Troy sat not far behind her, and she wanted to talk to him, have him next to her, her hand in his. On her way out, she greeted him, and he pulled her into a warm hug, his mouth kissing the top of her head.

"We need to talk soon," he whispered before letting her go when Edmond appeared by her side.

"Good to see you here, Summerton," Edmond said, dismissing him as he wrapped his arm around Skyla's shoulders and guided her away from the children in the direction of the limousine.

"I don't understand why you wanted to be here," he whispered in her ear. "That maniac doesn't deserve it."

She stared at him in disbelief. "I'm here for the children and his family. Don't you understand that?" she whispered back.

The grip around her shoulders tightened. "You have to think about yourself and not about strangers," he replied, narrowing his eyes. "They're not your responsibility."

He opened the car door and kissed her cheek before

helping her inside.

"We couldn't agree less, Edmond," she spat at him. With her sleeve, she wiped off the wet spot he'd left and closed the door.

When they came home, Skyla was exhausted from all the tension. Too tired to care any longer, she collapsed into bed and passed out.

That night, she found herself staring at the ceiling of her bedroom. For the first time since her rescue, she started to delve into her own feelings, instead of only thinking about the wellbeing of the children. Her life had changed in so many ways, probably in more ways than she could even imagine yet. She wasn't the same person anymore.

What do you want, Skyla? she asked herself. *How do you see your future? Do you still want to further your education in accounting? Do you want to go back to work?*

Don't make any rash decisions, she heard caring voices drone in her head. They were the voices from her parents and sister, her friends, and the doctors and counselors who'd come to talk to her in the hospital and at home. *You need time to come to terms with what happened to you. You've been through so much. Your scars and memories will remain, but you'll learn to live with the damage. Give yourself time. Don't let this destroy your life. You'll survive this. You're strong. Give it time.*

Throughout the night, restless thoughts ran around her head. Exhausted, she sat up in bed, her arms clasped around her knees, her eyes burning from lack of sleep.

They were right. A lot of things needed time, but one decision couldn't wait. It had to be made right away, to help her attain clarity and simplify her life.

Her future would evolve around the children. In that future, there was no place for Edmond. He didn't like children. He didn't pay any attention to them. He only talked about himself, and she couldn't deal with a demanding, ambitious, egocentric man, who never wanted to be part of the children's lives.

Besides, she didn't love him. In all honesty, she doubted she ever had. Confessing this to herself made her feel shallow and vain. It made her doubt her ability to decipher her own feelings.

Instead of dwelling on that knowledge and the many regrets that came with it, she pushed them far away into a hidden corner in her head. There were too many other much more gruesome memories and atrocious images etched into her mind.

Her battle to recovery had just begun.

CHAPTER

45

"I DON'T WANT to hurt you, Edmond," Skyla said. "But I've changed and don't see a future for us."

Afraid he might throw a fit and the children would hear him raise his voice, she'd chosen to sit on the front porch of the house. The temperatures were barely in the sixties and she shivered in her coat.

Edmond shifted in the deck chair. "I see," he said, staring at his leather loafers.

"I'm truly sorry and hope you understand," she continued.

When he looked up, she noticed relief on his face before he quickly lowered his eyes. "If you feel that's the best for you, I understand."

Although she was thankful that he took the news like a gentleman, she hadn't expected he'd so readily accept defeat. It made her wonder if he'd ever loved her either and if their relationship had been doomed from the start. "Considering what happened to me and my feelings for the children, I think it's the right decision for the both of us."

"Taking responsibility for your kidnapper's kids requires enormous courage," he replied. He cleared his throat and stood. "I admire you for that and wish you all the luck in the world."

His opinion didn't matter to her anymore. She'd always wanted children; and for her, Tom, Lexi, and Julia were much more than Rikkerson's kids. Haunted by the same sense of powerless terror and the horrific flashbacks that kept ambushing her at any given moment of the day or night, she saw in their faces the same distress she knew was etched into her own when she awakened from her nightmares. She understood and loved them even more for what they shared.

"Thank you, Edmond," she replied. "I appreciate that and wish you all the best."

Before leaving, he pulled her in a brief hug. "Take care of yourself, Skyla," he whispered and gave her kiss on her head. "And by the way, I love your pixie cut hairstyle. It suits you."

Tears gathered in her eyes as she watched him walk away, taken over by a dire sense of finality, her feelings raw and unsettled. Breaking up with Edmond ended one of many chapters in her life, her innocence, her trust, her sense of morality, and her confidence trampled into a million pieces.

She wondered what the future would hold. Would the hurt, cold, and emptiness entombing her heart ever lift, and was she strong enough to fight the desperation and evil still holding her in its grasp? Would one day this horrendous gale of emotions end, and would the sun come out again? She hugged her skeletal frame until she'd taken command of her mangled thoughts and felt strong enough to head back inside and face the children.

After another sleep deprived night, her mother took her aside for a heart to heart conversation.

"I realize you don't want to share your struggles," she said. "Maybe because you don't want to burden us, or maybe because you don't want us to know the details of what happened to you and the children. I understand, honey, I do. Even as a young girl, you always insisted on fighting your own battles, but this is something you shouldn't fight alone."

Her mother was right. She wanted to battle her demons within herself, the humiliations and abuse she'd endured too difficult to share with her loved ones. But she felt completely adrift. The clothes Pauline had brought her from their apartment hung loose on her body, the pants falling down without a belt. She'd lost a lot of weight, and she continued to lose, each bite a struggle to get down. The cold hollowed out feeling inside her grew colder and hollower with each passing day. She was in a downward spiral, the ghosts from the cabin haunting her, and her efforts to cast them out futile.

"You have to start talking to someone, Skyla," her mom said, almost in tears. "If you keep going on like this, you might end up in a deep depression, or worse."

Mentally defeated, Skyla gave in, her sudden mood shifts impossible to control any longer, the grief over the loss of her old life too formidable, the demons she battled too scary to face alone.

CHAPTER

46

THE STREAM OF endless visitors at the house came to an end. The phone stopped its incessant ringing. The public lost interest. Skyla's abduction and safe return had become yesterday's news. She couldn't be more relieved. The only people she wanted to see were her immediate family and close friends, her emotions too vulnerable to be in the public's eye.

She looked at the children. Their beds were set up so close to each other that they could touch one another when they extended their arms. Tom was the only one still awake.

"I really like it here, Skyla," he whispered. "Thank you for bringing us here."

"I love it here, too." She tugged the blanket close around him and gave him a kiss on his blond head. "Remember, if you get scared, all you have to do is talk into the baby monitor and I'll be able to hear you."

He shrugged his small shoulders. "Dad used to leave us

alone for days and I'm not scared."

She sunk down next to him on the bed. "There's so much you have to get used to, sweetie. So many new things to see and learn. I'm sure it can be overwhelming, and we can't be brave all the time."

Tom turned onto his back and looked at her with his big blue eyes. "Are you scared, Skyla?"

At the office of her psychiatrist, she'd found a brochure with tips for helping children cope after a traumatic experience. About making them feel safe, offering a listening ear, answering questions, accepting their feelings, and being there for them. Everything she needed herself.

"Sometimes," she replied. "But I'm talking to a doctor and it helps to share my feelings. She also gave me breathing exercises to help me relax." Skyla inhaled deeply through her nose and pursed her lips as she blew the air out. Tom giggled and tried to do the same.

She gave him another kiss and stood. "Good night, sweetie."

He yawned and rolled over to his side. "Troy promised to take me to the train store. I can't wait until tomorrow."

"That'll be a lot of fun." She waved at him from the door before she turned around and headed up the stairs. Her thoughts went to Troy. When she'd come home that afternoon, after her third visit to Doctor Nash, he'd just left. She'd listened to the enthusiastic chatter from the children, how they'd beat him in *Race to The Treasure*, Tom's new favorite board game, while Doctor Nash's words whirred through her head.

"Surround yourself with people who love and respect you,"

she'd said. "With people who accept you for who you are, and with whom you can be yourself without fear of being judged. Develop a safe team and environment."

In Troy's company, she'd always felt safe to voice her opinion, to share her inner thoughts, and be herself. She needed him in her life.

With the evening stretching out in front of her, Skyla joined her father in his study. "Is it okay if I sit here for a while?" she asked, checking to make sure the baby-monitoring app on her new cell phone worked.

"Certainly," her father answered from behind his desk.

She curled up in a chair. It was peaceful and warm in the office. The heavy oak furniture sturdy and solid, the carpet and paintings on the wall telling tales of times past. It was the place where she grew up and that she called home.

Her father leafed through a magazine. Now and then, he looked up and gave her a loving and reassuring smile. Her disappearance and his heart attack had aged him. His hair was completely grey, and he'd lost weight. Rikkerson had not only devastated her life, but also the lives of many others. She knew her parents had suffered greatly, making her feel guilty even though she knew none of it was her fault.

Fingering her necklace, she shifted in her chair. "I'm so grateful you opened your house to us, Dad. Thank you," she said.

"We would do anything for you, sweetheart," he replied. "This is your home, and you and the children can stay as long as you want."

"Thank you so much," she smiled. "Mom said the same and

that means so much to me."

In the companionable silence that followed, she felt her father's eyes on her.

"We're here for you in case you need to talk. You know that, right?" he asked.

Raw pain crushed over her in waves as the horrific details of what Rikkerson had done to her resurfaced. A soft moan escaped her throat. She couldn't tell her father what had happened. It would devastate him hearing words of assault, rape, and humiliation coming from her mouth. The urge to flee the room and take a shower, to wash off the dirt, made her get up.

Before she could leave, Harold rushed after her and took her in his arms. "You're so beautiful, sweetheart, inside and out, and I love you so much. Nothing could ever make me feel different." He rocked her back and forth as she cried softly against his shoulder. When she calmed down, she left the loving protection of his arms to dry the last of her tears.

"I love you too, Dad," she sniffled, recognizing again it was time to face the world and fight for her future. "And I promise, I'll come to terms with all that happened. I know I will." She sat back down in her chair, her father's handkerchief a wet wad in her palm. "It's just that..." She fell silent.

"What is it?" Harold said. "Please, honey, tell me."

Skyla folded her hands and pressed them against her chest. "It's just that I hear so little from Troy. Is he all right?"

"What do you mean?" her father asked. "He's been by multiple times, including this afternoon."

Another silence fell, but this time it felt awkward. Her father was right. Troy had stopped by numerous times at the hospital. He'd attended the funeral, spent time with the children during several of his visits at the house, and joined them twice for dinner. But on each occasion, he seemed subdued, perhaps even distant, and they were always surrounded by people, making a private conversation impossible.

"Oh, I don't know." She sank deeper into her seat, her shoulders slumped. "I have the feeling he's angry with me. Did he say anything to you?"

The worry lines on her father's face deepened. "Of course, Troy isn't angry with you. What's bringing this on, Skyla?"

She waved off his concern. "Nothing really, I was just wondering if he's okay," she replied, regretting she'd raised the subject.

Harold let out a deep sigh. "What's 'okay', Skyla?" he asked. "He's very happy you're home and to know you're safe, and he asks me every day how you and the kids are adjusting. While you were missing, he was a tremendous help. He couldn't have been a better employee or friend."

Skyla had heard about Troy's involvement in the search, how he'd dug up Rikkerson's file, and the extra workload he'd taken on. She loved hearing it again and moved to the front of her chair, not wanting to miss a word.

"I could go on and on about what a wonderful job Troy did," Skyla's father continued. "How grateful I am he found you in the woods. His endless efforts to find leads. His constant optimism you would be found. But he didn't do all that to help me. He did it .... He did it mainly for himself."

"For himself?" she exclaimed. "I don't understand."

Her father folded his hands and leaned forward. "He did it

because he loves you, honey."

She felt a flush warm her cheeks and avoided her father's inquisitive gaze. For years, she'd known deep down that Troy cared for her, maybe even loved her, but she had taken his feelings for granted. She'd felt comfortable in his company and considered him a dear friend. A friend who accepted her for who she was, never putting her in the position of having to prove herself or explain her actions. She'd enjoyed his quiet presence and admiration, his patience, his humor, and his support, while she'd chased butterflies, mirages, and Prince Charming.

She covered her face with both hands, deeply embarrassed. If only she hadn't been so naïve and foolish. If only she'd grown up sooner. Would Troy ever forgive her?

Her father drew her up from the chair and pulled her into his arms.

"Troy kissed me, right before I was kidnapped," she whispered against his shoulder. "All those months, I thought about it constantly. Whenever I tried to picture Edmond, all I could see was Troy's face." She freed herself from his arm and began to pace the floor. "How can you love someone and not realize it, Dad? How is that possible?"

"Don't be so hard on yourself," her father said. "You would have figured it out. I know you."

Skyla straightened her shoulders. "I need to tell him."

"Now don't rush things, honey," he warned her. "Take your time. You just broke up with Edmond, and you've been through so much. You may not know what you really want, and I don't want you to hurt Troy. He doesn't deserve that."

His words fell on deaf ears. Sometimes it was better to take your time and wait, but this was not one of those moments. She knew that as well as she knew her own name.

"I won't hurt him, Dad. I promise I won't!" she vowed.

CHAPTER

47

"DID YOU DRIVE out here on your own?" Troy asked when Skyla appeared at his door.

Until now, she hadn't ventured anywhere by herself and she'd forgotten her anxieties in the wake of her urgent need to talk to him.

She smiled nervously. "I didn't even think about it."

"Well, come in." He smiled and took a step back to let her enter. "I just finished dinner."

Skyla followed him into the kitchen and looked at the empty pizza box on the counter.

Troy shrugged. "I'm not much of a cook." He studied her for a long moment. "You look a little tense, but better. Can I get you something to drink, or maybe make coffee?"

"No, I'm good, thanks," she replied, pushing a strand of hair behind her ear, her nerves buzzing.

Troy tossed the empty pizza box in the garbage and wiped

the counter with a paper towel. "All cleaned up," he grinned. "Do you want to sit down? In the living room, maybe?"

Her timid eyes met his curious ones across the kitchen. She knew he wondered what had brought her here.

"I broke up with Edmond, in case you didn't know," she said, her voice coming out in a rush.

Troy walked to a cabinet, took a glass from a shelf, and filled it with water from the faucet. "I heard and was surprised," he said, giving her a fleeting glance. "What happened?"

Skyla shrugged, looking down at the ground. "Nothing happened. I just realized I never loved him."

"Never?" He took a long drink from his glass of water. "Well, that's a good enough reason."

And then she did exactly what she promised herself she wouldn't do and burst into tears.

"What's wrong?" Troy said. He put down his glass and took her into his arms, holding her close and rocking her as though she were a child. "Don't cry, Skyla." He sighed into her hair. "If you didn't love him, you made the right decision. You know that, don't you?"

He'd always treated her with unfailing kindness, tolerance, and respect; always ready with a benevolent word of support, to give her advice, and help out when needed. She'd always trusted him implicitly. Her secrets were safe with him. His undemanding, laidback friendship throughout the years proved to be even stronger than the one she'd had with Pauline. She was lucky she knew him, and that he knew her.

"I love you, Troy," she whispered against his shirt. "I love you so very much."

She felt his muscles stiffen before he stepped back from her. She immediately missed his embrace.

"What did you just say?" he demanded in a tone of disbelief, his eyes drilling into hers.

"I love you," she said, this time with more conviction.

He turned away from her. "You're upset. You don't know what you're saying."

She grabbed his arm before he could walk away. "I know you love me, too," she said. "You told me so over and over again out there in the forest."

He clasped both of her hands in his and looked down at her.

"It's true. I love you with everything inside me, and I nearly went out of my mind when I thought I'd lost you." His voice started to crack. "I would've turned over every rock on this entire planet to find you, if I'd only known in what direction to look. But that doesn't mean I'm going to believe it when you, out of the blue, declare your love for me. Skyla, you've been through such a traumatic experience. You need to heal and not make rash decisions."

"Why does everyone keep saying that?" Skyla replied. She didn't know if she was angry, disappointed, or sad. All she knew was that she didn't need time. There was already enough wasted of that. "You kissed me in the parking lot! Why didn't you kiss me years ago if you loved me for so long?"

Troy released her hands and started pacing the floor. "When I met you, you dated Jasper, the musician. He was followed by Nolan before you started dating Edmond. During that time, I knew you liked me, appreciated me, maybe even cared for me, but not as a lover," he said, throwing her quick side glances.

She followed his every move, his tall, lean body dressed in a white T-shirt and faded blue jeans instead of the usual suit and tie. He looked amazing.

"I had the feeling the time wasn't right for me to make a move," he continued. "That I would've ruined our friendship by kissing you. Besides, I was eight years older than you. Therefore, I thought it would be best to wait. A decision I now deeply regret."

"I wish you hadn't," Skyla said. "Your kiss opened my eyes and during all those months in the cabin, I relived that moment, dreamt about it." She stepped forward to block his path so that he had no other choice than to stop. "Kiss me, Troy," she said and slid her arms around his neck, taking in his beloved features. "I know you want to."

"My God, Skyla," Troy sighed against her mouth, his hands on her hips. "What are you doing?"

"Something we should have done years ago," she smiled, her voice soft and filled with love.

"I love you so much," he replied and moved in closer.

His kiss was tentative at first, his lips gently exploring the soft curves of hers. Then he drew her closer, his love for her, hidden for so long, bursting free and overpowering his senses. "I shouldn't do this," he groaned. But he didn't stop, his fingers stroking her hair, his kisses scorching her skin wherever his lips touched.

She reveled in the tenderness of each touch, each caress. In his arms, she felt at home, her love for him deep and strong.

"Can you forgive me for not realizing earlier it was you I loved, and not Edmond?" she asked, touching the side of his face with her fingertips.

"We all have our regrets," Troy said, kissing her palm before he drew her with him to the living room. "My biggest regret is leaving you there by yourself. If I'd stayed, or at least waited until you were ready to leave, nothing would've happened to you. You would've been safe."

"That's not true," she protested. "I wasn't a random victim. He'd targeted me, and he would've waited for another opportunity. I was never safe, no matter what."

"Maybe," he replied with lingering doubt on his face. "But I'll never leave you again like that." He shut his eyes to fight the tears that stung behind his eyelids.

"Nothing could've stopped him, Troy," she tried again to convince him. "He'd already followed me around for several days. He knew where I lived, worked, shopped. He was just waiting for the right circumstances."

Troy sat down on the couch and pulled her into his lap. "Thank you for trying to make me feel better about it." He buried his hand in her hair and kissed the tip of her nose, his thumb caressing her cheek. "I came to the hospital, as promised, to tell you how much I loved you, but I found you in Edmond's arms."

"I saw you leave, but Troy, you have to understand I was such a mess," she said, noticing from up close the pain in his eyes, the wrinkle between his brows. Before continuing, she swallowed hard. "Edmond's questions had brought on a panic attack as I relived the terrifying moment before you found me. When I heard someone calling my name, convinced it was Rikkerson who'd followed our trail. That he was going to beat us, kill us. I was so frightened, the memory so vivid that I broke down. All he did was try to comfort me."

Fighting her tears, she breathed in a long, shaky breath. She didn't want to fall apart again. Not now. "I've cried every day for the last four months and don't want to keep doing that," she said, struggling to smile, her emotions twisting inside. "I want to heal, to forget, to move on."

"And you will," he vowed, taking her hand and placing it over his chest, his muscles firm and sturdy under her palm. He was such an incredibly good man, his skin warm and his heartbeat strong. She could feel his love through every gentle touch of his fingers.

"I knew you needed to process so much. I decided to keep my distance for a few days longer, so you could catch your breath. But I was coming for you," he said with a grin. "To work my way into your heart. To fight for you. To use any means at my disposal to leave Edmond in the dust, wondering what happened while I swept you away. You mark my words."

"I know you would have," she agreed, glad to see a hint of the old Troy reappear. Then she slid off his lap to settle beside him. There was something very important she needed to say, and his reaction would determine their future together.

Troy's brows immediately knitted in concern. "Are you all right?"

She placed her hand on his knee and squeezed it. "Do you know I testified in court against Rikkerson six years ago?"

Troy nodded. "I went through the entire casefile more than a few times, word by word."

"I was young at the time," Skyla continued. "I hated him. Hated him for cheating the system and cheating on his wife. He was scary, cornering me in the gym, putting his hands where they didn't belong. So, when the opportunity arose, I jumped on it. I wanted to hang him. I wanted him to pay." She gave a short, bitter laugh. "But I never thought about the consequences for his family. Not once did I give it a second thought to where they would live or what would happen to them."

"Oh, my love. Don't blame yourself for testifying," Troy said, lifting her chin so he could look her in the eyes. "Don't you realize he put himself and his family in that situation? He was the one abusing the system. He was the one chasing other women. Everything that happened was all his own doing!"

She felt so raw, the guilt so strong, that she struggled to think clearly. "You may be right," she moaned. "But I want you to realize I've been dirtied, used...."

A heaving sob escaped her throat before she could continue.

"There's so much I need to overcome, and after what I shared with the children during those terrifying months, their future is my responsibility. If you want to continue what we started tonight, don't forget that those three children are part of the package." Pent-up hurt and grief flooded into her. "It won't be easy, for the both of us."

He drew her into an intimate embrace.

"I love you more than anything in the world, and promise to always be there for you, Skyla," he whispered. "I'll help you bury your demons and do whatever it takes to help you forget. I want to stand next to you, fight for you, and do anything to make you happy. I want to marry you, have a family with you, and I already love Tom, Lexi, and Julia and want to raise them as my own."

He laughed through his own tears. "Is that enough of what *I* want, or shall I continue?"

She knew there would be many hurdles to overcome, for all of them, but with Troy by her side, it would all work out.

"No, that's plenty," she grinned, and nestled against his chest.

Also from Ramcy Diek

Storm at Keizer Manor
A Multiple Award-Winning
Historical Time Travel Romance

Eagles in Flight
An Award Winning
Romantic Suspense Novel

About the Author

Ramcy Diek fell in love with the United States during her
travels with her husband.
The Pacific Northwest became the Dutch couple's home, where
they built their RV Park and raised their two sons.
During this time, Ramcy also made a slow transition from
reader to multi-genre writer.
Her debut novel *Storm at Keizer Manor* received multiple
awards. This inspired her to spend more time doing what
she loves most: writing stories.
Visit Ramcy's website at www.ramcydiek.com for updates on
more new releases and to sign up for her mailing list.

Made in the USA
Middletown, DE
03 January 2021